Coming to Life on South High

Praise for Lee Patton

Nothing Gold Can Stay

"*Nothing Gold Can Stay* is a 14-karat gem. The characters, both major and minor, are extremely well drawn…as a work of romantic gay fiction it is absolutely priceless."—*Jone Devlin, Triangle*

Every Summer Day

"No matter where a reader lives, it's always a delight to discover a book that sets a gripping story in a recognizable ZIP code…DU alumnus Lee Patton delivers that compelling blend with his latest novel, *Every Summer Day*."—*University of Denver Magazine*

By the Author

Nothing Gold Can Stay (as Casey Nelson)

Love and Genetic Weaponry: The Beginner's Guide

My Aim Is True

Every Summer Day

Coming to Life on South High

by

Lee Patton

2021

COMING TO LIFE ON SOUTH HIGH

ISBN 13: 978-1-63555-906-4

This Trade Paperback Original Is Published By
Bold Strokes Books, Inc.
P.O. Box 249
Valley Falls, NY 12185

First Edition: March 2021

Credits
Editors: Jerry L. Wheeler and Stacia Seaman
Production Design: Stacia Seaman
Cover Design by Tammy Seidick

Acknowledgments

I'm grateful to novelist Tracy Smelser and poet Patty Holloway for their chapter-by-chapter feedback and especially their enthusiasm and heartfelt reactions; to George Ware for all his support with the first complete version; to Jerry Wheeler for his astute, rigorous, and thorough editing; to Greg Francis for his comments on the final chapters; to Kristen Hannum, John Serini, Jack Long and Joanne Mackey for their input and suggestions on earlier sections. The first chapter, "Straight People and their Problems," appeared in *Danse Macabre*'s Stonewall edition in slightly different form.

For My Father

Funny, gregarious, good company—a hell of a fisherman
and party animal, dedicated worker and great provider

It's better to have loved and lost
than never to have lost at all.

—Mary Rice Moore

PART I

CHAPTER ONE

Straight People and Their Problems

Slammed too many times during too many parties, the door between the house upstairs and the basement apartment finally broke from its hinges. It smacked the kitchen floor like a blitzed-out sorority girl.

Gabe had managed to nap through the soundtrack of the throwback *Playboy* scene downstairs. Old-school jazz and hard rock in shuffle play, giggles, and orgasmic screams echoed up the stairway from the subterranean lair. The landlord's son occupied the house's converted garage, an eternally dark studio apartment below the main floor. Clouds of pot wafted up the stairwell, casting their own seductive, dopey weather. On the living room couch, Gabe had been drifting on his own cloud, a billowing half-dream…a slow kiss…a zipper undone…a wild strand of brown hair tickling his cheek. Now, a perfect dreamer's track, a funkadelic take on "The Man I Love."

The crashing door startled him awake.

Then the girl startled him more. "Oh, Jesus! I didn't mean to break it!" She leaned as if to attend to the door's injuries, careful to hold her drink steady, and drawled down the stairway, "Don't worry, darling, my daddy will pay for it."

"That's good, Candy," Conrad called up, deep but faint. "Because mine won't."

A battered paperback of *Madame Bovary* slid off Gabe's stomach as he sat up. He watched the blonde's fingers graze the fallen door. "I'm sure sorry," she declared, "you poor old thing."

Like the other young women who'd accidently wandered up from Conrad's basement to appear in the main floor hallway, Candy was uncommonly pretty. Purdy as her languid Texas vowels. Even from the adjacent room, Gabe noticed her long, scary fingernails, the same pink as her pouty lips. Old-school as Conrad's music, she wore dark, heavy Cleopatra eye makeup. Her big golden coif was roughed with tufts, as if she'd spent the afternoon in lusty abandon.

In no time, she was standing over Gabe, wavering. In her drink—the same pink—ice clinked. The cocktail wavered in her grasp. She smiled, screwy and crooked, which saved her from being too Hollywood, cover-girl gorgeous. "You an art student, sweetheart?"

"No." Gabe stretched himself up, rubbing his eyes, then his legs. Off-white latex paint flecked his holey jeans. "Housepainter."

"Painting actual houses? In November?"

"Indoors. Now we're painting actual apartments."

"A real, live working boy!"

"As well as a scholar." He held up *Madame Bovary*. "Comparative literature."

"I love it! I swear, I'm going to change my major to literature next semester!"

"What is it now?"

"Undeclared." Candy's eyes roved up and down Gabe's jeans again. "So, you're an actual poor person, putting yourself through school and everything?" She hid her mouth behind her hand. "Sorry. I'm a little tipsshy." Extending the drink arm's length, she spoke carefully, as if trying to banish that slurred *ssh*. "Conrad makes these too strong. Texas Greyhounds. Vodka and ruby grapefruit. You're cute, but I gotta get along now."

"What were you looking for?"

"Oh. The toilet."

Gabe directed Candy to the upstairs bathroom, figuring he'd never see her again after she staggered back down to Conrad's netherworld.

❖

Later that evening, the fallen door got used as a stretcher to rush one of Conrad's blacked-out girlfriends—not Candy—to the campus clinic. Conrad freaked out, claimed he had to contact the girl's family, then disappeared in a stretch Lincoln that appeared, as if scripted, to scoop him down South High Street. So, each gripping one end, Gabe and his housemate Russ hustled the half-naked, semi-comatose young woman sprawled atop the door two blocks to Campus Urgent Care.

When Gabe visited the clinic to check up on her at six in the morning, the half-naked girl had already signed herself out. The door was never seen again.

❖

A few mornings later, Rain stapled an official Indiana state flag where the basement door used to be. "Conrad's music is just too random," she said, cocking her ear down the stairwell as she straightened the cloth. "Coltrane, then the Beastie Boys? Come on!"

Gabe thought the flag was gorgeous, explosions of gold stars and rays on a field of dark blue. He told his housemate, "Your father would be proud."

"No, he'd kill me," Rain said, laughing. Her father was state controller back in Indiana. "I probably broke twelve state laws, stapling that thing upside down."

"Then we're lucky we're in Colorado."

"That's what I say every morning, when I wake up one thousand one hundred and one miles from Indianapolis."

The starry flag wavered, as if caught on an indoor breeze. Someone was knocking on the doorless doorframe. "I thank my lucky stars I'm in Colorado, too," the knocker drawled, parting the flag and slipping though. "If you'll excuse me for breaking and entering again." It was Candy.

Gabe, in sweatshirt and boxers, and Rain, in nothing but a tie-dyed T shirt that stretched to her knees, signaled for Candy to come all the way into the kitchen.

Extending her hand to Rain, she smiled to say with odd formality, "A pleasure. I'm Candace Holmes. Candy." She was decked out in matching plaid tam o'shanter, vest, and miniskirt in the university's colors, maroon and yellow, plus glossy white cowboy boots.

Sweeping her hand toward Candy's outfit, Rain exclaimed, "How *gay*!"

"How do you mean?" Candy asked.

"She means 'joyful,'" Gabe intervened, "in Indiana-speak."

"I like that," Candy said. "It's so old-fashioned. I have always held we should win that word back from the homosexuals."

"Rain just uses it the old way," Gabe said, "to get on my nerves."

"Now, why would anybody want to get on your nerves, darlin'?"

"Because Gabe's a big homo," Rain said, sitting at the counter. "Would you like some granola, Candy? A muffin? Russ made some brownies last night, too."

"I wouldn't go near these brownies," Gabe said, holding out a blueberry muffin for Candy. "You look like you're going someplace respectable."

Candy glanced down at her getup. "Oh, I'm just serving coffee to old geezers in bolo ties. Donors to the scholarship fund."

"Good," Gabe said. "Keep 'em happy."

"You're the eye candy?" Rain asked.

"So to speak," Candy said. "My daddy's on the board of trustees. He wants me to 'give back.'"

"My, my, my," Gabe said, trying to whistle. "You're giving those geezers something, all right. That skirt is very, very short."

"Are you really gay?"

"I'm afraid he is," Rain put in. "He's got this annoying crush on my boyfriend."

"I do not!" Gabe lied.

"I wanted to apologize…" Candy trailed off, eyes imploring as she munched on the muffin. "I didn't realize y'all's place wasn't part of Conrad's domain. I thought I was just going upstairs, not barging into your house. And I'm truly sorry I broke your door."

"It was ready to collapse any time," Gabe said. "Our absentee slumlord has promised to fix it a bunch of times, but…"

"He's absent," Rain said, shrugging.

"You mean Conrad's daddy?"

"He's usually in Vegas," Gabe said, "when he's not in Key Biscayne."

"My daddy would never treat his tenants like this." Her dark eyes, doe-shaped, heavy-lidded, and darkly lashed, narrowed now. "I should give Conrad a piece of my mind."

"No, Candy, no!" Rain exclaimed, then lowered her voice. "We don't mind being neglected as long as the rent stays low."

"We fix our own plumbing and send our tiny rent checks to an offshore management company," Gabe stage-whispered. "We'll gladly raise the Indiana flag over any number of doorless doorways."

"But then Conrad himself should look after you," Candy said. "You've got to wonder what he does with all his free time."

"We all wonder," Rain said. "We might make a funny brownie or two, but God knows what Conrad delivers in those stretch Lincolns."

"It's not called South High Street for nothing." Candy sighed, licking her fingers and easing against the flag barrier. "Thank you kindly for breakfast."

"Y'all come back now," Rain mocked, but not cruelly, "any time." There was a lilt in her voice—like she really meant it—welcoming and gay.

❖

"You don't mean it," Candy told Gabe weeks later, her finger tracing his ear's outer edge. "You'd never cheat on Rain with that awful Russ."

"Russ isn't awful," Gabe said in a hush, curled up on his bed, turning his bare back to her.

"You're a good boy, Gabe, but Russ is kind of slippery. As slippery in his own way as Conrad is." Candy tossed aside her half of the sheet and searched around in the dark for the pink cocktail they were sharing. Though they spoke barely above whispers, tonight's party down at Conrad's was the loudest ever. Above the laughter, screams, and occasional thuds, the bass backbeat shook Gabe's walls. It was two thirty in the morning.

Gabe shuffled onto the pillow, side by side with Candy now as she sat up to sip from the huge plastic *Go Pioneers!* tumbler she'd brought up from Conrad's. For the last few weekends, he'd looked forward to Candy's midnight appearances. Even though her body didn't excite him, her warmth and ardor, her scent, her loopy intellect seduced his affection. He loved how her sideways grin and her wild cackle undermined her careful Texas goddess makeup, making her seem almost an ordinary mortal.

She'd usually drift back downstairs after he fell asleep, but one time they'd wakened naked the next morning, tangled in each other.

Now he nuzzled her shoulder, combed her blond mass with his fingers, then reached for the tumbler to take a sip. "Russ might be slippery," Gabe said, "but I'm sure I would have sex with him if he made the first move. No questions asked."

"I have a question, then. Where are your morals?" Candy sank down to rest her head on his shoulder. She idly roved his chest and his nipples with her hand, heading south to caress the faint line of hairs around his navel. "Russ and Rain are a committed couple. Just because you and Russ are boys doesn't make it any different than what it is, Gabe." She slapped the smooth flat above his pubic hair. "Adultery. Practically."

"Ouch! Don't burn me on a pyre of Bibles yet. I haven't done anything."

Russ had been doing something, though. During a recent dinner at their favorite Mexican joint, Gabe had just sat there, nerves afire, as Russ kept rubbing Gabe's thigh with his knee, soft and subtle at first—as if it was accidental—then aggressive and constant. The whole time, Russ dangled his arm around Rain's shoulders. Then last night, at a whiskey-fueled poker game with the rest of the painting crew, Russ had none-too-subtly angled to sit next to Gabe, even enduring cracks about "cheating with his roomie," only to start his leg-pressing routine during every slack hand or break in the game. Before the last ante, he raised the stakes forever, daring to reach under the table and slide his hand up Gabe's thigh, stopping just short of his crotch. Before anyone noticed, Russ lifted that same hand to toss his chips into the pile.

"I'm a Methodist, darlin', not a Puritan," Candy said, caressing Gabe's thigh herself. "We don't burn people at the stake. Or burn Bibles. But I do believe you are a prime-grade bullshitter. You have all these fantasies, and you like to think you're so very bad and amoral and sex-crazed, but you could never cheat on Rain, no matter what you say or think."

"Why are you obsessed with *cheating*? Believe me, when I look into Russ's big blue eyes, I'm not thinking one thing about *Rain*. I love Rain, but this has nothing to do with her. How can I *cheat* when I've never agreed to your straight people rules?"

"Is this what they're teaching in Comparative Literature? This cheap moral relativism?"

"Quite the contrary. I'm learning all about straight people and their problems. I study novels all about you heterosexuals and all your high morals about *cheating* while you all fuck like bunnies. The novels we're studying are always about families, mommies and daddies and babies, midwives, abortions, and deaths at childbirth. Meanwhile, daddy screws the upstairs maid. Of course, everyone's always punished for *cheating*. That's the Great Lesson of All Literature. So rest assured, Madame Bovary, morality is alive and well! But there's nobody like me in the thousands of pages I've read since I started my major. It's all about you, Candy, and I'm reading it in your honor."

"You are not!" Laughing, she slapped his stomach again. "And if I may say so, you are definitely reading everything the wrong way."

They fell silent and pressed closer, Gabe raising his long, skinny leg over Candy's smooth thighs. Down at Conrad's, the music and voices grew mellower, while across the hallway in Russ and Rain's room, the boom-boom grew louder. Only silky hunks of fabric hung in each bedroom doorway, creations of Rain's, batiks of children holding hands in a golden field. As ever, in the middle of the night, Russ's panting and grunts grew as loud as Rain's oh-my-God yelps and screams, bestial and rhythmic at the same time. Gabe was sure they were biting the pillow, restraining their outcries, and imagining they were subduing passion for their roommate's sake, but it still sounded like they were fucking right inside his ears.

"There they go again," Candy whispered, giggling. "Doesn't it give you ideas?"

"Yeah." His hand pressing her back, Gabe pulled her naked breasts against his chest. He kissed her, slicking her lips, tangling her tongue with his. "Makes me wish you were Russ."

"What would you do, exactly?"

"I dunno. I always fantasize about kissing him, just like this."

"Just kissing?" She pulled back. "Lord, Gabe! You've never been with another man, have you? You're a virgin! Lordy, Lordy, you're twenty-one and a virgin! That's more shocking than anything I've ever heard from those libertines downstairs."

"Okay, I admit it." He broke away, reaching for the pink drink. "I'm a virgin. So burn me on a stack of Bibles."

❖

As Thanksgiving approached, it dawned on Gabe that everyone associated with the house on South High Street was adrift, cut off from family and home ground. Except him. He'd spend this Thanksgiving, just like all of them, with his parents, who lived in Denver's northern suburbs. Candy adored her father but was estranged from her stepmother. Russ and Conrad both had distant, drive-by parents who drank too much. Rain was self-exiled from her illustrious Hoosier brood and earned her independence in Denver the hard way, cutting all family financial tethers and working as a janitor on campus.

Russ, Rain, Conrad, and Candy were all around twenty-five—to Gabe the ripe, full maturity of adulthood—yet each had their college careers "on hiatus" while they cast around for "the perfect major." Not one of them could explain to Gabe's satisfaction what was so damn hard about actually finishing a bachelor's degree.

"Our house is so gay in the November light," Rain proclaimed, standing in the living room the morning before Thanksgiving. "I love the sun slanting in the windows from the south. Before it became a student crash pad, I'll bet a happy family lived here."

"Is that some kind of hint?" Russ said, emerging into the living room in boxers and a black tank top, his long brown hair sticking out in five directions, both hands cupped around his coffee. "You wanna start a family, Rain?"

"Not while I'm cleaning urinals and you're painting over bloodstains in Mafia slums."

"You're so conventional." Russ kissed Rain's cheek. "For a hippie chick."

"They're not really Mafia slums," Gabe said, sipping coffee, already in his painting clothes. "They're just tiny Sheetrock boxes owned by ordinary slumlords." He watched cars prowl for parking on South High while students jogged toward their last classes before the holiday weekend. He was trying to avoid the sight of Russ's long, muscular bare legs, still bronzed from summer's laps at the outdoor pool.

Rain smiled, stretching her face into the huge window's lemon-colored sunbeams. "For a bunch of poverty-stricken working stiffs," she said, closing her eyes in luxurious gratitude, "we sure are lucky to have this place."

Despite its battered walls, doorless doorways, cracked windows and groaning floorboards, the old house did have its charms. Flagstone steps led to its only remaining original door, then into a formal foyer. A grand old stone fireplace stretched between two huge arched windows. Off the living room, a breakfast nook snuggled into a bay window. The nook was so pleasant and sun-kissed, looking out on a giant Norway maple—the only surviving life form in the bare-dirt backyard—that the three roommates gravitated there for all meals. Their dining furniture was a card table with mismatched folding chairs, which sometimes made Gabe feel they were still kids, shuffled aside, while the real adults feasted elsewhere.

But since he started college, he'd never felt more at home anywhere than here on South High Street. Like Rain, Gabe liked to imagine the family that lived here before the house was converted into two units, with Conrad's apartment still a garage, built into a small hillock under the house's main floor. He enjoyed the surviving touches of its middle-class heyday in the twentieth century, like the milk delivery hatch opening into the walk-in pantry.

Sometimes, dozing or daydreaming on the couch between a shift of painting apartments and trudging to evening classes, Gabe stared at the rusty ruin of a swing set outside in the dirt and could almost hear children's squeals, or spot the ghost of a schoolgirl posing by the fireplace in her prom dress, or almost catch kids playing in the stairway, high-pitched screams rising not from Conrad's downstairs orgies but from a game of hide-and-go-seek—steps that once led to a real basement for storing skis and toys, a real garage for a family station wagon.

Though Russ had complicated things, Gabe still fantasized the three of them might stay on here even after he finished his degree in June. They could fix up the place and create some semblance of a family that might even include a baby. Mornings like this, with the sun streaming in and the smell of fresh coffee, reawakened the fantasy. Because without it, his future looked a hell of lot like the backyard, that broken swing set, that bare-earth dead zone.

He tuned back in to reality. Russ and Rain nuzzled by the window, their coffee chilling on the stone sill.

❖

That afternoon, cleaning paintbrushes in a bare one-bedroom apartment, Russ and Gabe got even more light-headed than usual. Lacquer thinner fumes overpowered the usual latex stench. They'd had to prime the plywood patching in a wall bloodied and punctured from some evicted tenants' brawl. "I think the boss is buying some really cheap thinner," Russ said, screwing the top back on. "Man, I'm dizzy."

"Let's get out of here, Russ. We can't finish until after Thanksgiving anyway, and we need fresh air. Rain says being cooped up with paint and solvents all day is going to kill us both."

"And nobody is ever as right as Rain." Russ laughed, held open the door, and slapped Gabe on the butt as he passed into the breezeway.

Down in the parking lot, Gabe watched kids playing in the cold evening, chasing each other behind cars, chanting, "Crime scene! Crime scene!"

"Wow, we've got a spare minute to ourselves, now, don't we?" Russ asked, getting behind the wheel of his pickup. "You don't have any classes tonight." He turned out of the complex onto a boulevard thick with bumper-to-bumper holiday traffic, a procession of taillights stalled in the smoggy twilight. "Damn, now we're going to die of carbon monoxide poisoning. Let's see if we can wait out this traffic jam somewhere."

Gabe figured they would pull into one of the beer-and-pool taverns lining the boulevard. He looked forward to a beer and being alone with Russ in a dark booth in a deserted corner. Now that they'd be alone in the booth at last, maybe Russ would try some grand gesture like locking his ankles around Gabe's. He still felt light-headed, whether from the thinner fumes or the smog or the anticipation of Russ's touch. His stomach felt hollow, his guts air tossed, as if they were on a humping country road rather than stuck in a jam. Gripping the seat, he dared to glance over to Russ, who stared grimly ahead.

They crawled forward, past the taverns. The strip malls gave way to dark, spiny brush and bare trees along the Bear Creek greenway. Russ turned abruptly onto a lane that led into broad, airy acreage. They passed an open gate and its sign, "Park Closed After Dusk."

"I had to get out of that traffic, catch a breath," Russ said. He didn't sound natural, as if he were under-rehearsed, trying out lines. "Ever been here, Gabe? It's kind of cool."

The truck's high beams scanned a deserted soccer field and a row of bare cottonwoods along the creek. Russ drove to where the park's lane dead-ended in a empty parking lot. Before Russ killed the lights, Gabe glimpsed a concrete pond and a dried-out waterworks wrapping around the lot.

"In the summer, it's so cool," Russ said, in that same fraught, off-tune tone. "Water gushes up from all those pipes." Now he killed the engine and rolled down his window a crack. "At least we can get a little fresh air while we wait out the traffic."

Out of the blue, he said he was horny. He reached down and rubbed his crotch, back and forth, back and forth, finally unzipping his jeans and stroking through his shorts. "Gabe, hey. Go down on me."

Frozen with shock, Gabe mashed himself against the passenger door. He swallowed hard and looked into the dark glimmer of dry pipes poking from concrete. "I've never done that before."

"There's nothing to it, man." Russ yanked at the hard bulge in his shorts. "Just get your mouth down there before I come all over myself. Come on, kid."

"I'm sorry, man." No matter where his fantasies and dreams had taken him, Gabe was wide awake and didn't want to be here. "I just…I wish we could, like, kiss first?"

"*Kiss*? Are you shitting me?"

Hopping out into the thick, smelly air, Gabe fought the impulse to puke. Just in splattered work jeans and short-sleeved T-shirt, he didn't really know where the hell he was going. Red taillights bunched on an expressway, freeze-framed behind the cottonwoods. Gabe crossed a footbridge onto a paved walkway that followed the creek. Dry leaves scrabbled underfoot. Coyote willows splayed, naked, against the bright windows of a condo complex across the greenway.

In one of the plate glass squares, a young couple unpacked groceries at a kitchen table. The wife, with baby hitched to her side, passed a frozen turkey to her husband, who caught it in his arms and pretended to drop it, as if it weighed more than his arms could bear. She laughed, waving her arm as if to dismiss his antics, until he caught her hand and pulled her into a kiss, the frozen turkey tucked under his arm like a football, the baby yanking at his hair.

Gabe wandered farther down the greenway. Leaves crunched on the path behind him. Of course, it would be Russ. Russ, carrying Gabe's hoodie. Russ, placing it around his shoulders, patting down the fleece as if to protect Gabe from the chill. Then, Russ wiping away the tears. "I'm sorry, man, I was an ass…"

But no. The crunch was from a stray dog, sniffing through leaf piles along the creek's banks. When Gabe turned back, Russ's headlights spotlit the high branches, then his taillights joined the massive, creeping procession on the boulevard.

Hunched against the cold, Gabe kept walking past the last yellow-bright condo windows, no choice but to follow the creekside path the miles back to South High. Under giant cottonwoods, he could see nothing but darkness ahead.

❖

In bed around three the next Sunday morning, Gabe told Candy about the incident in the pickup. He did not reveal that his antagonist was Russ. "I don't get it," Gabe whispered, sighing, idly caressing the small of Candy's back. "All that under-the-table seduction for a quickie blow job?"

"Don't try to understand straight men. You might as well waste your time analyzing rabbits."

"But if this guy—the crew member—was really straight, why was he even messing around with me?"

"Rabbits, Gabe. Nasty, self-interested jackrabbits. Tell me, do you approve of abortion?"

"Wow." That was a hell of a subject change. "I don't really approve or not approve. It's not for me to decide."

"That's a cop-out."

"Why are you asking?"

She rose up, crooking her arm on the pillow and smoothing Gabe's hair. "Guess."

❖

Crossing to his late-afternoon European Novel class—Adultery 101—Gabe skirted the campus childcare center just as parents stopped by to pick up their kids. Tykes bundled up in bright jackets and too-big mittens toddled across thin, crusty snow toward outstretched arms and laughing faces.

A few days before, Candy had told him she deserved her predicament. She knew what the risks were with someone like Conrad, plus being sloppy about protection after too many drinks or too many lines or too many hits. "I have the same background as Conrad," Candy had proclaimed with a certain hauteur, as if affluence entitled a person to be more randy and irresponsible and tragic than other mortals. "So, I know where this goes, and I don't like the destination one bit. I have no plans to tell him about this, and I will slay you if you say a word to him or anyone else."

"I won't, I promise," Gabe had told her. "Listen," he added, surprising the bejesus out of himself, "why don't I marry you?"

When Candy laughed, Gabe shocked himself even more and insisted he wasn't joking. She should consider his proposal seriously. They would raise the child together, with Gabe finishing his degree before the baby was due in midsummer. He imagined himself teaching Freshman English on a fellowship while he started grad school, and after a long day of discussing The Politics of Gender in Moliere's Comic Universe, he'd pick up their little girl at the childcare center. She would be adorable in a tiny plaid overcoat—a prodigy who would play the piano at three, but kind of a tomboy, too, climbing trees and playing fire trucks with the boys, a natural beauty who would break into a wide smile and wild giggles when she was happy. Which would be often.

When Gabe reached the Language and Literature building, Candy was waiting for him just inside the main entry, warming the back of her bare legs at a heat register. She wore the tam o'shanter and the maroon and yellow outfit under an open overcoat. "I'm working a holiday meet 'n' greet at the theology school." A brooch fixed to her coat twinkled red and green, red and green. "Can we take a minute to talk before your class?"

Her eye makeup was smeared. Her skin looked pale and veiny in the foyer's fluorescent light. Still, Gabe's freshman roommate Ben, passing upstairs and catching sight of Candy in her miniskirt and boots, gave thumbs-up to Gabe and smirked.

"Not bad for a lit major," Ben called down. "Good going, Gabe."

"It's not what you think," Gabe said.

"Then too bad for you," Ben said, disappearing into an upper hallway.

Gabe tried to kiss Candy, but she caught his chin in her hand and pressed a finger over his lips. "Your proposal was a very sweet gesture. And I did think about it long and hard, believe me."

"It wasn't just a gesture, Candy."

"We can't get married. When we're alone in bed together, I'm like a doll you play with. Just like I played with mine, fascinated with their plastic breasts, the blank space between their smooth legs. It was an idle fascination, Gabe. We both know you're just kissin' me for practice, dreaming of some guy you have a crush on."

"I don't have a crush on any guy. I really don't. I can learn to be a better lover."

"I should never have climbed those stairs and trespassed into your bed, Gabe. Or your life. I shouldn't have let our little slumber party get to this point. The truth is, some nights after you and I played around, I'd drift back to Conrad's bed at four or five in the morning, and he would reach for me, embrace me, kiss me. Then he'd screw me, Gabe, and I would close my eyes and pretend it was you."

❖

Gabe hovered by the Indiana flag, pushing it back a bit, waiting for the girl's chatting voice downstairs at Conrad's to go silent. Rain passed by with a bag of groceries. Russ followed her into the kitchen with a six-pack.

"What's going on, Gabe?" Rain called, opening cabinets. "We hardly see you at all any more. Why don't you join us for dinner?"

"Yeah, kid," Russ said, popping a beer open. He held it out for Gabe. "Why don't you? Just like old times."

Gabe waved the beer away, trying to smile. "Thanks, but I can't drink tonight. Gotta study. Adultery 101, you know, the final."

"You've got to eat, though, Gabe," Rain said, twirling a package of spaghetti. "You're getting so skinny."

"I don't think we've told ya," Russ said, gulping the beer. "We're getting married, Rain and me."

"Don't say anything, Gabe." Rain pressed two fingers to her lips. "I know, I must be out of my freaking mind."

Gabe knew he should widen his smile and say congratulations, but he clutched the flag's seam, cocking his ear downstairs. It was quiet down at Conrad's. He excused himself, parted the flag, and stepped down the dark stairwell.

Conrad's bar edged along his entryway, dim in the reddish light of a lamp covered with a silk scarf. Conrad began to button a shirt over his bare chest, which was creamy smooth as a boy's above his protruding belly. A girl stood up, emerging from an armchair in a dark corner, grabbing a purse, and yanking the red scarf off the lampshade. "Hi!" she called when she noticed Gabe, then stretched the scarf under her eyes, harem-girl style, and laughed.

Gabe stared at her, squinting. Wasn't she the half-naked girl he and Russ had carried to the clinic atop the broken door?

"I'd make you a cocktail," Conrad told him, "but we've got some urgent business." He left the top three buttons unfastened and grabbed a jacket.

"The limo's here," the girl said, waving through the plate glass window to the Lincoln, which pulled close, as if about to crash into the ghost of the old garage door. She hurried outside, struggling into her coat. "Come on, Conrad!"

Gabe backed into the doorway to cut Conrad off, scattering plastic tumblers underfoot. "I wanted you to know something, Conrad, okay?"

"It's really not okay. I've got a big…meeting, a session with some of my dad's clients, and if I'm late, I'm gonna be in big trouble."

"Candy has a serious medical condition right now." Gabe stretched himself even taller, height his only advantage over Conrad's burly bulk. "I just thought you might want to know. Maybe go see her?"

"A *medical condition*, huh?" Conrad smiled, tossing his house keys in his palm. "No offense, but you've got a lot to learn about women, Gabe. Candy just partied a little too hard." He placed his free hand firmly on Gabe's shoulder, pressing him aside. "Now she has to get cleaned up, you know, down there."

"No, it's not—"

"I know what it's not. I also know about every bed she's crawled into."

"Conrad, it's serious. You've really got to see her."

"Your concern is downright charming," Conrad said as he shoved, then passed Gabe to gain the open door. "It makes it even harder to have to tell you the unhappy news. You're going to have to find a new place to crash."

The shock hit Gabe like a punch, but he recovered fast enough to try a blasé tone. "I was planning to."

"I'm going to miss you, white trash prince, even if you are kind of a dick." He roughed Gabe's hair. "But your sweet Candace was a bad girl, and now she has to take care of her own messes. Just like I do," Conrad said, pulling the jacket over his shoulders like a shawl. "Or my father might kill me." He hurried out to the idling limousine. "And I mean *kill* me."

❖

"What if I raise the kid?" Gabe drove Candy's ancient black BMW up Downing Street toward a family planning clinic on Capitol Hill. "You go on your merry way, and I adopt the baby? I'm serious."

"So I carry this fetus around inside me until next summer, push it out, grunt, scream, hold my helpless squirming child in my arms, then hand it over to you? I don't think so, Gabe."

Candy didn't look at him as the street broadened into a parkway along the Denver Country Club. Peering out the window, she seemed to concentrate on a vast stone house, its life-size figures of the Holy Family in a swanky manger decorating the circular drive. "Please don't make this any harder. Please stop with the Boy Scout routine about raising the damn baby. I know you're trying to help, but you're not. I just want to get this over with."

Heading closer to Capitol Hill, Gabe's guts twisted. Under the brilliant December sky, bare crabapple trees cast long, spindly noon shadows over snow. He felt like he'd volunteered to be the getaway driver for a crime he hadn't foreseen or understood. He didn't know why he reacted this way, not just reluctant but panicky. He'd never been anti-abortion and wasn't opposed to Candy's decision on principle, only personally. As the blocks became older and shabbier, converted Victorians crowding close, he could not shake the sensation that he was a trespasser complicit in some looming disaster.

"Don't be sad, Gabe." Candy touched his shoulder, then caressed his arm. She stared over now, imploring. With no makeup and her hair pulled into a ponytail, she looked impossibly young and pure—a schoolgirl in a pink hoodie, jeans, and sneakers. "Your life is going to be so full, so free, once you really get started. You're going to meet some wonderful guy who actually deserves you, and you won't believe how much fun you'll have. You won't have to be tangled up with straight people and their problems. Promise me one thing, though."

Gabe's stomach flipped as the Beamer slip-slid on a patch of ice in the alley. They'd planned for this, parking at the back of the clinic on the advice of Candy's family planning counselor. At the back entrance, they could avoid the permanent cohort of protestors, the strident ones who shouted "Don't murder your baby!" or the maternal ones who tried to intercept the young women with offers of adoption, free counseling, or biblical pamphlets. Gabe hurried around to help her negotiate the mud glaciers on her side of the car, offering his arm. "I love you, Candy, I really do. I'll promise you anything."

"Just tell all your lovers that I was the one who taught you how to kiss."

Hand in hand, they found their way down a surprisingly dark, rickety flight of stairs into the clinic, which occupied a rambling old red brick mansion. The chanting out front, on the sidewalk, "Jesus loves you, loves your precious child!" grew faint as they descended, step by step.

Halfway down, Gabe blocked her way, stepping in front of her, still squeezing her hand. "How do you know, though, that I'm not the real father? What if we actually went the whole distance while we were sleeping?"

"Or maybe when I was passed out? Is that what you're really saying?" Candy breathed an exasperated sigh. "You've got a lot to learn about women, Gabe. Like I wouldn't know. Like it would be *nothing* to me?" She freed her hand to push him aside and hurried down the final steps, then called back to him: "Don't you have any idea how I feel about you, you son of a bitch?"

Framed signs showed the way into a series of basement hallways under low ceilings, ductwork overhead, all steamy warm. Inky, antiseptic odors intensified. Gabe caught up with Candy at a bright, open reception, and saw tears in her eyes.

A smiling clerk in a Santa hat checked a ledger and directed Candy to a doorway. She lingered at the opaque swinging doors, then shoved them hard, passing through.

When he asked if he could accompany Candy, the too-jolly clerk almost laughed. "No, no, no, young man. It just wouldn't do." She informed Gabe he would have at least a half hour to do as he pleased, and indicated a couch, a tiny winking artificial Christmas tree, and a stack of magazines. And a pamphlet, *Responsible Family Planning: A Guide for Men.*

The reception area was overheated and stuffy, so Gabe retraced his steps back to the sunshine. He picked his way along the alley's icy ruts and emerged on a side street dominated by an old brick public school in the same ornate but dumpy condition as the clinic.

Recess was just ending in a sunny, snow-cleared playground, the kids scattering back to classrooms. One boy, though, a crew cut towhead, maybe first grade, lingered on the monkey bars, laughing when a bigger kid tickled his tummy, trying to make him loose his grip. Fingers gripping the chain-link fence, Gabe realized it might be even better if their child had been a boy. The crew cut blond looked a lot like Gabe when he was little, complete with missing front teeth and freckles.

He would really love that damn kid. He would be a kind and considerate father, one who said "please," not just yelling out orders like a drunken drill sergeant. His little blond boy would flourish under his easy generosity. His teachers would adore his son so much that Gabe would blush with pride at parent-teacher conferences. Other parents would whisper, "And to think, that poor young man is raising that wonderful boy all by himself…"

When Gabe snapped out of the daydream, the crew cut boy was gone, the playground deserted. A teacher shut the exterior door with a hard, latching slap. In the slam of silence, the protestors' chants grew audible again. "It's not a choice, it's a child."

Gabe sidled through the narrow gateless entry to the schoolyard and sat on a swing, rocking himself in the warming sun, aware of his elongated, solitary shadow. Where was he going to go now? He studied the rows of chintzy conversions surrounding the school, the cramped blond-brick postwar apartment houses, and wondered what kind of lonesome tiny Sheetrock studio apartment he could afford.

He glanced at his watch, noting the minutes he had to kill before he urged his feet down those dark stairs to rejoin Candy. He would have to accept the reality he would never play dad to any tomboy pianist or freckled towhead.

Instead, he would offer his hand to Candy and guide her up, into the daylight. Forcing a smile, he would try to be gay.

Chapter Two

Sexual Transmission

So far, as he faced the end of the last semester of his senior year, Gabe wondered if he just wasn't very good at being gay.

Or at keeping friends. Rain and Russ had moved out of the house on South High soon after Conrad sent Gabe packing. Upending traditional heterosexual practice, the couple learned Rain was pregnant *after* they decided to marry. They abandoned their pretense of striving for degrees and moved back to Indianapolis.

But one friend actually reappeared, saving Gabe from solitude and maybe homelessness. His freshman dorm roommate, Ben, offered to rent the bedroom vacated by a mid-year graduate at a good price. Ben's apartment was only a few blocks farther up South High Street from Conrad's and even closer to the heart of campus. One of those mid-fifties motel style designs that pretended Denver was Miami Beach, the building had gaudy turquoise trim with open breezeways and flimsy single-pane windows as if six months of freezing nights was a pessimist's fantasy. Like so many of its mid-century Denver counterparts, the apartment house was named after a female special to the builder, her first and middle names scrawled in jolly cursive over the entry: *Edna Victoria.*

Furnished only with folding chairs and books, Ben's apartment was swanky by student standards, the bedrooms and living room opening onto a long balcony from wide, sun-facing glass doors. "This would be great," Gabe told Ben, "but I've got to tell you something first." The words he wanted dried out on his tongue. He realized he'd never really told anyone but Candy. The words felt even more desiccated, told to another guy. "I'm, uh, gay. It's cool if that's not going to work out for you."

"Wow! Gabe, we shared a dorm room for a whole year, and you never told me?"

"I wasn't sure back then. I was still hoping I wasn't."

Ben stared, nodded, then smiled. "Didn't you ever want to get it on with me?"

"What kind of a question is that?" After all, he had endured a whole year of Ben's lights-out midnight monologues of frustrations and fantasies about girls. He'd always been dogging after pretty girls, and even openly panting after some who weren't so pretty.

"Come on," Ben said. "I'm not ugly, I'm always horny, and you saw me naked or half-naked all the time. It must have occurred to you. Sex, I mean."

"Maybe a little, but not really. It's not like that, always sexual in the cut-and-dry way it seems to be between straight men and women. And don't get the idea I was all hung up on your looks." In fact, Ben was kind of a dreamboat, strong-jawed, blond, the nebbish literature major uneasily coexisting in his tall, well-built, athletic body. "You weren't interested in me," Gabe said. "So, why would I make a move? You'd never shown a flicker of interest in gay sex. Plus, even if you are beautiful, you're just not my type."

With a cocky smile, Ben didn't act as if he cared whether or not he was Gabe's type, but he obviously relished being called beautiful. Ben's beauty was blunted by his personal style, though, itself a weird combination of bluntness and blunder. With an unheard of gift for numbers in a literature major, he minored in math and had been a computer and chess geek in high school. By college, he'd evolved into a bookish boor and a clumsy jock, never overcoming his foundational geekiness. The sly, sexy wolfhound he imagined himself to be was actually a puppy who peed on every carpet.

"It's not going to be a problem, Gabe." Ben extended his hand to Gabe for a manly shake. "It's going to work out just fine. It might even be interesting!"

"No, it won't be." But Gabe smiled, relieved. He'd been pretty sure Ben wouldn't outright reject him—guys like Ben who were so ardently straight, so obsessive in their adoration of females, usually weren't too homophobic. "My love life is nonexistent," Gabe said, "and probably always will be."

❖

But Gabe's love life actually did get interesting. To his own bewilderment, by mid-April it was humping along. At twenty-one, he was discovering what his straight friends had figured out at fifteen or sixteen: sex could be mighty compelling.

In the early spring, Gabe worked up the nerve to check out the scene. He was too freaked to try hookup sites, so he eased into gay bars on weekend nights. He'd shelter by himself in the safety of a crowded bar with a midnight drag show. Gabe never got why lip-synching to ancient pop diva tunes was worth more than a minute's passing interest, nor why dressing up as an unconvincing, outlandish parody of a woman was such an accomplishment, nor why the other guys in the audience would hoot in appreciation. Turned off, he'd stand apart at the bar, nurse a cheap beer, and go home alone.

After a few barren weekends out, he tried a huge club in River North and hid his lonely-ass self among the multitudes lining the dance floor. He noticed a cute guy noticing him, glancing sideways from his gaggle of buddies, then smiling directly at Gabe and pointing to the dance floor. He already liked the guy's easy laughter and confidence as he took Gabe's elbow and led him out to join the airless mass of dancers. When they finally kissed at closing time, Gabe wondered if he'd been granted entry into Real Life at last. Without much thought in a mind already addled by beer and seduction, he invited the guy home to South High Street.

❖

Gabe had never known anything like that first night with Adam, his first man. Embarrassed by his lack of experience and still stung from his humiliating crush on Russ, Gabe didn't dare tell Adam he was a virgin.

Afterward, drinking beer on the balcony in their jackets, braving three in the morning in early April, Adam told him what a great kisser he was and how much he'd like to try that again.

"I learned it from a Texan," Gabe said, leaving out that the Texan had been a girl, or that Candy's Texas soul kisses were his only amorous expertise.

Adam caressed Gabe's arm. A grad student with a research fellowship at Colorado State, he told stories of recent trysts, including a recent "surprise fuck" with the hired bartender at a biology department party. Awed by Adam's exploits, Gabe grew more apprehensive. His futon beckoned just beyond, bedroom door wide open, awaiting the inevitable. Adam eased his fingers past Gabe's wrist, then clasped his hand, crushing the beer can with the other.

That first time hadn't been too bad. Adam led Gabe to the futon, undressing him effortlessly, buttons and zippers and elastic dispatched. He started out hard, pressing Gabe down as he kissed, beery and aggressive. But they ended up just playing like two horny Boy Scouts, stroking each other to quick climax. Caught in Adam's arms, Gabe breathed relief.

Adam gently smooched Gabe's cheek, then lay back. "Sorry, buddy. I guess I've had too much to drink tonight. Got too excited."

"It's cool," Gabe said, as if he needed to be magnanimous. In truth, he couldn't imagine how he would ever be able to take Adam inside himself. Jesus, how did anybody—male, female, anal, vaginal—ever manage that? A raging hard-on might be central to the human sexual universe, but being on the receiving end seemed impossible. "It's great, really," Gabe said, "just lying with you like this."

"Amen," Adam said, pulling Gabe closer. It was so dark that starlight and a sliver of moon cast a faint shimmer across the futon. The still, chilled air made their body heat and tangle of naked, sweaty limbs feel even warmer. When he learned that Gabe was about to graduate with a degree in literature, Adam asserted that, despite his science studies at Princeton, he devoted every other free credit hour to the humanities. "I just felt if I ignored philosophy and literature, I really wouldn't be educated. I'd only know these heartless hypotheses."

Before sunrise, they would drop the names of David Hume and Immanuel Kant, and read aloud, out of sheer perverse freedom to roam, from Gabe's disintegrating paperback of *Zen and the Art of Motorcycle Maintenance*. Having studied philosophy in a yearlong freshman course, Gabe loved the chance to bullshit about the elusiveness of reality. At some point, he got fired up about Henry James's short fiction—"some of it's actually readable and semi-concise"—and pressed on about his favorite, "The Beast in the Jungle," in which a man avoids his curse, the Beast, a horrible, unknown fate. "The man cowers in his rooms, shrinking from all experience, until, grown old, he realizes he's actually met the Beast after all. It's the life of safe inaction he'd chosen to live."

"Wow," Adam said, "wow, baby, I don't think either of us are in danger of meeting that beast," and kissed Gabe, gentle and lingering as the sun rose. They slept until noon, cradled in each other's arms.

The next Saturday night, Gabe finally lost his virginity. "Relax, babe, relax," Adam kept growling, harsh and whispery. Gabe bit the pillow, trying to concentrate on old Donald Duck cartoons. He ultimately managed to survive it, but without getting anywhere near ecstatic abandon. Though his heart craved this ultimate connection with Adam, his tender butt thought it was insanely unnatural.

Still, they soldiered on. Every Saturday night that April, it was actually Adam who grew more relaxed, probing and pounding away while Gabe gnawed on pillowcases. In truth, Gabe held a secret far scarier than his sexual fear and discomfort. He was falling in love with Adam.

He played this overpowering secret close to the chest, poker-faced as he spent the first weekend in May in Fort Collins with Adam. They smuggled rum and Cokes in giant plastic cups into Adam's cousin's baseball game, then drove up Poudre Canyon, sun-kissed in May's first warmth, top down and bare-chested in Adam's battered, vintage MG coupe, sharing beers and shamelessly pontificating about Wittgenstein or the fraudulence of trickle-down economics.

Gabe could perform this high-toned bullshit easily, offering his share of grand abstractions and wild laughter but staying silent on the real depth of his feelings. His love for Adam attached itself to everything surrounding them, the narrow passages of tortured, lip-pink canyon wall, in the scrub oak's first green buds, the snow piles melting on Cameron Pass. At the top—10, 278 feet—the aspen were still bare, the lakes crusted with ice.

Back down the canyon, Adam led Gabe on a favorite hike through former ranch land now preserved as open space, up a side stream where his family used to picnic for birthdays and holidays. Up the trail, Adam told Gabe about his family's deep roots in Colorado, his great-grandfather a two-term governor and his great-great grandmother among the first women to cast a vote when Denver became the first city to grant universal suffrage.

"Republican, of course," Adam said, smiling. "That's the curse of these illustrious old families. They're conservative as hell." But he confessed he'd come back home to Fort Collins after Princeton due to family matters. He easily won a fellowship at Colorado State. "My folks wanted me to come home."

The stream's course broadened into a marshy gap full of the stunted stalks of last season's wildflowers. Under a small reservoir once serving the ranch, the steady outflow created a boggy zone, mucky in its arid surround of juniper, oak brush, sage, and prickly pear.

"Over here, Gabe," Adam said, leading him along a faint path raised above the marsh—rotting old planks—"there's a dry spot on higher ground, a kind of secret meadow. I've explored this area in summer to study marshy toadflax for our research."

There, on the yielding, just-greening sod, Adam stripped Gabe with hushed deliberation. Belt, socks, shoes tossed away in slow motion, then his zipper undone, millimeter by millimeter, his pants shucked until he was a naked boy enmeshed in Adam's naked aggression. After a short, sharp stab, Gabe took Adam's thrusts easily, pain-free at last under the man he loved.

❖

"I lied." Adam had escaped from his grandparents' dinner party one weekend to steer his MG down I-25 and spend midnight with Gabe in Denver. "I told the family I had to get back to the lab. That the toadflax scum in our petri dishes would curdle, killing our research on immortality."

"Why not just tell 'em you had a boyfriend waiting for you in Denver?"

"You don't know my family, do you, bucko?"

"You've never introduced me."

"Someday. Maybe. Some day."

The next weekend they left a rowdy gay pub on Capitol Hill and strolled past Poet's Row up the exterior stairway to the capitol. On the top steps, they surveyed the panorama of downtown high-rises and cranes atop skeletal, higher high-rises to come; the art museum's castle ramparts; the City and County Building's Depression-Deco grandeur. Adam stood under a statue, shooing debris off the figure's bronze spats. He pulled out the whiskey he'd snuggled into his windbreaker, raising the flask before he sipped. "Hope you're not too dry, Great-Grandpa. Wish I could give you a sip."

Gabe studied the statue's face, highlighted in streetlight. Just like Adam's, bland as a catalogue model's until you noticed the jut of jaw, the determined gaze under the broad brow. Then, taking a sip from the offered flask, he noticed the name on the plaque and almost spit whiskey. "My God! He's an Adam, too."

"You didn't know?"

"I'm not up on my Colorado governors. But doesn't that make you Adam Schneider the Third or something?"

"The Fourth. But I hate that WASP-y shit." He laughed. "Especially when we're all Saxon and no Anglo."

"What was old Adam like?"

"Hell if I know. According to legend, I barfed on his lap when I was a baby and he was dying of lung cancer at National Jewish. Funny, cause he was a notorious anti-Semite. Typical right-wing fascist of the time. Ordered the state militia to suppress a miner's strike in the Mosquito Range. Cheated the *braceros*. Probably bashed a fag or two in his time."

"He must've done something good."

"Well, the royalties from his Mosquito Range claims are funding my PhD, leaving me free to advance the cause of gay rights."

"How?"

"Let me demonstrate." Adam opened his arms, then enfolded Gabe in his windbreaker. "Here, let me warm you up."

Pressed chest to chest, they breathed together, their exhalations elongated among the antique lamps and men immortalized in bronze. An empty bus rumbled down Lincoln Street. This late, the city lay emptied, almost motionless, as if Governor Schneider had commanded an evacuation. Their lips found each other—kiss enough, Gabe fantasized, to reignite the whole cityscape.

"I love you, okay?" Adam pulled back, whispering. "I confess it. I love you more than anything."

On these long-awaited words, Gabe's psyche took a little detour while the earth opened up, his feet plunging into the molten mantle. Then his head soared into the night sky, up to Orion, whose sexy stars winked, diamond-hard. But Adam didn't need to know how easily Gabe could lose his cool, how far gone he was, how his hopeful heart had been careening, out of control, in orbit since the moment they met. "I hope your toadflax research team discovers the secret of eternal life soon, Adam, because I want to kiss you like this forever."

❖

But forever metastasized into never. In the middle of May, just before finals, the end came via the now-expected daily call from Fort Collins. During a surprise snowstorm falling on the budding maples and oaks like nature's embarrassing cum shot, Gabe took Adam's call, joking, "Why don't you give up immortality and come live with me in Denver?"

In response, only a heavy sigh. "I'd love to, but the research team has other plans for me." Adam sprang how he'd be spending the summer term in Massachusetts. His mentor's huge grant had come through, and they'd be dividing their time between a lab on Cape Cod and a research facility at Harvard. He'd be leaving right after Memorial Day. "I've got to pack up my current research, wrap up tutorials, and throw my entire life into a suitcase. All in the next two weeks."

Over the next few days, Gabe did his best to absorb the shock, puzzled by the story's off-notes. Did prestigious research grants really come in such a big, sudden rush? Were entire academic teams relocated in summer rather than in the fall?

But nothing prepared him for what came next. Gabe's hopes had been reduced to inviting Adam for one last Denver weekend, then planning long-distance visits before their fall reunion.

But over the lines, he could almost hear Adam shaking his head.

"Maybe we shouldn't see each other, Gabe. Not until I know where I'm really going with my life."

"Not see each other?" Gabe could not understand the phrase. It might as well have been spoken in Apache or Farsi. "*Not see each other*?" In the silence, echoing after his babbled repetition, he could hear a door slam, the tinny TV noise going up, and a strangled laugh. Out of desperation, he asked the only question that made sense, straight from a TV script. "Adam, is someone else there with you?"

"Yeah." Adam repeated it, as if convincing himself. "Yeah."

"Can I at least come up, just to say goodbye?"

"No. Let's not drag it out. I can't see the point of that."

Just as he'd had no experience of falling in love, Gabe had no preparation for its complete descent into nothingness. People talked about "getting dumped," but Gabe found the phrase repulsive. That was too casual, too comical to describe the vacancy inside him. Barren, alone, he woke to hopelessness through the last weeks of the last semester.

He decided to call one last time, just before Memorial Day. Adam was even more distant and abrupt. The chilly, awkward call ended even colder. "Don't ever call me again."

In the wake of that, Gabe sometimes schemed he'd drive to Fort Collins and confront Adam, consequences be damned. But he always banished that plan, and not only because it made him feel even more pathetic and powerless. There was just no arguing with *I don't see the point of that.*

Over and over he wondered how Adam's profession of love sank to contempt in a matter of days. The only thing that made sense was Gabe's clumsiness as a novice lover. Adam must have found a sex partner who knew the right moves, the ease he'd craved through the months of breaking Gabe in. Really, it was simple. He'd found someone who gave pleasure without whining and whimpering like a scared kid. What did Adam really need with some lanky sack of klutzy arms and legs now that he was bound for Cape Cod? Why keep trying to make a grown-up lover out of that overgrown kid down in Denver?

Gabe survived finals still flummoxed that Real Life had forced such a—not a detour, but a closed route ahead. He sometimes day-dreamed that his real self had gone east with Adam, where they lived a beautiful, sea-swept life together on Cape Cod. More often, he got twisted into nightmares, only worse, since when he woke, he had to go on living through reality's pitiless narrative.

❖

As May in old south Denver ripened with bright, long afternoons, Gabe felt marooned on windswept plains that had never known a sea breeze. One welcome distraction, though, was Candy's reappearance in his daily life. She'd declared her major to be Comparative Literature in the spring semester, and though he'd seen her regularly in their Nineteenth Century Russian Literature seminar, she now suggested Ben and Gabe join her for a finals study group. The three met a few evenings at Edna Victoria, anticipating the whacked essay questions likely to arise from their professor's obsession with *The Brothers Karamazov*, which he regarded as "a Holy Scripture of morality arising from erotic energy."

During one break from the seductions of Russian morality, Ben asked Candy why she'd quit her decorative welcome hostess gig at the university's alumni center.

"I got sick of being pinched by old guys who think, just because they've given a bundle to endow the university, they're entitled to my endowments."

"But who could blame them?" Ben asked. "The center made you wear that little microscopic skirt, and you're gorgeous."

Candy stared at him, her expression pivoting between outrage and gratitude. "That's nice of you to say, but I was supposed to be a hospitable guide to programs and opportunities. Besides, I'm an old bag now, not sex bait for donors."

Since their painful errand the day of Candy's abortion, Gabe noticed how she'd become more serious, immersing herself in Great Literature, dressing more simply, wearing her hair in an uncomplicated bob, and drinking far less. Even her Texas drawl was surrendering to Colorado's flat vowels. "But I learned one benefit of my delayed progress as a student. Since I'm an elder of twenty-five, I didn't have to be a graduate to get a housemother position at a sorority. So next year, I'll have a gorgeous place to live and a whole gaggle of giddy Greek gals to look after."

"So alliterative," Gabe said. "I reckon you've fallen under the spell of this here liter'ture stuff."

"Yes, I've discovered my calling—literature, not house mothering—so late in life."

"I happen to be drawn to older women," Ben said.

Somewhere between finals and Gabe and Ben's graduation, an underwear trail led to Ben's bedroom most nights: a bra here, a pair of briefs there, a pair of panties dropped on the way to Ben's closed door as if Hansel and Gretel had run out of crumbs. The subsequent squealing, panting, and yelping, unmuffled by the cheap Sheetrock walls, took Gabe right back to those doorless nights listening to Russ and Rain.

Gabe writhed alone in bed, lonesome as a Russian Orthodox monk, the erotic pandemonium also taking him right back to those brief months with Adam. During the rush of his progress in sexual experience, he deluded himself that he'd finally become an adult, a man—a *real man* despite the iconography of pansies, faggots, and fuck boys. Yet now Adam's rejection unmanned him again. Once the hurt began to ache a little less, his humiliation only deepened.

What made his solitude endurable, what made psychological survival possible, was how Gabe's unlocked heart seized up like a crappy subcompact with thrown rods—a complete breakdown. Some natural anesthesia, like a psychic twin of physical shock, dulled his pain. His shame gradually eased, too, and with it, his ability to feel anything. This state of suspended emotion allowed him to hit the bars again without a second thought and create a profile on hookup pages.

Gabe spent the summer after graduation in the lowest phase of his life. By day he was an inky drudge, lucking into a temp position copy-editing a state health department project, the definitive study of Sexually Transmitted Diseases in Rural Colorado.

But most weeknights and every weekend, he would rove the vast plains and serrated ranges of sexual transmission itself. He never called any of these hookups afterward and could barely recall a face, a voice, or a gesture, let alone whatever adventure they'd had in bed. He started out inviting them to his own room, just for the grim satisfaction of answering Ben and Candy's panting with two males' even lustier, deeper moaning.

If one of those lusty guys dared to message him afterward with the civilized goal of a movie or dinner out, they'd learned that Gabe had a previous engagement. If one of those guys dared to say, "I really like you, I really think we ought to see where this goes," they felt the humiliation of Gabe's silence, the stab of his shrug.

All that sex became no more erotic than a soldier going through the motions of a drill on some bleak, frostbitten dawn. Without it ever being clear, except in retrospect, without it being a "game" or anything so calculating, let alone fun, Gabe became toxic. From April's clumsy virgin to July's promiscuous operator, he existed as a real-life gay cliché, the slut whose only sexual problem was how to get rid of his partners as soon as possible in the morning. He solved that by learning to have sex only at the other guy's place, so he could slip away in the middle of the night, no kiss goodbye, no note, just the fluorescent hiss in a strange Capitol Hill elevator at four in the morning.

And though some remnant of the dreamy, clumsy Catholic kid still had the grace to feel kind of guilty, Gabe craved control—the power to kiss off this parade of attractive, accomplished young men without even a kiss. He made sure he was the one who was lusted after, the one who was adored, the one who held the power to tell them all to fuck off, *there was just no point.*

One late Saturday morning in August, Gabe had made the after-sex mistake of falling asleep in the narrow bed of a Mexican-American ex-Marine who was genial and skillful but far too short. Having endured the ex-Marine's instant coffee, stale bear claw, and awkward up-reaching hug farewell, back on South High Gabe found an unexpected visitor who reached his apartment house's doors just as he did. A tiny, thin woman in hospital scrubbies awaited, wrinkled and enervated in later midlife, her olive skin gone sallow, and her dark hair invaded by wiry, gray-white intruders. It was his mother.

Gabe was immediately embarrassed. At the sight of his mom, the promiscuous operator was reduced to a boy fresh from some unholy mischief. He wondered if she could smell the sex on him. The sun was already punishing, glaring down on his mom's crucifix so it glinted through the opened top buttons of her scrubbies. His mother offered a hug. Gabe planted a kiss on top of her head.

"Fancy meeting you here. I just got off my all-night shift. Was hoping you'd be home."

"They have phones now, Ma. In real time, you can inquire if the desired party is present in his residence."

"Like you ever answer. I don't like to talk into that voicemail. Anyway, Tony's coming, too."

"I'm always glad to see you. Come up, I'll make some coffee. Where's Uncle Tony, then?"

On the question, Elena's brother appeared down the street, parking his massive black SUV and lumbering up South High bearing a brass lamp and a wood chair with a sagging wicker seat. "I just got all this stuff and there's no room in my storage unit." Tony owned a suburban apartment complex and sometimes acquired left-behind furniture. "Last time we were here, I noticed a distinct need for furnishings."

The need was distinct—besides the folding chairs, Ben and Gabe only had a dirty-pink, holey sofa found in the alley, and their signature décor, plank and concrete block bookshelves. Gabe used the card table left behind in Rain and Russ's evacuation as his desk. "Nice of you, Tony. A real chair!"

"There's more in the pickup. It's part of a dinette. It's more civilized than slouching on the floor like savages."

"Your pizza and frozen burritos," Elena put in, "will taste even better, sitting down."

"Great, let's bring it up. Imagine setting down coffee cups on a table top instead of the floor."

Within minutes, Gabe, Elena, and Tony were setting beer glasses on that beautiful fake woodgrain table. It already felt too hot to drink coffee, so Gabe broke out the last of the beer. Tony was going on about his son's best friend's little brother—didn't Gabe remember Jeffrey's brother Marty?—who was back in Denver now, after having studied in Italy.

"Yeah, I remember Marty. He was still a middle school kid when Jeffrey and I were in high school."

Tony and Elena exchanged a smile. They had the same sly Croatian smile, a little sinister, Balkan Mafia, wolfish, showing too many teeth.

"He's not a kid anymore, Gabe," Elena said. "And is he ever tall. Almost as tall as you. And handsome!"

Gabe stared both of them down. “And you’re telling me about Marty because?”

“No reason,” Tony said. “I just figured you’d be seeing Jeffrey around and would want to know.”

Gabe sat back, finishing off a long draught of beer for fortitude. His mother and uncle were too giddy over this bit of once-removed gossip. Was he being outed by his own mother and uncle? He’d assumed his mother was utterly clueless, deep in her heterosexual paradigm, though she had once taken Gabe aside in high school to say, “It’s okay to bring your girlfriends home, you know,” by way of asking *why the hell don’t you have a girlfriend?*

Tony, though, man of the world in his Saturday-casual khakis and pressed dress shirt, was savvier and had asked Gabe repeatedly where the girls were. Gabe was always able to deflect these lines of questioning by mentioning his father. That silenced them. What sane guy would bring a nice girl home to endure Patrick Rafferty’s sullen glares and scorn?

Elena’s maybe-matchmaking smile vanished, as if she, too, was thinking about her husband. “By the way, your dad…”

“That’s another reason we stopped by,” Tony said.

“He has these pains,” Elena said, “in his stomach somewhere. He won’t tell me about it. Just gets mad when I ask.”

“We wanted to tell you in person,” Tony said. “He’s drinking a lot.”

“How can he drink any more,” Gabe asked, “than he already does?”

“On weekends, it’s all day long,” Elena said.

“I found him filling a glass with straight whiskey,” Tony said, “at nine thirty in the morning.”

“I think he’s trying to kill the pain,” Elena said. “He won’t see a doctor.”

Good! Maybe he’ll kill himself! Gabe thought, enjoying the first buzz from his beer. “I hope the old man’s not suffering too much,” he lied.

Chapter Three

Like Coursing Blood

After Elena and Tony's visit, Gabe thought he ought to go home to see how his father was doing. Maybe that was the first sign he needed to recapture some common sense after his good judgment had been addled by too much sex with too many guys he couldn't name.

He sounded out the notion of this voluntary visit on Ben, who'd met his father a few times. What Gabe really wanted was for Ben to remind him of his father's nature, absolve him, and so derail the entire idea of visiting him. But, of course, Ben had to be perverse as well as obtuse. "Your dad needs you now, and you shouldn't let him down," Ben advised as they passed down the apartment house breezeway. "Your dad's a real working-class hero, Gabe."

"He's working class all right, but why is he a hero?"

"He works hard. He speaks his mind."

"And when he opens his mouth to speak, it reveals that his mind is full of shit."

"We can't all be effete lit majors."

"Why not? The world would be much improved."

Ben turned on the sound of a door opening at the end of their floor. Two women, one in her early thirties, the younger about Gabe and Ben's age, emerged from their apartment. Laughing, they stopped to exchange quick greetings with Ben, but each cast longer glances at Gabe. Mary Anne O'Malley, the older one, asked how his copy-editing job was going and teased, "I imagine you're up to date on sexual transmission, Gabe."

"That's a hell of a way for a nice Catholic girl to talk," Gabe said.

He'd known the younger woman, Jamie Anderson, since their freshman philosophy survey and had gotten acquainted with Mary Anne over the summer. "And yes, I certainly am up to date. Ask me anything about age and race indicators for clap infections in Costilla County."

Jamie laughed, still staring at Gabe brazenly. "See? Isn't he clever?"

"Maybe he's smarter than he looks," Mary Anne said with a smile, cocking her head and fingering her chin as if to appraise Gabe's overall mental and physical worth. "Nice build, too. Sturdy. You're Irish, aren't you, Gabe?"

"Half. And half Croatian. Two sad Catholic backwaters on the fringes of Europe."

"Good genes, though," Mary Anne said. "Tough. Warlike."

"Good at losing wars," Ben said. "Hey, what about me, ladies?"

Jamie laughed. "You're kinda cute, too, Ben."

"Kinda cute? I've been told I'm the best-looking Jew on campus."

"That's a small competition, but I would never dream of taking that title away from you," Mary Anne said. "Well, lovely running into you, gents."

Ben watched them vanish down the stairwell. "Damn. That was condescending, huh? I'm not used to hot women ignoring me like that."

Gabe laughed. "They're gay, Ben. Get over it."

"No way. They were inspecting you like you were a prize quarter horse. Didn't you notice the way they were flirting with you?"

"Their interest in me is biological, but not sexual."

"Why not me, then? I'd love to get it on with lesbians! That's one of my favorite fantasies."

"That's why, Ben. They don't want some straight guy getting mixed up in their private affairs."

Ben leaned on the breezeway railing and gazed down at the two women until they drove off in a battered 4x4. Ben looked wistful, the warm morning breeze stirring his wild golden hair, women out of his reach for once.

❖

The next Saturday, Gabe found himself on his parents' patio under the locust tree his Uncle Tony planted to celebrate Gabe's birth. From a shaky mesh chair, he stared into its fingery, banner-like leaves until he spotted the birdhouse he'd made for his mother in middle school, so crooked and off-kilter he had never seen a bird go near it. Gabe appreciated the locust's merciful, wavering shade but was horrified to realize the tree was almost full-grown already. Hell of a thing, having your life span measured by a tree. Would he grow old and gnarly at the same rate, his branches rotten and hollow?

Gabe had navigated the short drive home to Butcher Creek full of dread, not so much about his father's health as his father's certain irritation and denial at being asked about it. Gabe now sat dazed, momentarily alone while his mother rooted around in the kitchen for beer and chips and father worked in his garage workshop, making an angry racket with a table saw. Gabe had lost the will to—what was the right word for their relations?—*tolerate*? *confront*? *suffer*? the old man.

It was far more agreeable to sit under the locust tree and toast his mother with a can of cold beer. "Thanks, Ma. Glad you didn't have a Saturday shift today."

"I'd rather be at work, tell you the truth." She nodded toward the table saw racket out back. "Your father hasn't been much fun today."

"That's a surprise, when he's always so sunny and pleasant."

"Funny, Gabe. Sorry I forgot to laugh."

He studied his mother, struck by his failure to consider how harrowing it was for her to coexist daily with the creature Patrick Rafferty had mutated into. Gabe was usually so busy tolerating, confronting, or suffering his father, he had little bandwidth available to consider his mother's plight.

As a devout Catholic, Elena believed divorce was out of the question. But she had found a benevolent and flexible adaptation. Through an immigrant neighbor, a skilled nurse who'd become a good friend, Elena got a job as a nurse's aide in a sprawling family clinic. The neighbors carpooled together to Denver until Elena could afford a used car, which gave her the ability to volunteer for overtime. Lots of overtime. To blunt Patrick's disapproval not only of Elena's sudden independence but also that "ugly Indian wetback illegal bitch next door," as he generously characterized their naturalized Guatemalan American neighbor, his mother insisted her job was only temporary.

It had been temporary for more than a decade. Unknown to

Patrick, Elena worked side by side with Latinas and African American nurses for years and would now cruise off to her Denver attachments, including her brown and black godchildren, under the guise of going into the clinic for an evening shift.

Elena Rafferty would always be the kind of grown woman who said things like "that's so funny I forgot to laugh," the kind of high school dropout who didn't know Gilgamesh from Anna Karenina, who knew almost nothing of the world literature that composed Gabe's world. She was a slight, skinny woman who'd long lost the looks that were "never much" according to her own assessment, a woman of repeated platitudes who'd never startled anyone with an original insight. But looking at her now, her prematurely crinkled face dappled in deep summer locust light and shadow, Gabe adored her. So did almost everyone who encountered her. Elena's heart pumped an improbable innocence, an effortless integrity most bishops and cardinals would die without ever finding in their veins.

"I'm gonna buy a new patio set, did I tell ya? And you and Ben can have this table and chairs for your balcony. I know they're old and ugly, but they'll be better than nothing."

Gabe looked at the shaky mesh chairs and cracked glass-topped table with new eyes, acquisitive. "That would be great, Mom. We've been sitting out there on folding chairs."

"I know. I saw 'em when Tony and me came over. That's what gave me the idea to pass this on to you. You'll be doing me a favor, so it doesn't end up in Pat's workshop with all his other crap."

Reminded of that weird conversation the day Elena and Tony brought the furniture, their heavy hints and offhand matchmaking, Gabe wondered if he should just come out—so to speak—and tell her. He never really considered it through all the virginal years when gay sex was no more than an idle fantasy, an abstraction. During those brief months with Adam, he did sometimes flirt with coming out to his family. Then, when Adam shut him out without warning, Gabe decided there was no reason to go through the hassle. And what was he supposed to do now, recount the summer's anonymous hookups to his own sainted mother? Deep in misfiring synapses of his Catholic indoctrination, it crossed his mind again that all that sex would never wash away, sticky as dry jizz on the skin of his soul.

But now, relaxed in the beery shade, a new thought crossed Gabe's mind. Wouldn't it be kind of, well, *loving* to be honest with his mother? He chugged a deep draught for courage, cleared his throat, reminded his mother of that conversation about Jeffrey's adorable brother Marty, and informed her he was gay.

"I wondered when you'd finally tell me."

"So, it's no big surprise?"

"I always wondered, that's all. You had your nose in a book, off by yourself, when your boy cousins were watching the Broncos. Stuff like that."

"That's what marked me as gay? Literacy?"

"Huh? You know what I mean. But then, when the game was over, you'd shoot hoops with them, so I wasn't sure."

"Ma, I hate football—it's a stupid game—but I've always liked basketball. It's no big mystery and doesn't have anything to do with being gay or not."

"Well, it threw me off. Anyway, it doesn't matter to me whether you like boys or girls."

"Are you sure, Ma? Don't you want me to get married and make grandbabies?"

"Have you ever heard me say that?"

As a matter of fact, Gabe never had. Patrick and Elena weren't exactly advertisements for heterosexual fecundity—they'd married in their mid-thirties, the first time for both of them. They'd waited three more years to have Gabe, then called it quits on baby-making.

"I got my godchildren," Elena declared, "that's enough for me. But you know, one thing I worry about. Older men, they'll take advantage of you. I know what men can be like."

Gabe suppressed a smile, recalling an older guy he'd taken advantage of a few nights ago. "It's not like that, Ma. Seems like it's usually more equal between guys."

"Tell me something, while we're on the subject. Another thing I wonder about. Was it something I did? To make you gay?"

"It's not like that either, Ma. Come on. It's more like being born with blue eyes instead of brown ones."

Elena blinked her dark brown eyes. "Like you got Pat's." She and Gabe sat in silence for a while, listening to the snarl of Patrick's table saw. "You ought to go check on your father, huh? It might put him in a better mood."

"To see me? Since when?"

"Since you were born. He's so proud you graduated college. With honors!"

"Be nice if he told me."

"That's not his way." Elena sighed and began to deadhead the spent geranium blossoms in one of the plastic pots near her chair.

Gabe finished his beer, hoping it would lubricate his way down the concrete path to his father's workshop. He passed from Elena's side yard garden, under her vainglorious old rose on a trellis, into the desolation of Patrick's domain, the weedy, thirsty remnant of the lawn and the metal mini-warehouse-garage that had obliterated more than half of the backyard.

What his father called his workshop was a monument to his failed dream. He'd once hoped to break free of the refinery and freelance as a handyman-carpenter while custom designing wood furniture. Despite his skills, his side business never took off, thanks to his personality and lack of social connections to potential clients. He'd gone into considerable debt to buy and equip the steel monstrosity, debt that kept him trapped in a Butcher Creek that he no longer recognized on a cul-de-sac that, in his own words, "might as well be fuckin' Mexico."

Hesitating outside the open doorway, Gabe studied the fragment of horizon visible from their lot, a squeezed vista of the alley and beyond, the marshy flatland of holding ponds and caking mud that led to a line of far cottonwoods lining the South Platte River. Butcher Creek itself was an intermittent toxic seep that trickled toward the river. It ran reddish after a rainfall, absorbing the bottomland's red clay, looking like coursing blood—which must have inspired some trapper or pioneer to grant its charming name.

The subdivision occupied a floodplain dotted with stagnant oxbow ponds left behind when the river's spring runoff seeped over the banks, then got marooned by late summer. Postwar developers built small blond-brick boxes and lured white, working-class Denverites out to this discount promise of suburbia, wedged between the ponds to the west, a gigantic oil refinery to the south, and Commerce City to the east. When Patrick got a job on the refinery's maintenance crew, he mortgaged one of these now-shabby boxes and lived here all his married life. He loved to repeat how, when he first moved to Butcher Creek, "I had I-70 between me and every nigger in Denver, and I-76 between me and every spic in Brighton."

But a funny thing happened: Patrick's white pond evaporated. More and more whites jumped to bigger, newer stucco boxes in more distant suburbs as more and more Latin families moved to Butcher Creek. Once his refuge from Denver's diversifying hordes, the subdivision had become a sore point of resentment for Patrick. Many of these Latin *paterfamiliases*, whether from Colorado families who'd arrived in the New World centuries before the Rafferty clan or more recent arrivals, ironically could have made great pals for Patrick. A few could be as bigoted and coarse as he was, but Patrick never bothered to discover his new neighbors.

Gabe peered into the workshop, his sun-wracked eyes adjusting to the inner darkness. The snarling saw was stilled now as Patrick measured two identical wooden slabs. Unlike Gabe, his father was a compact man, but he had bequeathed his son his thick brown hair—graying now—always helter-skelter in maddening waves, and his extra-long arms, which now reached around one slab to snap his measuring tape in place. "Hey, Dad. You building furniture again?"

"Kinda."

That would be a good sign. If he was taking up the long-abandoned craft again, he must be feeling better. "What is it gonna be? A chest of drawers? A sideboard?"

"What the hell's a sideboard?"

"Never mind. So, you feeling okay?"

"Why wouldn't I? What did your mother tell you?" For the first time, he looked up from his crouching pose around the slab to look at Gabe. "That woman sure has a mouth on her."

"She's just worried. About your stomach pains."

"They come and go. It's probably her cooking."

Gabe, reluctant to move from the doorway, laughed without wanting to. Elena was famous in the extended family for her home-cooked Croatian and Italian fare, recipes inherited from her grandparents, whose village in ex-Yugoslavia was spiced by nearby Trieste. "Yeah. Like getting a stomachache when we eat too much of it."

"It's too damn rich. I'd be happy with meatloaf and boiled potatoes."

"Nice problem to have, though."

"You'll know, when you're stupid enough to get married, just make sure she can cook regular American food."

"I forget, what is American food?"

"I just told ya. Meatloaf and boiled potatoes."

Gabe sidled inside and leaned against a cluttered workbench placed under the only natural light in the entire complex, a tiny window that looked back to Elena's side yard. Had Patrick, cutting lumber, been glancing at Gabe and his mother as they chatted under the locust, missing out on the big coming out? Of course he stayed out of it. Extended conversation was for women and faggots. And slick operators like Uncle Tony.

Gabe wondered if he should take this rare, semi-agreeable moment to get it over with, just blurt out that he was gay and let the wood chips fall where they may. But why was he rushing headlong into this? He really had no pressing need to let the old man know. He didn't exactly have a long-term partner—not even a boyfriend, not even a casual new interest. Not even a fuck buddy, just a continuous undressed parade of guys he expected he'd never see again.

Maybe Patrick could actually relate, maybe he'd had his own serial un-intimate intimacy with female partners when he was stationed at Fort Carson in his early twenties. If Gabe did decide to be honest now and let his father know there would never be any "she" who would cook him meatloaf, he'd never have to go through it again no matter how bad Patrick took it.

Patrick seemed to be circling the same topic. "So, a couple days ago," Patrick said, penciling a measurement on a slab, "I was lying down on the couch while Tony and your mother were blabbing away like usual. I wasn't feeling so great, not quite asleep. They must've thought I was in my death throes or something, but I was listening. I got the idea they were thinking of fixing you up with some girl. But…I wasn't sure. It didn't make sense. They kept bringing up the little brother of somebody."

"Yeah. They mentioned him to me. Marty Montgomery."

"That's what I'm saying. If you're a queer, I don't want to know about it."

"I guess there's nothing for me to say, then."

"Nice-looking kid like you, smart, tall, built like a brick shithouse—I always wondered, where the hell are all the girls?"

"I know why. But guess I can't tell you, huh?"

"Better not, huh? Faggot sex makes me want to puke my guts out."

"Straight people do most of the same things, with some of the same orifices."

"I didn't set out to raise no fag, sonny-boy."

"What a drag for you, daddy-o! Apparently you raised the faggiest fag in all of Butcher Creek."

"So, do me a favor and keep whatever you do with *orifices* to yourself."

"With pleasure, sir. Well, sure been nice talking with ya." Gabe shoved off from the workbench, wondering why he'd even bothered. The old bastard had never given a damn about him, anyway. Everywhere he looked, he avoided touching some scheme-in-progress with tools he could barely name—was it a C-Clamp or a U-Clamp? A swivel base or a screw handle? *It's no wonder I turned out to be a typical, unskilled fairy with you for a father, you fucking self-centered son of a bitch.* Gabe swallowed the words, as usual, but not the resentment. Unlike his father, Gabe couldn't bevel trim boards or tie cool knots, because Patrick didn't "have time." Despite Patrick's craze for tools, Gabe had to learn about them in seventh-grade wood shop, when he produced that birdhouse scorned by all but his mother.

He'd learned everything essential for being a Coloradan from Uncle Tony and his son Karlo: hiking and mountain biking in the backcountry, backpacking, skiing, climbing 13'ers and 14'ers—as well as inheriting Karlo's discarded equipment. So even that rugged Shangri-La fifty minutes from this putrid cul-de-sac, the Rocky Mountain wilds he'd learned to love, had created a wedge between son and father rather than a shared passion. Patrick scorned everything more sublime than Butcher Creek as a "tourist trap."

Gabe took one last, appraising look at his father, still crouched around the two wood slabs. Now he saw the larger, rectangular section already cut, neat, behind them. "Glad you're feeling better, Dad. I'll see you later, okay?"

"Wait. How do you like the wood grain?"

In the doorway, anxious to leave, Gabe shrugged at the odd question. “Okay, I guess. I’m not exactly an expert.”

“What about the height?” He stood, finally, holding the twin slabs against his thighs. “’Bout right?”

“Seems like it, but I don’t really get what it’s gonna be.”

“Well, your mother told me you were using a card table.” Patrick scowled at Gabe, then smiled. “It’s a desk. For you, stupid!”

Chapter Four

The Great Divide

This is what Gabe had been missing all summer so far, this sensation of standing on a rocky crest at 11,000 feet, staring down an inert marmot on a rock heap and staring up at jagged peaks still ridged with snow at the end of July. Little white clouds puffed over the Divide. The map in his head told him he stood in the geographic center of Rocky Mountain National Park, perched on a boulder overlooking Hallett Peak. He hadn't done the Flattop Trail since Tony took Gabe along with Karlo, when they'd both just started ninth grade, to complete the whole exhausting, exhilarating loop.

Now Gabe remembered having this exact sensation back then, how the cool, clean, blue sky and the dizzy heights jarred him into realizing that no matter how tiresome it might be to trudge uphill in Karlo's ill-fitting hiking boots, it was more than worth it to experience this, to know the mountains could erase the way he felt down in Butcher Creek, sweltering in the smog and inhaling the refinery's stench. They didn't call it the Great Divide for nothing.

Today, Gabe was hiking again with Karlo along with his best friend, Jeffrey, from a prosperous Castle Pines family whose fortune came from financial services—Tony said it had just made a list of the fifty most prominent black-owned businesses in North America—and Jeffrey's much-discussed younger brother, Marty. The three were lingering over lunch just down the trail while Gabe went ahead the short distance to soak in the overlook. He always wanted to gaze at the serrated summits longer than anyone else, so he took some time alone.

But not for long. Marty appeared beside him and soaked in the summits with obvious yearning. After a while, he said, "I never thought I'd be so glad to be back in Colorado."

"Did you get a chance to hike in the Alps while you were in Italy?"

"No, but I skied them. Cortina. It's fine there, but the Rockies are in my blood. My family spends a lot of the winter on the slopes. We grew up on skis, practically."

"Yeah, I know. Remember that time, years ago, when I stayed at your condo in Vail? That weekend with Karlo and Tony?"

"Kinda, but all those ski weekends blur. But I do remember *you*!"

"Jeffrey and I were freshmen. You were skiing with your middle school friends. But you guys were already doing expert slopes. I was off by myself, trying to survive my first intermediate runs."

"I didn't recognize you at first, Gabe, when you and Karlo pulled up this morning. You got so much taller."

"I wouldn't have recognized you, either." Marty did have the same angelic face but without the baby fat. His athletic body was sleek as a jaguar's. "You're not a little kid anymore."

Marty smiled. "No. A grown man of nineteen. Almost twenty. Not far behind you."

He looked even younger, with his hair cut short and his long-lashed brown oval eyes. Heavy-lidded, they had a sleepy, serene quality that contradicted his alert demeanor, his game readiness for whatever might wait around the next bend.

He studied Marty's eyes for a sign of attraction. Now, with the peaks crowding close overhead and clouds pushing eastward over the summits as pure as benediction smoke, Gabe craved to sample Marty's lips. Marty kept staring back until he broke into a wide smile. The silence between them wasn't awkward. It was inviting, so Gabe bent closer.

"Man, what a view!" It was Karlo, with Jeffery close behind. "But we gotta hustle, boys, don't you think? Those clouds are starting to mass up for the rainstorm sure to form by late afternoon. And we've still got miles ahead of us."

❖

They stayed that Saturday night at Tony's summer home on Fall River a few miles above Estes Park. Fringed by firs, the deck overlooked chewy, spewing rapids. Leaning against the railing, Gabe savored the rush of cascading water. He soaked up its coolness as if he could save it up, then spend it against Denver's assault of heat when they got back Sunday evening. The other guys had crashed after a downpour forced them to trudge the last miles wet and chilled through mud and over slick rocks.

Gabe was bewildered. After Adam shut him out without warning, he intended to guard his heart against any future temptations. Eventually, he figured, he would become completely heartless, immune to more wounds. But the afternoon with Marty had undermined his plan. Instead of clutching shut, his heart's valves seemed to open up. Instead of lust as the usual main attraction, he felt tenderness. In both its meanings—a swift fondness for Marty as well as an abiding ache, as if from an inflammation.

"I was sent here on a mission," Marty said, coming through the open glass door. "Karlo gave me orders to tell you to get ready for dinner in town."

"Hey, I'm the only one who didn't take to my fainting couch after the hike. I've been ready."

"Well, I'm not." Marty was still wrapped in a heavy guest bathrobe, his hair still wet. "I still have to get dressed." Instead of going back in, though, he joined Gabe at the railing. He stared at the river, smiling. "I just can't get over this. After my semester abroad, it's like I keep seeing Colorado with new eyes. The Rockies just feel so wild, like you could still step where nobody has ever set foot before. Italy's beautiful, but it's so tamed. It's been trampled over for thousands of years."

"I've got to admit something, Marty. When you mentioned Cortina, I remembered it from the library maps I used to pore over when I was a kid." It felt important to get it out there quick, who he really was. Nobody—a working-class, untraveled bumpkin from nowhere. "I loved to study the world's places, but I've never really been anywhere."

"Cortina's even more self-satisfied than Vail, and the runs aren't nearly as extensive. They held the Olympics there in the fifties, and they still brag about it."

"Well, Utah is the most exotic place I've ever seen."

"I love Utah! Given the choice, I'd go on a hike in the Canyonlands instead of the Italian Alps."

"And I'd give anything to go to Europe, but I'm working for a pittance as a copy editor this summer. Maybe after grad school, if I ever have any money."

Marty wanted to hear about his plans. Gabe had applied to the International Relations master's program at the university, and to his surprise, they found his undergraduate studies in world literature plus his courses in philosophy and political science actually made him a viable candidate. "I figure international studies will be a good bookend to my world lit major. A little more practical, maybe, a little more employable? But for now, I can only afford one course."

Marty tightened his robe against the river breeze. "So, maybe I'll see you around campus?"

Gabe gripped the deck railing to guard against an urge to reach over and loosen Marty's robe. He hoped he not only saw him around campus but saw a lot more of that lush territory under his robe. Lust now threatened to crowd out tenderness.

"It's funny, Gabe. Since Karlo's your close cousin, and he and Jeffrey are best friends, I wonder why I didn't see more of you the whole time I was growing up."

"I guess it's the two-year age difference, huh? It's such a big deal when we're younger. When I'd go with Karlo and Jeffery on adventures, we'd usually head out from Uncle Tony's place in Cherry Hills. Never at my family's place. Butcher Creek is so far from everything. Just northwest of hell."

"Well, I'd love to see Butcher Creek some time. I've never been to that corner of the metro."

"It ain't exactly Venice. Nobody goes there unless they're doomed to live there." Gabe watched the rapids, satisfied that what he'd told Marty was at least partly true, but feeling the old twinge of guilt over his lie of omission.

At twelve, Gabe once escaped the refinery's stench for a long stretch, a Fourth of July vacation with Tony's family, along with Jeffrey, here at Tony's Fall River "cabin." When the clan delivered Gabe back home, Jeffrey got out of the car to help Gabe with his gear. He asked him if Butcher Creek always "smelled like dead cats."

After days along the pine-scented river, the reek overpowered Gabe, too, and he was sorry to see his parents didn't notice it at all. He looked at his father, who seemed to be ignoring his arrival while he sealed a crack in the driveway. "You're right," Gabe said with dawning astonishment. "It does smell like old carcasses."

"Inside a pile of burning inner tubes!" Jeffrey scrunched his nose while he carried Gabe's pack to the front porch. "P.U.!"

As soon as Jeffrey returned to Tony's van, Patrick rose from the cracked concrete to confront Gabe about his injury to civic pride. "So, you've been out in the boonies with that nigger."

Meaning Jeffrey. After their slaphappy weekend with Karlo's family, the hikes, rock climbs, and rope swings, Gabe had forgotten Jeffrey was black. If he'd remembered, he could've made sure he didn't come near the house.

"But, Dad, Jeffrey's not—"

"Not a nigger? Coulda fooled me. You let that little nigger contaminate our property, then agree with him that we stink?"

"Not us. The refinery. And the rendering plants."

"Are you gonna take that back?"

"Come on, Dad!" From their standoff in the driveway, Gabe heard a stumble nearby. Jeffrey, who'd hustled back from Tony's idling minivan to hand Gabe his left-behind cap, stood staring at Patrick, then ran back to the minivan without glancing back.

"He heard you say that!" Gabe watched Tony drive away, out of sight around the corner. Then he faced his father. "No. I'm not taking it back. It's true. It stinks here."

"It does, huh? I guess you just took your last trip to Tony's cabin, nigger lover."

"Sweet Jesus, I love the air up here!" the flesh and blood, age twenty-two Jeffrey declared now, ten years later. "It might be thin, but it smells so pure." He emerged on the deck wet-haired as Marty, but fully dressed for dinner in Estes Park style—shorts, boots, and a hoodie. "That was a hell of a hike, boys, huh? But I thought I was gonna die the last two miles."

"Was nothin' to me, big brother," Marty said. "A walk in the park."

"Well, walk in there and get your smart ass dressed, little one. I'm starving!"

After Marty went inside, Jeffrey joined Gabe at the railing. "So, I can see what's happening, all right? Just know Marty's one volatile little cat. Be careful, Gabe."

❖

Gabe tried to be careful, he really did. But he didn't fixate on Marty's volatility so much as his purity. He wasn't used to a gay guy who seemed so ethereal, so removed from the fleshy suck-and-fuck of the whole sticky scene. Marty could pull up an image from a Botticelli painting and discuss its place in Botticelli's oeuvre as well as its significance to Renaissance art, not like an art snob but in the excited way another guy might discuss the prospects of any given Colorado Rockies outfielder. All of it was a huge turn-on just when atheist, existential, ex-Catholic Gabe had started to imagine himself a monk, chaste on his simple single bed. He yearned to clean up his act, learn the piety of Saint Francis, leave his summer of anonymous sex behind, and get closer to Martin Montgomery.

Gabe fantasized he would leave the hookups behind. The virgin turned slut would turn, obligingly, into the straight-arrow steady. His daydreams were suddenly G-rated—he and Marty would ride bikes to Washington Park, lying side by side beside Lake Grasmere and finding lambs, Miss Piggys, and Jesus-on-a-tortilla roiling in the puffy clouds. Even the contrails would spell wonder across the blue yonder, writing the unexpected haiku of a long, lush, forgiving season.

By August, he and Marty actually went out, catching Film Center stuff with subtitles, zero background music, howling arguments in Romanian or tense-but-suppressed confrontations in Danish. He also fell for Marty's family, stunned as he was that Marty invited him, the only non-relative, to a quiet family celebration of his twentieth birthday in their Castle Pines castle. Ever the Butcher Creek guttersnipe, Gabe was helplessly impressed with the discreet, easy graciousness of the affluent and well educated.

Copying how Marty or Jeffrey wielded an unfamiliar fish fork or fruit spoon, Gabe loved how the Montgomery family joshing was gentle. Around their table, even strong opinions were polite. The shy and restrained were coaxed to participate with respect and humor. Most astonishing, Marty's father didn't start a topic to showcase his grievances or greatness, but to glean responses from every mind around the table, young, old, black, white, whether new friend ("There is no such thing as a *stranger*") or feeble-minded young'un ("Cuz, we heard you survived your sophomore year at East High. Tell us how you mastered those biology exams!").

Could this ever be a perfect match? Marty had glided in Benzes through a plush, cushioned childhood while little Gabe once went airborne out the rusted-out passenger door of Patrick's belching, extinct Econoline. Marty's father's way of handling the paucity of Gabe's experience of the finer things was as plush and cushioned as those luxury seats. Offered wine, Gabe decided he wasn't going to pretend he knew his way around this refined table. He admitted he was more of a beer guy, and not much of a connoisseur of brews, either. "Whatever's cheapest at the supermarket," he said, smiling, trying to joke. "My mom always has wine with dinner, but I'm afraid the bottle usually has a kangaroo on it—which is a splurge. It usually comes out of a box."

Marty's father poured a half goblet of deep red wine from a carafe and passed it to Gabe. "This is a nice Malbec that goes well with the roast. Try a taste, son."

Gabe had never tasted wine so smooth, so rich, so lacking in the aftertaste of turpentine. But he was more blown away that such an accomplished man would call him *son.*

Anxious as he was to consummate his friendship with Marty, Gabe wanted just as much to hold back. Maybe actually continue *dating*, whatever that was. Maybe go see another Bulgarian tragedy at the Film Center on a Saturday night, crossing South High to join Marty, then escort him back afterward, with no more than a chaste kiss at the steps of his residence hall.

The Saturday after Labor Day, though, Gabe woke up aroused, naked and alone on his futon in his room. His bare bedchamber could easily stage his monk's-cell fantasy, but what was he going to do about this morning hard-on? What would Saint Francis do, pretend he didn't have a dick? Or share it, lovingly, with some cute friar down the hall?

He imagined kissing Marty's lips, which would taste exactly like that Malbec, while slowly unbuttoning his shirt, revealing that luscious flesh inch by inch. He was about to open the buttons all the way south, past his navel, and work on Marty's belt buckle when a high-pitched laugh pierced his open sliding door. It was Candy, just outside on the balcony, teasing Ben. "I can just see you, in one of those visors with a transparent bill, under a green banker's lamp, lost in somebody else's taxes. What a waste!"

"Keep it down, baby," Ben said, "Gabe's still trying to sleep. Plus, it's still too early to torment me."

What the hell time was it? The wind-up alarm on the floor said it was well after ten. No wonder it was already so warm, despite the open door, the September sun pounding on the glass. Gabe gave up on sleepy autoerotic temptation and climbed into the same tank top and boxers he'd worn for beers with Ben and Candy and Jamie and Mary Anne the night before. He fixed an instant coffee and slipped onto the balcony, ready to enjoy the sunlight from one of the folding chairs, since Elena had not yet surrendered her old patio furniture.

"Well, well! You finally dragged your slug-a-butt out of bed," Candy said, leaning against the rail. She wore one of Ben's extra-large T-shirts, which at least covered her crotch. "Thank God you're somewhat decent, since there's a lady present."

"Where?" Gabe asked. "I just see the same old nasty chick who's sleeping with my roommate."

"Jealous? Just 'cause you slept the whole night alone in your own bed? For once."

"I worked all week poring over rates of syphilis among young adults in Mesa County, and I'm ready to try celibacy."

"We'll see how long that lasts," Ben said.

"You've been a very bad boy," Candy added, "this whole summer."

"I've also been very bad at keeping my intimate affairs secret from you gossips." He thought again of Marty, who'd been to some family gathering the night before and stayed the night in Castle Pines. Gabe wondered what sublime blend from tropical climes filled Marty's coffee cup this morning. It sure wasn't this granulated instant mud.

He hadn't told anyone about Marty yet. Was there really anything to tell? He'd been so tempted last night, on his third or fourth beer, to confess his crush to his friends, all of them hooked up in monogamous liaisons. But fighting back that temptation had its own Franciscan satisfaction. Plus, if nothing came of this, he'd at least saved himself from more embarrassment and shame, a first for this whole degenerate season.

"Candy's been giving me shit about my accounting classes," Ben said. He'd been accepted into the graduate program, leading to a CPA certification, on the strength of his near-perfect math score on the GRE. "We can't all be daddy's girl forever, though."

"Good chance I won't be. My new stepmother is pressuring Daddy to cut off my allowance. She thinks I'm an eternal undergraduate."

"And there's not a grain of truth in that?" Ben asked.

"There's a whole boulder of truth to it, I admit. But I'm serious now. I'm going to finish this literature degree, I swear. I already love my new classes. But, Ben, are you really loving yours? All those dreary numbers?"

"I love 'em. Besides, it keeps my father off my back."

"That's just it, darling. You can't be daddy's boy forever, right? What right does he have to pressure you? They're your studies. It's your life!"

"But it's his money. He footed the bill for my BA, even though he didn't like my major. He's a man's man, he doesn't get literature, and he sure doesn't get how I'm supposed to make a living at it. And he has a point."

"So you're gonna be a *tax accountant*?" Candy asked it with the same distaste she'd use for *sewer inspector*. "I'm going to miss all our wonderful midnight bullshit sessions about Voltaire and Thomas Mann!"

Gabe smiled, imagining these two sex fiends interrupting their raucous midnight humping to compare *Candide* with *Death in Venice*.

"I'm not going to stop enjoying literature, for God's sake!" Ben said. "I'm just going to be able to savor it without starving. And dealing with my dad's guilt trips and disapproval for the rest of my life."

Captivated by their debate, Gabe realized that not having educated, successful parents actually had one bright side. Dropouts themselves, Elena and Patrick never interfered in his choices after he finished high school. Since they weren't paying any of his bills and believed a college degree was a magic ticket to comfortable affluence, regardless of major, they were so wowed by his scholarship, then his magna cum laude degree, they never hounded him about his future. God bless the working class.

His phone rang. A voice, no less, from comfortable affluence itself—Marty, who was waving up from the opposite sidewalk on South High. He wanted to know if he could come over.

Gabe waved him up, overcome with exhilaration. Or was it validation? Maybe this was gonna be a thing, this beautiful guy just stopping by on any given Saturday.

Then he was overcome with trepidation. Marty was already hurrying up the breezeway stairs, and Gabe had no time to tame his thick, rowdy, bedhead mane, no time to change out of his wrinkled rags, no time to straighten up the beer can, corn chip chaos of the living room, untouched since last night's little party. Here Marty was, smiling, hugging Gabe hello, and the only thought Gabe could form was a faint hope he didn't smell too bad.

Marty didn't—a subtle, delicious scent, something distinctly unavailable at Safeway. He was perfect in a pressed, white short-sleeved shirt arrayed with gold peace signs, khaki shorts, and those ergonomic sandals posh people wore. Even though he held a backpack overflowing with books, he carried even more, big art history volumes. "I was just at the library, getting lost in Italian art. Then I saw a pic of Michelangelo's *David*, and I thought of you."

"Boy, are you gonna be disappointed," Gabe said, "should you ever see me naked."

"You're not far from it, now." Marty stepped back, smiling, to take in the galoot in boxers before him. "And I'm not disappointed."

"Good, because this is the real me. A barefoot bum who lives in a crash pad." Gabe gestured around. "Welcome. We're having instant coffee on the balcony. Can I make you some?"

"Sounds great." Marty noticed the Vermeer print Gabe had taped up over the alley-discard couch. "I love that one. It deserves a frame."

A *frame*! Like he could ever afford such sumptuous luxury. While the water boiled, Gabe led Marty out to the balcony to make introductions, praying Ben and Candy would behave. They didn't, but Marty was unfazed, returning Candy's over-eager hug with equanimity. "Forgive my attire," she said, pulling the T-shirt farther down her thighs. "But I swear, I'm wearing panties, so no worries, right?"

"None at all," Marty said. "Your legs are gorgeous."

"Oh, Gabe! No wonder you weren't afraid to reveal Marty to us," Candy said, "even in daylight. He's beautiful."

"Not like all the others," Ben said.

Marty laughed but Gabe cringed, grateful to escape inside when the teapot whistled.

He brought out one of the dinette chairs with Marty's coffee, since the other folding chair was broken. Ben sat cross-legged on the floor, Candy kicked her legs like a Rockette from the railing, and Gabe sank in the other chair, despairing of the scene, the disarray of this poverty, with Marty sitting gamely on the kitchen chair, holding the coffee cup with nowhere to put it down. *Some people are denied a place at the table*, he thought, *while others don't even have a table.*

The three chatted about their first week of classes, but Gabe couldn't claim any academic goals except a single night class at the International School. That was all he could afford. Without financial aid, a master's was out of reach for now. So, he was not even a real grad student, just a lowly copy editor, a mere long-term temporary contractor. Just another oxymoronic nobody. He felt the stain of his background—its cheapness, crudeness, ignorance, and prejudice—darkening this sunny moment. Thinking back to that moment his father had called Jeffrey a nigger, Gabe felt flooded with shame over the hurt and anguish it must have caused him. Jeffrey had never mentioned the insult, but he also never again visited Butcher Creek.

Gabe vowed never to expose Marty to that. He had the feeling that despite Marty's equanimity and his casual cool, he had little experience of real American ugliness. He'd been spared the racist shit Patrick smeared at every opportunity.

"We were just discussing the most important topic in creation," Candy told Marty. "Whether to live a life of getting and spending or to devote yourself to the finer things."

"Yeah, in Candy's case," Ben said, "the finer things are sex, hair dye, and spending her father's money on booze and drugs."

"But I'm a changed woman, Marty. An acolyte of the world's finest literature."

"Maybe it's the getting and spending that gets us to the finer things," Marty said.

"Yes," Candy said, looking sideways at Ben. "As long as the get-and-spend doesn't end up being the end-all."

"I'd never have been able to study in Italy or work on an art history degree if my dad hadn't built a network of financial services in African American neighborhoods. He got his fingers dirty with cash so I could spend it gazing at Raphael's angels."

"You just sit there, keeping still, angel," Candy told Marty, "so I can keep gazing at you."

Chapter Five

Whatever Weird Scene Awaits

"I'm reconciled to my faith," Mary Ann said, snapping shut the sliding door to her balcony against a gust of cold wind. "Why should I worry about what a few rigid goons think?"

"Because there are lots and lots of rigid goons, and if you dared to be open about your relationship with Jamie, they'd ax you as an administrator at your very Catholic charity." On the sofa, Gabe looked out to the gathering clouds. "Then the church would excommunicate you. Beware. Catholics have no charity."

"Jesus, Gabe, I'm talking the majesty of God as worshipped in a universal religion, not ecclesiastical idiocy. Sure they could ruin me, but no matter how much hell they raise, a few dogmatic males can't ruin the eternal faith."

"Colorado's archbishop is doing his best to ruin it, though. Just another right-wing extremist in vestments. Ecclesiastical drag. He's anti-female, anti-choice, and anti-gay. How can you stay loyal to a church that despises you?"

"Because the archbishop is just another little man occupying a seat in a corrupt bureaucracy for a passing moment in the church's long story."

Mary Ann was one of the few Catholics Gabe knew who was actually interested in ecclesiastical non-idiocy, which was why he spent more and more time enjoying her company. With a probing interest in theology and world religions, she approached topics of faith with a searching, open fascination, as if every passing idea about God—or not-God—was crucial to investigate anew in friendly debates. "Meanwhile,

I do worry about your complete lack of faith, Gabe. It seems to me your existential atheism is becoming more hard core."

Gabe shrugged. "Faithlessness is my faith. Been that way since ninth grade."

"I'm afraid you're going to degenerate into nihilism."

"We live for a *passing moment*, then we die. That ain't nihilism, that's just the life of any mammal. Or insect. Imagine if ants or earwigs believed they'd live in heaven with God after their little existence was over."

"Maybe they do. It's not that humans are so exalted, Gabe. It could be the opposite. Maybe we're no more in God's eyes than a bug, or a germ. How can we comprehend God's vastness?"

Gabe didn't have an answer for that. He hadn't meant to get into religious philosophy—again—with Mary Ann, but he enjoyed the challenge of probing her steadfast devotion. He'd actually stopped by Mary Ann and Jamie's apartment on Saturday afternoon to collect the sleeping bag they'd borrowed for a July camping trip. Gabe hoped to use it as blanket on the first cold night of the season. Caught unprepared, he didn't yet have any warm bedding. Gray skies massed over the mountain horizon, quickening the end of the already quick-ending October afternoon. The first cold winds had inspired Jamie to make hot chocolate and encourage Gabe to stay for a visit.

The childish drink made Gabe feel virtuous and innocent, though he had an unvirtuous plan to keep warm when night fell. Marty was coming over late to watch *Saturday Night Live*, and Gabe was finally going to invite him to stay over on the futon. All these weeks of celibate dating had proven their point and worn out their purpose, and it was past time to exchange chastity for carnality. "I don't know how you can overlook the church's hypocrisy, Mary Ann," he said, "and all its negativity toward sex. Especially gay sex."

"I'm not overlooking it, I'm dismissing it as the narrow work of males obsessed with celibacy and terrified of the power of female sexuality outside of procreation. It's all the work of men, Gabe, not God."

"Yeah, God has got to be one sexy son of a bitch," Jamie said, sipping her hot chocolate and snuggling beside Mary Anne. "I mean, look at his creation. Species-wide, it's sticky with attraction and reproduction."

"Speaking of which, did we tell you we've decided to have a child?" Mary Ann asked, her arm around Jamie's shoulders. "We've been saving up. Maybe we'll even get a real house."

"With a real yard," Jamie said. "And a real second bedroom for the baby."

"In vitro? Turkey baster?"

"Don't be gross, Gabe," Jamie said. "We're thinking of doing it the old-fashioned way, with a man."

"Who's gonna be the biological mom?"

"That would be Miss Jamie here," Mary Ann said, laughing. "I don't know if I could deal with all that icky heterosexual wrestling."

"From what I understand, straights don't exactly wrestle," Gabe said. "I know this much. They get naked, the man lies on top of the lady, and a baby ensues."

"Yes, exactly!" Jamie said. "I actually tried it a couple times back in my former life. I had a few boyfriends before Mary Ann ruined me."

"Ruined or not, it's got to be Jamie," Mary Ann said. "I'm past thirty, so my eggs are getting quite elderly."

Jamie, though, was only twenty-three. Boyish, but not butch. She kept her hair cut short but dressed up in skirts and girly blouses for her work. Jamie had been working as a copy editor, too, for *Planet Quarterly*, a journal affiliated with both the university's literature department and its much more prestigious International School. Ben said Jamie was alluring, and Gabe had to admit she attracted him, too, more than most girls, especially on weekends when she wore jeans and T-shirts and seemed even more boyish. "Speaking of sex," Jamie said, "how are things going with your new interest?"

"Beautifully. But no sex to speak of, not yet."

"Aww! That's cute, Gabe. It must be true love. Have you brought him home to meet the folks yet?"

"Not my dad. If you'd met him, you wouldn't have to ask. Trouble is, Marty keeps asking. I've met his father, and now he wants to meet mine." Gabe told the story of Patrick's ancient insult to Marty's brother, Jeffrey. "I sometimes wonder if Jeffrey told him about that, and Marty's just taunting me, testing the depth of our connection."

"If Marty really knows what happened to his brother, he wouldn't want to experience that kind of ugliness," Mary Ann said. "No black person would."

"That's the problem. Marty isn't your average black guy. He's been sheltered, kept innocent."

"I doubt that, too. He can't have come of age in our society without knowing how racist we are."

"I don't know, Mary Ann. He might be an exception. It's like he's some kind of emissary from a better world than ours. I don't want to spoil that, and my father will. In ten minutes, he'd demolish Marty's beautiful delusions."

"Is it your role to safeguard his delusions, then?"

Gabe was taken aback by Mary Ann's question. It sounded incisive but didn't seem fair to put that way. "Is it my role to expose him to cruelty?"

❖

It snowed that night, a badly kept October surprise. Gabe set a candle on the windowsill, and it, plus the red ember of the joint he passed to Marty, were the only glimmers in his dark room. The snowfall sent hurried, projected shadows of snowflakes plummeting against the far wall, their rhythm as random as the jazz on shuffle play. After enduring the last lame *SNL* skit on Ben's TV, they'd gotten this far—side by side on Gabe's futon, stripped down to their boxers and snug under the opened-out sleeping bag.

Marty had surprised him, bringing the joint. "Jeffrey passed it to me just for this occasion. He says it's the finest Denver greenhouse weed."

"I'm beginning to feel that weedy delirium already." Gabe pulled back the sleeping bag to study Marty's compact chest, his flat, taut stomach, all that golden skin in candle shine. They kissed between tokes, while Gabe caressed that chest, then that stomach, then moved downward to pull down his boxers.

They proceeded to lovemaking with stoned effortlessness, a huge relief to Gabe. Another surprise, Marty was unhesitating, even aggressive—an insistent operator, versatile and experienced—far from the bashful innocent of Gabe's many fantasies. He pulled off Gabe's shorts in a single swoop, tossing them across the room.

Pulling Marty's legs around his hips to start with classic face-to-face humping, Gabe shoved in rhythm with Marty's moans of pleasure.

Marty pulled Gabe into a long kiss, then pushed him off and over. Marty climbed on top, shuffled between Gabe's legs, and grabbed his hips for a good old-fashioned assault from behind. Gabe's face was mashed into the pillow, muffling his laughter until Marty's hard-core backdoor pounding reduced Gabe to yelps and howls.

These easily exchanged localities of sex seemed zoned only for them, first jokey, then wild. Despite Gabe's months of promiscuity, he'd never spent all night in revitalizing sex like this, topping and bottoming each other over and over as if that ganja was laced with carnal magic. They'd sleep, then reach for each other to screw each other awake. Then, spent and helpless with laughter, they'd fall asleep again.

Under a clearing sky near dawn, with a couple inches of snow on the window ledge, drowsy, entangled, they began to form their groans and grunts into actual words.

"I wonder," Gabe said, scanning his bare room, "if you feel like you're slumming when you come over to my place."

"You've seen my dorm room. Most prison cells are more lavish."

It was true. Just across South High, Marty's residence hall was an ordinary mid-century brick rectangle where single rooms were dark, small, and spare, a narrow bed and built-in desk between bare concrete walls, as if confinement would lure residents into studying.

"That goes with student life," Gabe said. "But I'm supposedly an adult, you know, out here in the real world."

"The real world that's across the street from campus? You and Ben and Candy are still hugging close to the student life. Hell, you *are* students. Still."

"Yeah, but I'm not really a real student anymore. I can barely afford my one graduate class. How long can I go on as a lowly contract worker for the health foundation? The hours suck, the pay's terrible, and there's no future." Gabe swept his arm to indicate the room's empty walls, the clothes stored in plastic bins, the card table impersonating a desk. "I'm not getting anywhere financially, as I'm sure you've noticed."

"You're the one hung up on this. Have I ever said one word about your financial state or your background?"

"You don't need to. That's the privilege of privilege. You get to be all serene and cool and content. Working-class knuckleheads struggle to catch one fleeting moment of self-possession like yours."

"Truth is, your working-class Irish, scholarship boy vibe is a total turn-on."

"So, you *are* slumming." Gabe smiled. "And I'm just another Mick with a dick."

"Not unless I'm just another uppity Negro prick."

"Jesus, Marty! We can't talk this way."

"No, but we are. Not that I'm taking anything away from your big Mickness, but you're brilliant, too!"

Gabe loved that, flattered he wasn't just a hack but a serious, brooding adult of almost twenty-two, discriminating with literature even if Butcher Creek would forever course, half-savage, through his bloodstream. "But don't forget," Gabe said, "I'm not just any old Mick. I'm half-Bohunk, too."

"And all hunk," Marty said, laughing and kissing his chest in a long double helix, as if tracing with his lips Gabe's outer-outskirts-of-Europe DNA. "Despite your tragic chromosomes."

Laughing, then barely suppressing a gauche gasp, Gabe kept studying Marty's body in the dawn light, overwhelmed by its beauty. Sleepy, Marty kissed him, whispering, "Hardly anything is ever like you hope it will be. But last night was perfect. Thanks." In a few moments, eyes shut tight, Marty lay back and babbled to himself in deepening sleep, crimping his fingers like a little boy lost in the spell of a happy dream.

❖

Gabe had it all planned. He'd checked the granola box the night before and verified it was almost half full, along with half a quart of milk. When Marty finished his shower, he was going to have everything ready, served on the dinette with folded paper napkins, matching bowls and spoons, plus two servings of instant coffee. This was the South High high life all right, a semi-perfect breakfast to follow the perfect night.

He pulled on sweatpants and a hoodie in a concession to the snowy morning and went out to the main room to set up the feast.

At the dinette, Ben was emptying the last of the granola into his bowl. He finished off the milk, too, saving the last ounce to swig from the carton. Listless, Candy swirled a spoon around her cereal as if considering whether it was ladylike to actually finish off any given serving of food. Her messy blond hair was tied in a sloppy bun with a pencil stuck in it, as if she were playing Sexy Librarian. "Aha!" She smiled when she noticed Gabe. "It must have been wonderful with Marty. Finally."

"It sure sounded like it," Ben said.

"It was, but we're hungry now."

"There's almost nothing in the fridge, though," Ben said. "A couple beers and some ketchup. That's it. We gotta go to the store one of these days."

"You ought to splurge on a big breakfast at the Greek diner," Candy said. "There's nothing like greasy spoon eggs and potatoes after an all-night, um, assignation."

"I don't think you're using that word right," Gabe said. "There was nothing secret about it. Obviously." He checked a phone message from Uncle Tony: *Be warned. Elena and Patrick are dropping off some things later this AM, snow be damned.*

Damned indeed. He heard the shower shut off. He had to get Marty the hell out of here.

❖

So, it was an oleaginous, heavenly splurge served by a gorgeous middle-aged Greek waitress, a dead ringer for Erato, the Muse of erotic poetry. She winked at Marty and Gabe and seemed to intuit why they each wolfed down an Athens Omelet Special, then followed it with a shared, gooey serving of Olympian Ambrosia Waffles. After breakfast, Gabe slow-walked Marty through campus, claiming it was "dazzling" after the first snow, though it was actually dreary and watery, melting in slushy puddles.

When they reached Marty's dormitory, Gabe spotted a familiar rusting pickup across South High, parked in the loading zone in front of his apartment house. Loaded with a heap of patio furniture under a heap of softening snow and a boxy shape under a plastic tarp, it looked like Ma and Pa Joad had detoured north from the Dust Bowl.

Marty hadn't noticed the pickup, so Gabe made haste to block the sight of it, leading him into the lobby. "It's still chilly outside, and I want to kiss you."

"I wanna kiss you, too, right here."

A girl in thick black glasses manning the reception desk looked up from her book and smiled. "Can I watch?"

At the elevator, Marty smiled back and said sure, pulling Gabe close for a smooch. "I'll see you around, buddy."

"There's always tonight."

"If I finish my paper on JMW Turner."

"I love JMW Turner. I can help you with it."

"Like help with how his whole color palette brightened up when he left London for Venice?"

"Yeah, from grays to sun-kissed fireworks," Gabe said, "like he fell in love with Venice."

Marty kissed him again. "Venice has nothing on Denver."

"That's 'cause," Gabe said to the closing elevator doors, "Venice has been deprived of you, Martin Montgomery."

Gabe hustled across South High, anxious about whatever weird scene awaited upstairs. This particular weirdness had Elena and Patrick, still in their damp jackets, drinking instant coffee around the dinette with Candy, who seemed to be entertaining them in her best alumni center reception mode. "Gabe is absolutely exemplary around here, Mr. and Mrs. Rafferty, a model for us all," she was saying with a big ol' Texas grin as Gabe came in, "generous, studious, hard-working."

"We're very proud of him," Elena said, turning at Gabe's approach.

"I'm afraid he sometimes works and works all night long," Candy went on, relentless. "On his edits, I mean. For the health foundation. He's been teaching all of us what he's learning about the dangers of certain diseases, related to, well, sexual transmission."

"As if he would know," Patrick said, fingering the cap in his lap. Gabe realized his father had never before set foot in this apartment. He'd missed Gabe's graduation in June, sending Elena and Tony with the excuse he was having stomach trouble. Today he was quieted and looked kind of shrunken, skinnier in the shoulders and chest.

"Gabe," Elena said, "you never told us about Candy. Living here."

"She's not quite *living* here," Gabe said, putting his arm on Candy's shoulder, "but she often *breakfasts* here."

"It's nice to have a girl around, isn't it?" Patrick asked.

"A delight beyond measure," Gabe said. "But she's Ben's girlfriend, you know."

"Though Gabe and I have long had our own precious bond."

"Where is Ben, anyway?"

"Getting into some warm clothes. To help you bring up the furniture your parents have so kindly delivered."

"I saw the pickup out front. Hell of a day to deliver patio furniture."

"They'll be plenty of sunny October days left to enjoy it," Elena said. "You know, Colorado weather—wait a minute." She looked at Patrick. "Anyway, your father insisted we do it today."

"I gotta work tomorrow. I wanted you to have it before all the warm weather is really done for."

Gabe let them know he was grateful. He was grateful, too, that Marty had been spared this perplexing delivery of cast-off chairs and a rusty mesh table in a snowstorm. It perplexed him, too, that his father only supervised the delivery, with Ben, Candy, Elena, and Gabe all hauling up pieces as Patrick leaned on the pickup's bed, coughing as he gave muffled orders about the best methodology. Ben and Gabe struggled with the last, tarp-covered, boxy thing. "Keep it covered, damn it," Patrick called, staying put. "Don't let any moisture get into it."

When Ben and Gabe had managed to haul it into Gabe's room, Elena slipped in as Ben slipped out to help Candy arrange the patio pieces on the balcony. Gabe looked with a flash of terror at his futon, the messy sheets and open sleeping bag left in flagrante.

"Your father is acting even stranger than usual. I'm worried about him, okay? We're gonna head out now." Elena kissed him and left him alone with the boxy thing, shoved against the window.

Gabe gingerly removed the wet tarp, tossed it to the balcony, and studied the desk. Its finished surface gleamed. It proved that Patrick could have had that career as a furniture maker if only he'd reached out to, then actually communicated with prospective clients without curses or insults.

The desk was flawless. Three side drawers, with room on top for his computer and a few reference books. He moved them from the card table, which he ceremoniously folded and put aside.

Outside, through the sliding door, the sun was flirting through the gray clouds, illuminating canopies of street trees flashing yellow-gold as they shook off the snow. On the balcony, Candy and Ben had arranged the patio furniture into hopeful groupings that yearned for warmer, drier days.

Gabe pulled his folding chair up to the desk's opening, positioning his computer, dictionary, manual of style, and thesaurus. He ran his palm against the smooth wood grain, back and forth, in awed disbelief.

He didn't know why he was crying.

Chapter Six

Fruit Compote

Through October and November, Marty started staying with Gabe more and more. "I feel like I outgrew living in the dorms a long time ago," he said one night a week before Thanksgiving, entwining his legs with Gabe's. "I don't think my parents trust me to manage on my own. They won't pay for an off-campus place."

"Just for school expenses, a bed, a roof, and three meals a day. Poor thing."

"This poor thing really likes sleeping with you."

"Are you really talking about sleeping?"

"Yeah. Plus, you generate a lot of body heat. Plus, plus, it's always fun to forecast what weird shapes your hair's gonna form by morning."

"Stormy, with intense waves."

Before long, Marty slept with Gabe almost every night. Imagine the opulence—he kept a duplicate set of personal stuff in the bathroom along with several changes of clothes in Gabe's closet. For his part, master host Gabe raised the futon onto a platform, splurged on real blankets, a bedspread, and two used, mismatched nightstands. He surprised himself with how much he liked having Marty over, under, and beside him, how harmonious they were together in close quarters. When he spotted Marty's toothbrush or hair pomade in the medicine cabinet, it always made him smile. So, this is what it was like to share your space, your life. This was intimacy. Nice.

Marty wanted Gabe to be more involved with his family and invited him to Thanksgiving dinner in Vail. "They're buried in early snow up there. It'll be a blast, skiing all day over the long weekend."

"I'd love it, believe me, but I can't abandon my mom on the holiday. It'd be pretty grim, just her and my dad and any stray guests she can rustle up to shield herself. My dad doesn't behave well at the table."

"But do you really want to spend all of Thanksgiving weekend apart?"

"'Course not, but I don't really have a choice."

"Well?"

"Well what?"

"Invite me to your Thanksgiving, then!"

"Oh, Marty. You don't want to trade Butcher Creek for Vail. Or the company of my dad for yours."

Marty turned away and stared through the glass door of his residence hall. "You're ashamed to bring me home to your family?"

This shocked a laugh from Gabe. "God, no. I'd show you off, man. Anyway, you've already met most all of our little clan already—Uncle Tony, Karlo, and my mom, right?" Gabe had made a point of inviting family-obsessed Marty along to his periodic lunches with Elena before or after one of her shifts at the clinic. They'd gone well, too, Marty easily tuning into Elena's loopy wavelength.

"What is it, then, about you and your dad? What's the big secret? You're not out to him?"

"That's not it, either." Gabe sighed. Since the agonizing September coming out with Patrick in his workshop, Patrick pretended to forget Gabe was gay and would taunt him to "set him straight" about it again and again. "There's no big secret, except that my dad's a complete asshole."

"I can handle assholes. They're even interesting, sometimes. Amusing."

"Not this particular asshole. He's about as amusing as a punch in the gut. I've tried to dodge his bigotry all my life. There's no way to ignore it, you know, just suck it up and suffer it."

"If only my great-great-great-grandmother knew how much you've suffered, Gabe. Before she perished from, you know, her owner's rapes and beatings."

"Okay," Gabe said. "Maybe *suffer* is the wrong word." He sank under the blankets.

"After all, how well can I ever know you," Marty said, caressing

Gabe's arm and bussing his cheek, "if I'm not allowed to meet your father?"

Allowed. That sounded all wrong, too, and Gabe didn't know how to get the point across. He just didn't want Marty to endure Patrick's raw racial animosity, as Jeffrey Montgomery had so long ago, and couldn't stand to see Marty get hurt. But how could he do that without seeming patronizing, acting like the White Protector, and making Marty feel belittled or dismissed or incapable of handling the situation?

"Just let me see how this Thanksgiving goes with him, the first one since I've come out," Gabe said, realizing how lame it sounded. "Then we'll take it from there. Okay?"

"At least come up to Vail Friday or Saturday for turkey sandwiches and a couple days of skiing."

"You got a deal," Gabe said, kissing Marty's neck while wondering how much debt from Vail lift tickets his new credit card could bear. Whatever price, it was worth it if going to Vail deflected from the torture of any further disputations about meeting Patrick.

❖

Oil tankers clackered by while Gabe's Tinkertoy compact idled behind the tracks. Behind them rose a huge billboard, a recruiting pitch for the U.S. Army with pretty young men and women seated at computers. New Skills for a New Millennium. On his way to Butcher Creek for Thanksgiving dinner, the billboard made Gabe wonder what the pitch was that had lured Patrick into the post-Vietnam Army years ago. Uncle Sam Wants All Bigots? What was his father like back then? Had the Army somehow ruined him, or had he almost ruined the Army?

Patrick had cared enough about an Army career to earn his GED. Even during his whiskey brag-outs, he gave few details about his service except that the highest rank he attained was as a corporal, serving on a maintenance unit. Gabe never learned what caused him to leave the Army, which Patrick seemed to have enjoyed as much as he enjoyed anything. Why didn't he seem to have any military benefits or old buddies?

After the oil train passed and Gabe drove closer to the south end of the refinery, he went under a plume of smoky fog. Odd, since the holiday had dawned sunny and unusually warm. The road followed electrical towers until it crossed a concrete ravine, an artery of brown wastewater. As the sunshine was blotted out, a bridge over the wastewater marked the entry to Butcher Creek. Diagonal with the wastewater canal, kids played in yard after identical yard, each caged in by chain-link fences. At a red light, using his windshield wipers against the odd, thick fog, Gabe watched a young father tease his giggling little boys, faking them out under driveway hoops, maybe killing time while the turkeys cooked on this eerie, warm Thanksgiving.

Father and sons at play on one side and wastewater churning on the other, Gabe indulged his regret that by the time he wanted to play sports, Patrick was well over forty and had pretty much abandoned balls, bats, racquets, and hoops. Once, Gabe had finally prodded his father to play catch in advance of baseball season. His father made an effort, even embellishing a few tosses with outbursts like "curveball!" and "watch yer follow-through." After a few minutes, though, when their neighbor yelled over the fence about his new circular saw, Patrick deserted his last toss to Gabe in midair.

The father and sons quickly abandoned their hoops in the fog. The boys put their hands on their heads, as if to verify the sudden moisture, then ran inside behind their dad. It gathered on Gabe's windshield, but his wipers only spread the sludge—it was not moisture but a thick, mud-like mess. He emptied his windshield washer reservoir just trying to find his way the few blocks home.

The fog was dissipating around the house, allowing faint streams of sunlight to reveal what was raining down: flecks of clay-like ash. It settled on the sidewalk and gathered on the fence posts. His parents and a large man about Patrick's age ventured out of the house just as Gabe approached, not to greet him but to assess the harm. Like Gabe's subcompact, Patrick's pickup was covered in the clay ash, as well as Elena's sedan. A fine mire gathered on the rooftop and clung to the bare branches in Elena's side garden.

A dispute seemed to be under way as they stood in the driveway. Shaking Gabe's hand, the large man theorized that "a holiday skeleton crew of wetbacks who don't know shit" had accidently released the rain of clay flecks at the refinery.

Patrick blamed "the niggers, who were dogging after Thanksgiving overtime and fucking up the whole operation without decent supervision."

Elena said she just got off the phone with a neighbor who'd heard it was an accidental emission. "Automatic alarms failed. The refinery's calling it an 'opacity event.' An opacity event! I told ya, Pat! Just like when they released all that poison gas last year. A bunch of double talk. They never did tell us the whole truth."

"Jesus, what are we breathing?" Gabe asked.

"Just the usual shit," Kenny, the large man, said. "Looks like it's over now."

Elena said their neighbor told her the refinery was already promising everyone free car washes. She practically spat *car washes*. "How they gonna clean our lungs?"

"Beers," Patrick said. "Come on, Kenny, let's get back to 'em."

"And the game!" Kenny said, heading back into the house. "We probably missed the best touchdown of the day."

Gabe and Elena stayed outside, heading through the gate into the side yard garden. Clay muck and dust clung to everything, making the November-brown geraniums look gray. It was faintly apocalyptic, Elena's new patio furniture dulled and dusty. "Now I got to hook up the hose and give everything a good dousing. I'm afraid of what's really in this dirty fog. It's not going to do your father any good, I'll tell ya that."

Elena told Gabe Patrick was continuing to complain about stomach pains as well cough a lot and drink too much. "Thank God you're here, Gabriel, that you didn't leave me alone with just your father and that stupid turkey."

"Come on, Ma, you always invite any stray neighbors Dad hasn't insulted yet. Anyway, who exactly is the stupid turkey?"

"I didn't mean Kenny!" Elena swiped Gabe's arm. "He's an old Army friend of your father's. He just moved back here from Idaho or someplace, so we invited him."

"Great. Wow, Dad has a friend!"

"They belonged to some outfit together at Fort Carson. I mean, some club or something outside the regular Army. Two peas in a pod, I'll tell ya."

❖

At the head of the holiday table, his father turned to glance at the ever-blaring cable news. Deep into boxed white wine, Patrick was, despite his scant attention, a loud and proud authority on world affairs. During a pause toward the meal's end, he offered his opinion on a new outbreak of violence live from the barricades of Palestine: "So, what's that nigger know about the Holy Land?"

"That's what I want to know, Pat," Kenny said. "Since when do the networks send niggers to cover Palestine?"

"Pass me the peas," Elena responded. "Please."

"Didja hear what I said? How come they do a report from goddamn Bethlehem, Elena, the birthplace of your beloved baby Jesus, with this nigger blabbing in front of the cameras?"

"I heard you, Pat. Anna, can you reach the peas for me? Thanks. You're a doll."

Anna, a single neighbor on the cul-de-sac, doll that she was, tried to smile. Another of their few white neighbors got busy topping off wine and salting potatoes he'd already pushed aside.

"What it is," Kenny said, "is a takeover, pure and simple. They're pushing whites out. I can't believe what a cesspool Denver has become. In a few years, blacks are gonna be in charge of everything. A total nigger city."

"So, Kenny," Gabe asked, calmly as he could, "Mom said you and Dad were in a club or outfit or something at Fort Carson."

"Not really a club." Kenny glanced at Patrick with a happy, conspiratorial smile. "It was like an association of like-minded soldiers."

"White like-minded soldiers?"

"Exactly. We just banded together for protection, you know. It was kinda like advocating for fairness to whites."

"That's right," Patrick said, refilling his wine. "The niggers had all kinds of quotas—"

"*Affirmative action*, Pat," Kenny said with a laugh. "There were just so many of 'em."

"Niggers everywhere you turned," Patrick said. "We had to eat with 'em and shower with 'em and take orders from nigger officers."

Gabe surprised himself with an almost out-of-body composure. "So, was this group sanctioned by the Army?"

Kenny's smile vanished. Oh-oh. "What are you getting at, Gabe?" He pushed his half-finished pie aside. "Did you hear anything?"

"You gotta watch him, Kenny," Patrick said, starting to slur.

"I never heard a thing about it," Gabe said. "This is the first I've known of your association, that's why I'm asking. Did you and Dad leave the Army around the same time?"

"Exsh-actly!" Patrick cried out. "Exsh-actly the same time."

"Was there any particular reason you both left the service?"

"I'm not sure I like your line of questioning," Kenny said. "You seem like a good kid, Gabe, but you should stay out of things you don't know jack shit about."

"You're right, Kenny, I'm sorry. I don't know jack shit. But that's the whole reason I was asking. Dad never tells me anything about his experience in the Army."

"See what he's like?" Patrick shook his head, the put-upon patriarch at the helm of his family table. "I told ya. He's sneaky." He turned to Gabe. "You dig and dig just like one of these hotshot nigger reporters. Why don't you just keep your half-ass questions to yourself and leave Kenny alone?"

"Okay, Dad. I will. Can I please have the applesauce?"

"Never mind the appleshhauce. You know what I think about you."

"Oh." Still ultracomposed, Gabe wondered how far to go in front of the daunted, captive guests. "I think I do, Dad. That I'm a secret nigger lover?"

"Yep. That's what I think."

"Yep. You're right. I am. Literally." Gabe listened to his best self and against all impulse said nothing more. He set down his wine and stared straight into his father's glassy eyes. As silence widened and stretched around the table, Gabe basked in its nervous, triggered reaches. He sensed the others' embarrassment but did not feel it himself. He had arrived at a new stage, imperturbable, too wise to sink to Patrick's level and too confident to be the first to blink. The son had outmanned the father at last.

When Pat shifted his gaze back to the TV, Gabe rose and reached for the applesauce himself. Before he knew how, Patrick had snatched it out of his hands. "Like I said, you know what I think, smart-ass."

Deprived of the table's food like a dishonored guest, Gabe realized immediately nothing had really evolved, not within himself, and certainly not between him and his father. He remained standing, straightening, reconciled to the coming ruckus. "And you should know what I think, Dad." he said. "I think it's irritating to have the television blasting when we're having guests for Thanksgiving. I think it's cruel of you to embarrass them, along with Mom. Besides that, I got a few thoughts on this subject of niggers in Palestine. Wanna hear 'em?"

Patrick glared, breathing hard.

Gabe went on. "I was gonna explain about this one here, why he's broadcasting about the violence near Manger Square? See, he's been a Mideast correspondent for more than ten years, and now he's the network's international producer, and even if he doesn't know as much about Palestine as you do, Dad, he knows a hell a lot more than the rest of us, and that's why, to answer your question, he reported the news live via nigger satellite feed. Now, if you'll give me that applesauce? Thanks." Gabe grabbed the heavy bowl and in terror, for a suspended moment, held it over his father's head.

For a brief flash, Gabe wondered which would crack first and loudest, patriarchal skull or ceramic bowl? Restraining the urge to find out, he overturned the entire glommy mass onto Patrick's plateful of second helpings. Then he set the dish down, kissed the top of his mother's head, reached for his jacket, and rushed for the door, but not fast enough to elude Patrick's aim. Outside, Gabe stumbled to his car with the sticky sauce dribbling from the nape of his neck into his collar.

❖

Gabe swung back to South High Street to pick up his skis and swipe his neck. He made it to Vail before midnight.

Jeffrey answered the condo door, surprised. "We didn't expect you until tomorrow. Marty's already gone to bed. He and I skied most of the day, first time of the season."

Gabe eased into Marty's room and lay beside him. Startled awake, Marty smiled and kissed him. Sleepy, he asked why he seemed scented by "fruit compote."

Before Gabe could recount applesauce tortures, Marty was already back to sleep, exhausted. Gabe lit the scented candle on Marty's nightstand and studied him, inch by inch.

In the overheated condo's stuffiness, Marty had kicked off blanket and top sheet and lay naked, smiling through dreams. Gabe's gaze, then his hand, roved that compact chest, flat, taut stomach, all that golden skin in candle shine.

Gabe dreamed, too, dreamed of licking applesauce—*fruit compote*—off Marty's sweet stomach, feasting all the way down.

CHAPTER SEVEN

Feeding the Beast

As winter deepened and his student life grew more distant, Gabe's connections within the campus community actually grew more intimate.

As when, in the supermarket one bleak January day, he ran into Todd Morales, his youngish freshman philosophy professor and one of a handful of faculty who'd become social friends. He and Gabe often swam evening laps at the campus pool and sometimes shot hoops on a forgotten outdoor campus court. He and his wife had invited Gabe, Jamie, and other former students for dinner a few times over the years.

"You're appraising those tomatoes very carefully, Mr. Rafferty," Todd said, approaching with a smile.

"I'm pondering utilitarian ethics, Dr. Morales. These green and ugly tomatoes cost too much. So if I were to steal them, wouldn't I spare the next customer from enduring low quality at a high price? Greater good, right?"

"No. Just wait till winter's over and the quality improves. But are you really that hungry and destitute, Gabe?"

"Naw. I've always been a hungry beast. I'm a little worried, though. My editing job with the health foundation was cut to half time. Philosophical query—can wages that are almost nonexistent be cut in half?"

"That's, like, math. Not really my area of expertise."

"And sometime soon, Todd, my contract's ending completely. The grant that funded the whole study's ending. But I'll bet gonorrhea, syphilis, and HIV are gonna keep on infecting rural Colorado."

"I'm sorry, Gabe. For you and rural Colorado. I'll let you know if I hear of any job openings anywhere, but we don't hear much about many in Philosophy. Zeena does, though, all the time."

Todd's wife was a rare creature in Gabe's bookish sphere, an entrepreneur. She'd helped found a small company that sold security equipment. Most important, she was a brilliant cook. Todd often scoured the supermarket, raided their summer garden, and probably supplied random roadkill, anything to feed Zeena's culinary artistry. Gabe lingered at the tomato bins, hoping Todd might be inspired to have another dinner for his former students, especially the ones fallen into destitution.

At last, Todd was forthcoming. "I'll see if can persuade Zeena to feed the beast."

When the health foundation job really did end, Gabe's February account balance flirted with overdraft territory. He was embarrassed to let Marty know the full extent of his poverty. Marty continued to take his meals at the residence hall, then cross South High to sleep with Gabe, but when he tired of dorm food and wanted to dine out, he insisted on treating, which made Gabe even more wary. Now he was not only penniless but a mooch.

When one of the kitchen crew at the sorority Candy now housemothered was felled by a serious skiing accident, Gabe substituted for him, "slinging hash," as the archaic Greek world put it. He fended off lascivious sorority sisters at mealtimes, earning little in pay but gaining a solid month of free meals.

Another connection that deepened was with Mary Anne and, especially, Jamie. With idle time after his sub job at Candy's sorority ended, Gabe found himself more often wandering down the second-floor breezeway into their company. One night in early March, a more fertile spring seemed to be hatching, right on their queen-sized bed. Mary Ann had excused herself, heading off to choir rehearsal at her parish. She exited laughing. "When you two get this way, I'm glad to leave you alone."

Gabe lay beside Jamie as they passed a joint back and forth. He confessed he was a virgin as far as actual intercourse with girls. "You don't have any reason to feel nervous about it," Jamie said. "You've done this a lot for the past six months, just maybe not in exactly the same way as straight folk do."

"Not exactly, no."

"But it's the same. It's just the same old putting in and taking out. And there's no pressure. There'll be more chances down the road. We're not going to hit the jackpot on our first try." Jamie took his hand, squeezed it, then accepted the joint Gabe passed. "But we've gotta start somewhere."

❖

In March, Jamie was leaving her copy-editing job at *Planet Quarterly* for much more emerald pastures as a features writer and editor for a regional weekly. She offered Gabe hope of a position more aligned with his degree. "I know my boss is going to like you, Gabe. Just as with our little liaisons, I know you can do it. He dreams of expanding the quarterly's reach. And he's desperate now that I've given my month's notice."

"He can't be any more desperate than I am." Gabe knew another position as a mere copy editor would promise more maximum toil at minimum wage, but that was a lot less punishing than abject poverty. He was so broke he had to forgo taking even one class at the International School. Plus, he wanted to impress Marty, or at least dispel doubts he might be unemployed forever.

The new job was better than Gabe expected. *Planet Quarterly*'s head editor seemed to like and trust him and soon assigned Gabe some content editing tasks, plus introducing the verse of a Nigerian poet and interviewing a Cuban dissident in exile in Denver. On warming spring days, he would have brown-bag lunches with Marty at the outdoor tables outside his residence hall, with Marty smuggling some treat from the cafeteria to share.

"Let us eat cake."

"It's great to have a reason to hang around campus again." Gabe turned his face to the sun. "Besides walking my boyfriend to his dorm."

"There's a chance I may escape from this residence hall altogether." Marty's art history professor was recommending him for another semester at the satellite campus in Italy where he'd research his senior thesis on the earliest pre-Renaissance masters. "Imagine it, right in Florence, walking right up to Cimabue and Giotto whenever I damn well pleased."

"I'm happy for you, but not for me. A whole semester without you?"

"I wouldn't go without you. I think I can talk my dad into helping fund your travel, too. Just think, you could even earn credits at the satellite branch of the International School. Wouldn't it be great? We'll study together in some Florentine library, then make love right where Dante romanced Beatrice."

"I'd love it, man! Are you kidding? I've been burning to see Europe since I was little. But I can't expect your father to fund me. I'd be uneasy to ask for so much when I can't do anything to reciprocate."

"You're not going to ask him, I am. Dad is doing so well with some new investment partners and the expansion of his financial services, he could cut a check for you without a second thought. He appreciates how happy you make me. Isn't that enough?"

Gabe laughed, but shook his head. He didn't know what to say, troubled by the thought of Marty being so blithe with his family's money. More than once, at the Montgomery family table, he'd had intimations of some past shadow over Marty, some hint of unpredictable, extreme stubbornness along with an impression that Gabe was welcomed precisely because their relationship had banished that shadow. "I couldn't possibly, Marty. I couldn't take advantage of your family's generosity like that."

"We'll see, Mr. Rafferty, we'll see."

❖

Relations with the elder Mr. Rafferty had been shakier than ever since the applesauce incident at Thanksgiving. Gabe avoided Butcher Creek as much as possible, venturing there only when his mother lured him with a guilt-inducing plea and promise to cook. "Your father is still not doing well, feeling weak and losing lots of weight, so I need you to help me move a few things. Plus, I'm thinking of making my special lasagna."

By April, extreme pain had finally driven Patrick to get a diagnosis. Those chronic stomach pains grew from an aggressive and metastasizing intestinal cancer, spreading to his colon and possibly kidneys. A self-assured VA specialist prescribed a month of radiation treatments. With convincing certainty, he persuaded Gabe and Elena that zapping Patrick's stomach with powerful death rays would give him "the best chance of stopping the tumors' spread."

"But will he be better?" Elena asked. "Will he recover fully?"

"Our radiation gastrectomy gamma ray is the best technology available, Ms. Rafferty."

Instead of his usual reflexive skepticism, Gabe found himself convinced the treatments would succeed. It was not a rational confidence but something more like the unquestioning faith he'd felt as a little boy—*yep, that stale wafer is actually the very body of Jesus H. Christ himself.* He and Elena immediately joined forces to drive Patrick back and forth to the radiation lab, with Gabe filling in for Elena when she had to work a twelve-hour shift or couldn't juggle her schedule at the clinic. He would take a morning off at *Planet Quarterly* then make it up, editing while he sat in the waiting room and taking his unfinished work home in the evenings.

As the spring's last snowfalls melted into its first thunderstorms, Gabe felt trapped in this track, back and forth every two or three weekdays from the campus in south Denver north to Butcher Creek through the thick morning commute. At the lab, Gabe would act as Patrick's interpreter, bookie, and oracle. "The docs say I'm looking a little better," his feeble, drained father would report after a session of having his internal organs sizzled.

But nearing the final week, inquiring about the schedule, Gabe gleaned from a visiting specialist that his father's cancer had "overwhelmed the pace of our therapy."

Driving Patrick back to Butcher Creek, Gabe worked up the nerve to paraphrase the doc's language. *It may not respond to further treatment.* Patrick cracked a fresh 7 Up, nodded, mumbled "I'll be damned." That was it. Within minutes, he was back to bitching about Gabe's driving and advising his son on delicate matters of driving etiquette. "Don't let that asshole cut you off like that. Flip him off!"

Gabe usually took the shortcut past the oil refinery. Razor-wired on both sides, the road sliced through the bowels of industry like a gamma ray. Columns of smoke scraped the cloudy sky. Maybe betraying an ounce of sentiment, Patrick suggested they visit the old job site. Gabe obliged, pulling into the maintenance office that served the refinery.

Patrick cried out to a group of men as they ambled toward lunch. He strutted toward them as best he could, straightening to his full bantam altitude, calling, "Hey, you palookas!" Though the black men waved to Gabe, who'd worked alongside them one summer, they ignored Patrick and made themselves busy farther away. Patrick's white ex-colleagues slapped him on the back and tousled his hair. One guy cried, "Look at this, Pat's still got these goddamn silver locks."

"You were hopin' it'd all fall out?" Patrick said, rubbing the man's bald spot. "Well, you got another think coming. I'm taking radiation, not chemo, you dumbshit."

There was some uneasy laughter, then a silence, until the balding man asked, "So, Pat, is it going to be okay?"

Patrick's hand went to his stomach. Gabe tried to read his father's pale blue eyes. A temptation toward self-pity? A denial of undeniable fate? Then Patrick's sudden smile broke all the tension. "I'll show those goddamn so-called experts. Plan on me coming back here and supervising you poor jokers."

Driving Patrick back home, Gabe took what pride he could that at least the white guys had been willing to talk and show a little concern during the hostile camaraderie. Then Patrick, of course, rushed to obliterate the moment's faint savor. Looking back as Gabe drove out the refinery gates, he exulted. "Those guys always thought I was a good worker, you know? Now that I'm gone, they feel it, don't they? Always knew they couldn't do without me. Even the niggers, though they won't admit it."

During one of their sunny, early May brown-bag lunches, Marty admitted he was upset. "Now, your dad's fighting a terminal diagnosis, Gabe, and I still haven't met him. I'll never have a chance to see him as he truly was. Think about it—I've involved you in my family. Open book, right?"

"The book's closed on my father. He's a miserable prick. Your dad is a gentleman."

"I just found out my dad is accused of collaborating with fund managers who aren't gentlemen at all. Jeffrey told me he's being investigated by a state financial agency. The investors he's working with, Wall Street types, are charged with some shady deals."

Trying but failing to imagine generous, courteous Mr. Montgomery involved with corrupt characters, Gabe wandered back the short distance to the *Planet Quarterly* office. It occupied the second floor of a squat brick rectangle, moldering in a shadowy bog beside the campus power plant. Sophie, the editor's assistant, smiled when he came in but ran an exasperated hand through her pile of frizzy hair. "I just sent you a revised article. It's got to be proofed for the next issue pronto."

"Something dazzling, I hope, as I suffer over every comma and apostrophe?"

"A gay writer facing torture in Uganda. Maybe death."

"Gee whiz, Sophie. This'll make my day."

"Don't look at me. I just do as I'm told, buster, with no authority or agency—no mental activity whatsoever. A mentally defective robot will replace me in a year or two."

"God, I hope not! I love you."

"Get to work, Gabe." Trying to hide her smile, Sophie turned her gaze to her computer screen. "Apostrophes await."

Gabe's tiny office actually had a small, high window since the space used to serve as the shared bathroom of a former dormitory. Rusty impressions of the shower stall and toilet still haunted the linoleum. Settling at his computer, he glanced up before surrendering all his attention to the screen, just in time to see a little cloud scud across the spring sky. It was shaped like a perfect apostrophe.

Just after Marty's last final of his junior year, he and Gabe decided on a high-country hike to cheer on summer's arrival and the end of Marty's incarceration in the residence hall. Gabe had a private motive, too. He was going to ask Marty if he wanted to move into Edna Victoria for the summer. When they found Ben at the table, finishing off the last carton of milk, they insisted he come along to celebrate his CPA certification.

A luminous white horizon had stared down at them all spring, and they were desperate to submit to the Rockies' cool embrace. They chose Eccles Pass, despite knowing they might find snowfields above timberline in early June.

"This is it!" Marty cried after they'd barely hiked a hundred yards on the squishy trail beside surging Meadow Creek. "Rushing snowmelt, the scent of pines!"

"Boulders!" Ben, marching ahead, cried back, "Birdies, Abert's squirrels!"

"Indian paintbrush, wild geranium, raspberry blossom!" Gabe added, running in delirious circles around Marty. A little farther up, though, all sunlight disappeared under a mass of gathering clouds.

After that, the first long section of trail was a monotonous climb through lodgepole pines, a monolithic monoculture that stamped out all variety on the sandy, barren forest floor. This segment was common on almost every high country hike, which Gabe cursed as *mirkwoods*. Old snow soured in piles beside the trail, becoming more frequent as they climbed. Daunted as a little hobbit, Gabe couldn't wait to end the gloomy ascent and reach the upper meadows, but meanwhile he grew distracted by Ben's tale of woe. "Candy just won't let up labeling me some dreary sellout. She's really become the worst kind of academic snob. From party animal to insufferable literary artiste in one school year."

"The girl can't help it, Ben. She's discovered the thrills of Zola and Balzac."

"I don't give a flying fuck about old Ball-sac. Candy and I used to have so much fun. Now it's nag, nag about my supposed boring future. Our relationship's becoming a torture chamber."

"Man, I'm sorry to hear that." Gabe had taken note of Candy's increasing absence at the apartment but assumed she had been spending more time mothering the sorority, ushering the younger girls through Hell Week, and studying for her own finals. "You guys have always seemed like a great couple. Great at raising the right kind of hell."

"You're both pretty, too," Marty said.

"I'm afraid we're gonna be pretty over, pretty soon. Candy just doesn't appreciate the pressure I'm under from my father. Her father just keeps funding her flights of enthusiasm, but mine hounds me and always has. And I don't want to stay in academia forever. There's just no money in a lit degree."

"Tell me about it," Gabe said.

"But I thought you loved your work at *Planet Quarterly*," Marty said. "Especially when they let you branch out from copy editing."

"I do, I do! But I can't live on my earnings. I just can't. I might have to get a side gig bussing tables at the Greek diner or something."

"See what I mean? That would be the future for me, or worse, if I'd stuck with the humanities. If I don't get into a high-earning profession, my father's threatening to make me pay him back, the total cost of my undergraduate tuition. For real. Then I'd be his indentured servant for the rest of my life."

"It's a drag, the way our fathers can upend everything," Marty said, powering ahead alone, his expensive new hiking boots oozing in the wet trail.

"Poor dude, another year of study in a palazzo in Florence," Ben said, waiting until Marty had rounded the bend ahead. "I'd give anything to be *upended* by a father like Marty's."

Mention of Marty's upcoming studies at the Italian satellite campus threatened to upend Gabe's joy in the hike. Gabe searched ahead with concern as Marty disappeared into the endless Mirkwood. Now that Marty's father was under investigation for his association with the shady investors, all mention of funding for Gabe to join Marty had ended.

But the lodgepole Mirkwood wasn't endless after all, nor were the clouds. When he reached that bend, he saw an opening ahead, a sun-dazzled, snow-striated ridge under a cobalt-blue Colorado sky. Spruce and subalpine firs began to appear as the woods became more open and varied. Glacier lilies lined the trail in gaudy clumps. Gabe's heart began to thrum with the altitude and anticipation.

Remembered from a long-ago hike with Karlo and Jeffrey—still wearing the hand-me-down boots he'd inherited from Karlo—Gabe visualized the trio of high meadows ahead, each an emerald, blossom-choked bowl ringed by the Gore Range successively rising to Eccles Pass. When the trees began to shrink in size and quantity, he could see Marty far up, trudging across the second meadow toward heaps of trailside snow.

"You better hurry ahead," Ben said, "maybe something's flipped him out."

It seemed impossible to catch up, no matter how Gabe powered forward, taking hard breaths as the trail tilted up the meadows, but luckily Marty had slowed, then stopped at a snow mass ahead. When

Gabe reached it, he realized it was much more extensive and higher than he'd realized from below, an impenetrable glacier.

"Look at this, Gabe, the sign for the spur to Eccles Pass is almost buried. There's no way to find the trail under all this snow."

A carved wooden arrow on a forest sign pointed the way, but snow at least five feet deep choked the entire signpost. Snowmelt gurgled from under the mass, sparkling in the sunlight, as if it were forming a boundary between the blinding white heaps and blazing green at their feet. Gabe and Marty stood, stymied, at that boundary's edge.

Gabe had hoped earlier hikers had at least trudged a route of deep footprints above the snowfield, but no one had yet dared. "We'll have to wait until July for the view from the pass."

Marty stared upward, squinting into the blinding, virgin whiteness and above, to the crest of sky for the vicinity of the pass itself. "You said it was so unforgettable, such a panorama of the Ten Mile and Gore Ranges. And we're so close."

"There's no way we can get up there without snowshoes."

"I hate this," Marty said with sudden, spitting contempt. "Man, we've hiked so long, so hard, just to be stopped in our tracks."

"That's the way it goes at twelve thousand feet."

"Oh, Gabe." His tone shifted completely, the anger drained to dejection. Pulling Gabe into an embrace, he rested his head on his shoulder.

Gabe kissed his head. "You okay, baby?"

"It's just too much, being thwarted at every turn."

Gabe wanted to change the subject to his proposal about shacking up for the summer before Ben caught up with them. "Nothing needs to thwart our summer. I've got an idea."

Trembling slightly, struggling to hold back tears, Marty pulled Gabe tighter.

Watching Ben's progress below, approaching the third meadow, Gabe wondered if the altitude was affecting Marty. He'd seen it turn some strong hikers shaky and even weepy. "Did I say something stupid back there?"

"No, no." Marty pushed back, straightening himself. "I'm not ready to move back in with my folks in Castle Pines. Gorgeous as it is, it's not really home to me." Marty had grown up in Park Hill in a rambling Craftsman his father had bought when his business still consisted of two small branches in northeast Denver. "I'm a Denver kid. It's alienating down there in the suburbs. And I'm thinking about the distance between us being twenty miles, not half a block."

Gabe saw his opening. "That's just why I was going to suggest—"

"And I'm thinking about the mess my father's in, how he might have been swindled by slick operators just when he was on the verge of expanding. They're investigating his past transactions and talking heavy penalties. Maybe even stripping his commercial license. Down in the lodgepole, I started thinking about Ben's father's focus on material gain. And I started thinking about your father, brought down by cancer, maybe inflamed by the job that was giving him *a living.* Then, on this warm day in June, everything beautiful, we come up against this goddamn glaciated blockade."

❖

After the hike, Marty decided after all he needed to head to Castle Pines to support his father and his family during the investigation. Depending on the outcome, Marty hoped to spend as much of the summer as he could at Edna Victoria with Gabe. So, it was not an official cohabitation, but Gabe decided it was as good as he could hope.

In July, Tony decided Patrick and Elena's twenty-fifth anniversary was something to celebrate at the parish hall, especially with Pat's pain reduced since his radiation treatments had ended. Elena asked her brother to keep it down to a small family and friends party at the house, so Tony obliged, hiring a caterer and bartender.

Gabe swallowed hard and decided to take Marty, certain it would end in disaster but hoping it would forever cure him of asking to meet his father. As Gabe helped with the invitations by addressing envelopes at his apartment, Marty asked, "So, did I make the guest list?"

"You're always on my list. I'll bask in your reflected glory."

"That's sweet. But you're nervous as hell! You don't really want me to come."

"I am sweet, and I *really* want you to come." Gabe wasn't nervous, only distracted because he noticed Kenny's name on the list, and he was not going to include his father's white supremacist Army buddy. "You do need to meet my dad, after all this time. Just prepare yourself, okay? You've led a kind of sheltered life. Wonderfully sheltered."

"You typecast me as this delicate fairy boy when my family's falling into chaos? You think I'll wilt over some Archie Bunker rerun?"

"In the reruns I've seen, Archie Bunker was funny. My dad's just mean."

"Can he really be such a throwback? I thought racism was more sophisticated these days. I thought the old-school ranters had passed on."

"Maybe my dad's the last one. We have to prepare ourselves for a scene, that's all. I'm just afraid he'll get drunk and say something unspeakable to you."

"Oh, babe, are you afraid I'll ruin the party?"

"No, I'm afraid my dad will. You're too refined, too brilliant for an ignorant little man who's coping with cancer by drinking himself to death in a nasty corner of life I wish you never had to see."

Marty searched the floor before he looked at Gabe. "That isn't the most magnanimous invitation I've ever received."

As the anniversary approached, Gabe and Marty's conversation looped into more downward spirals. Their positions reversed, with Gabe insisting Marty come to the party with the same force Marty refused on the grounds that the invitation was half-hearted. Yet Gabe was almost glad, after the last guests staggered home and he was alone with Patrick and Elena, that his boyfriend wasn't there to witness the party's end. Despite a lifetime of practice with these characters, its crude finale made Gabe feel like he was the wilted fairy.

'As Gabe consolidated the leftover booze on the patio, Elena hurried through the door wild-eyed, her corsage askew, just as Patrick crashed through the doorway himself, crying out. "You can't tell me what to do, damnit!" He grabbed Elena's shoulders.

Screaming, she tried to shake him off. "You stop that! You're hurting me! Gabe, he's hurting me! He's been drinking all day."

Shoving away Gabe's restraining hand, Patrick yelled, "What the goddamn difference does it make how much I drink? I'm gonna die whatever the hell I do."

"Good!" Elena cried, ducking from his grasp and heading back inside. "Maybe you'll die a lot quicker this way. I'll live like a queen on your two-bit life insurance!" She laughed without humor, an ancient Balkan scorn that strafed into Gabe like cluster bombs in a pointless war. Elena meant to exit with a flourish when Patrick lunged at her, seizing her waist. He nearly knocked her through the half-open door but was so off-balance that he tumbled, landing hard on his rear while Elena scrambled inside, screaming.

Reluctant to help the old man up, Gabe restrained a powerful impulse to knock him back down and shatter his brain against the patio concrete. Would it look like applesauce? But with the rough tenderness the fathers of truculent children must feel, he ushered Patrick to his own bedroom. Gabe roughed his father onto the skinny bed, where he curled up without protest, burying his face.

As Gabe passed through the doorway, he heard Patrick mutter, then call out clearly. "So, this *friend* of yours I been hearing about, he's rich, isn't he? Why didn't you bring him?"

"What do you care?"

"Don't be an asshole. You ashamed to have him meet your old man?"

Gabe stepped back to lean on the doorframe, tempted toward a new chance to attack. He considered the sterility of Patrick's life—nothing like Elena's brood of godchildren, nothing like Tony's happy, prosperous family, nothing like Gabe's own little orbit of friends. Patrick's contemptuous personality had left him facing death alone. Was his racial animus and intolerance just a proxy for his failure to appreciate the variety and wonder of creation?

Gabe tried to will an infusion of Uncle Tony's good nature into his own. He scanned his consciousness for help from the soothing correctness of academia and the musty compensations of literature. But nothing materialized, and he couldn't find the goodness in himself it took to lie. "Ashamed? Of you?" he asked just before he shut the door. "Damn right I am!"

He found his mother cowering in the next bedroom. "Don't let him attack me, Gabe!" She clutched her mother's ancient cane. "He's not coming anywhere near me tonight!" So Gabe spent the night in the orange vinyl armchair in the TV den, on guard against his father.

By dawn, with Patrick pacified and Elena calm enough to start the coffee, Gabe returned to his apartment, craving real sleep. When he arrived, Marty had let himself in with his key and was waiting for him on the balcony. "I'm so freaked, Gabe. If I can't be fully part of your life, maybe our situation is past repairing."

Gabe stared, groggy, too stupefied to answer Marty's stilted hyperbole, which sounded like he must have been rehearsing. Gabe held back what he wanted to say, *Hey, I invited you,* as Marty went on.

"I don't even get to comfort you, Gabe. Or share this pain of yours. No, please don't say anything. It'll become another carefully edited story to protect your little black prince. How can I share your life if you'll just keep me in the closet? I don't see how we can be together anymore. Which is absurd because…" And there his determined voice broke. "I love you so much." He kissed Gabe quickly and hurried out.

Gabe, hardly believing what he'd just heard, now could not trust what his eyes saw, Marty hustling out Edna Victoria's entry and crossing South High, then disappearing into the residence hall. Talk about absurd. *I love you so much*? How could love walk away like that?

Chapter Eight

Forgive Me, Father

He'd left the sliding door open in hope that the cooler air of early morning would mix with his bedroom's stifling interior inferno. Naked, the sheet tossed aside, Gabe woke to Candy and Ben's voices, so loud and clear on the balcony they might as well have been in the room with him.

"You're just a different person, Ben, than the guy I fell for. Where is the beautiful geek who tried to seduce me with Rilke's poetry?"

"I did seduce you, remember?"

They weren't fighting, for once. Not even a facetious mock squabble. They were calm, sad, and sincere in a way Gabe had never heard between them, which made it more wrenching.

"I didn't even know who Rilke was then," Candy said. "But I loved your ardor. That's what seduced me. That's what I miss."

"So, it's final? You won't even consider coming to California with me?"

"I have considered it. And every time I do, I realize how much I want to stay in Denver, how much I want to finish my degree. I'll be done by next June. I have to stay and see this through to the finale. I just have to, Ben. I've been a flake and slacker for so long."

"This is nuts. You quote fell for me because of my love of literature. My so-called romantic soul. Now you're breaking up because you think you're too literary for me, the dull accountant?"

Candy laughed without humor but from somewhere recovered her own Texas soul, if only in self-parody. "That's about the size of it, pardner. I reckon I've got to make my own way in this big ol' world."

The voices stopped, then the sliding door to the living room slammed shut. Gabe lay facing the ceiling, gobsmacked by how his world had changed so drastically. He felt impossibly more estranged from his father, who—wracked by abdominal cancers and destroying his liver with alcohol—had never seemed so unreachable, his intolerance so intolerable. Marty seemed determined to destroy their joyful partnership over a fantasy of exclusion from Patrick, as if Patrick was worth it. Gabe had never understood Marty's impetuous complaint and how it became more insistent over the past few months, and now Marty might escape back to Italy without any resolution. Ben, his oldest friend throughout college, would be leaving for Sacramento in August for a starter position his father had arranged with a high-end accounting firm. And now that Mary Anne and Jamie had confirmed their pregnancy, they talked more and more about getting a house somewhere.

More practically, ol' Magna Cum Laude Gabe was not only left abandoned but beginning his adult life in unsustainable poverty. He wouldn't be able to afford the apartment without Ben. He'd have to scare up a stranger as his roommate or move to some godforsaken studio far from his campus workplace. As much as he disdained its flimsy Sheetrock, drafty windows, and wobbly sliding doors, he'd loved being nested at Edna Victoria for the past year, his friends coming and going in headstrong, random camaraderie.

He stared up at the ceiling's chintzy swirling plaster job, probably covering up a half century of student crimes, wondering how he could patch things up with Marty. Barely able to face how much he would miss his life here, Gabe rose to the day ever more anxious at the prospect of starting out from zero, alone.

Ben wouldn't owe any of the August rent, having packed his car and loaded a mini-trailer with his bedroom furniture on the first of the month. He offered to pay anyway, saying he felt bad about leaving Gabe in the lurch. Gabe accepted it only as a loan and that he'd pay it back in the fall if he found a decent roommate among the returning students. They stood on the balcony, staring down at Ben's rented mini-trailer. The ski rack on his car's roof carried Ben's downhill and cross-country skis, ludicrous in the already heated air of six in the morning.

Their friendship was on indefinite hiatus. Ben was Candyless and Gabe Martyless, each of their futures at best indeterminate—Ben back to constrained affluence in the hometown he'd once vowed to leave forever, Gabe working his ass off but straitened, facing bills he could barely pay. But they were modern American guys, so the talk was groggy banter about the route Ben would take and the suffocating heat wave that had descended on Denver, robbing it even of its cool nights.

Finally, as Ben finished his coffee, Gabe felt he had to say it. "Man, I'm sorry to see you go. All the hikes, the skis, all the times you emptied the last of the granola or the last drop of milk. I'm gonna miss you, buddy."

"Me, too. This really worked out, Gabe. Come and see me in Sacramento. I'll take you on some amazing trails in the Sierras."

Such was their man-farewell. They man-hugged, careful not to graze any delicate man-parts. Then Ben was down the breezeway stairs and off, his compact tugging his little trailer down South High and out of sight.

❖

"Are you doing better now?" Todd Morales asked Gabe from the next lane at the campus pool. He pulled off his goggles. "Can you afford a tomato, at least?"

"Not really, it's actually worse," Gabe glubbed, standing up and leaning against the pool rim. A few times in the spring, he and Todd had shot hoops and a few half-court games with neighborhood guys at the forgotten basketball court, but Todd never mentioned any open positions in his wife's company. "I'm thinking instead of starving, I can snatch slightly bruised produce from the dumpster behind the supermarket."

Saturday morning, Gabe had escaped to the recreational lap swim, unable to face the stifling, empty apartment. Worse, his father's condition was deteriorating fast, which meant long calls with his mother, who repeated his doctor's every speculation and diagnosis in blunt translations of doom and implored Gabe to come up to Butcher Creek right away. Gabe promised he'd drive up in the afternoon.

"I hate to give up my position at *Planet Quarterly*," he told Todd now, "I'm doing more and more editorial stuff, which I really enjoy.

But I've got to quit doing what I love and make some real money. It's absurd, huh? What would Sartre say? 'Being and nothingness.'"

"I'm afraid I'm responsible for feeding your freshman infatuation with existentialism. I ruined you."

"No, you saved me, Todd. You were kind of a deprogrammer for my Catholic indoctrination."

"I might be able to actually save you. Zeena's open to hiring now—she needs someone who's adept with language. It won't be poetry, Gabe, but at least it'll be something in communications. And SecureTek generally pays well." He slid up on the pool rim, then stood on the deck, leaning down to touch Gabe's shoulder. "We'll have you over for dinner this week to discuss it. Probably something with marinara—hate to rub it in, but we've got a bumper crop of tomatoes. You can take a bushel home."

All those deep dives into epistemology and ethics when he was only eighteen, when Gabe wondered what the hell all that abstraction really meant in real life, and now, coming up for air to find salvation from his freshman professor? He thanked Todd and shoved off to finish plodding his kilometer, counting, as he always did, each half lap as he reached the opposite rim, *fourteen, fourteen and a half, fifteen*...or was it sixteen? He stopped, gasping. He'd never forgotten his lap count before. It was a sacred ritual.

He looked at the clock. 10:57. Several varsity swimmers were practicing a few lanes over, executing butterflies, rippling the water wildly, making a hell of a slapping racket that echoed throughout the funky old pool complex. Suddenly, Gabe couldn't focus, overcome by apprehension. He shoved off again, deciding it was lap sixteen after all, to finish all twenty-one laps of his kilometer in complete bewilderment.

As he walked back through the emptied August campus to South High from the pool, his 10:57 apprehension, that jolt of forgotten lap count, hardened into a premonition. Gabe became aware his father was dead.

The premonition was not some New Agey blood-bond intimation. It had the freaky certainty of fact. Patrick was dead, dead at 10:57

a.m. as sure as if Gabe had finally given in to a thousand fantasies and temptations and perfect chances and killed his father himself.

Blotting the morning's blue sky, iron-gray clouds had massed. A warm rain began, light but steady. On the sidewalk in front of Edna Victoria, a thin blonde he recognized but didn't know began to weep, pressed against an older man's shoulder. In her sad ardor, she knocked over a suitcase on the curb as a taxi waited. "I always think of you, Dad." She wrenched herself from the embrace. "You know that. Goodbye."

Gabe hastened into the foyer. On the stairs, he tried to smile as he passed his new Thai neighbor, Tan, who grinned and bowed. Grateful that the rainwater dripping from his forelocks masked the moisture in his eyes, Gabe clutched the handrail as he hurried by.

"Gabe, you okay?" Tan called.

Gabe waved okay, okay, but dashing past the breezeway's wrought iron posts, he began prowling the cage of his own dread. *Oh God, not now, no bawling in public, not after I've faked fortitude in so many waiting rooms and labs for so long*. This was stupid—the old man didn't deserve his tears. He was entrapped in a cage of guilt, too, hating how he'd left things with his father, his last words to him. *Yes, I am ashamed of you.*

Now he'd never be able to say goodbye to his own father. Big deal, right? Gabe didn't want to care, but he did. Warm tears slicked through the raindrops on his face. What would a face-to-face parting with his own father have been like?

Nothing like that scene on the street, the blonde and the dignified father. Instead, zapped by morphine in his orange vinyl armchair, clenching the remote control, Patrick Rafferty would attempt to yell at Gabe for more of the ice cubes he now sucked in lieu of swallowing food or drink. But he'd choke on his own command. Still seizing the remote, he'd grab Gabe's arm, as if to yank his son under with him, a drowning man burbling his last words: "*Goddamn you!*"

Wiping his face, he checked his messages. After a long pause, a small, wavering voice. "Gabe, you better come. Now. This is your mom." Then his Uncle Tony in traffic, barely audible. "Just got off the phone with your mom…damn shame…see you over there, kid. Abandoned that schmoozer in Colorado Springs. Heading north now."

Both messages had been left only minutes ago, just after Elena must have found Patrick lifeless in that damn armchair.

He thought of his poor mother, stranded in the sudden silence, alone with her husband's corpse. She would be watchful, trying to recall anything her old country Slavic grandparents taught her about vampires and the undead, terrified of any sign of Patrick Rafferty's uncanny resurrection.

If Gabe sped home, he might beat Tony to Butcher Creek. In the gutter along South High, a dead slug floated. Wet head swirling, Gabe mustered thanks for the cancer's final swiftness. In the last few days, the malignancies clawing into Patrick's bladder, then his kidneys, had left the old man in such weakened agony that Gabe had to fight back the impulse to deliver him from his pain. *Pat*-ricide, with a pillow? Gentle as bedtime, he could've snuffed his father for good.

Finally there was nothing between Gabe and the old neighborhood but the wastewater canal. Gabe smiled, sideways and sardonic, at a newly excavated grave in the little Catholic cemetery that crouched just north of the refinery. The graveyard wandered a little hillock along a cut-off farm ditch, now weed choked. Its century-old elms, dying of thirst, were spiny skeletons, dead as the Catholics buried there. Was that tidy new six-foot pit already dug to receive Patrick Rafferty?

The tiny brick houses that lined the diagonal road were hardly larger than the 4x4 pickups hulking beside them or the old, slumbering RVs blocking their narrow driveways. As the sun strained to poke through the clouds, rainwater still steamed on the streets. Trashy sumacs and Chinese elms struggled, half-dead late summer canopies drooping in the steamy heat, as if they'd taken toxic sips from the decontamination ponds.

He pulled into the driveway behind his father's pickup, which faced the converted attached garage still known as "Gabe's room." Relieved there were no strange cars yet, no priest, no mortician, Gabe entered through the patio, into Elena's tiny garden. Hollyhocks, cosmos, and daylilies sank in the rain around the locust tree.

The kitchen looked immaculate, as usual. A tray of ice cubes melted in the sink.

He set the tray back in the freezer and avoided the TV den by taking the hall. A seam of light bounced through the wedged bathroom door, the shower pounding. Gabe knocked, then pressed himself against the door. "Ma! How you doin'?"

"I just felt all hot and grimy, you know?" she called. "Like I had something crawling on my skin. So, you got the message I put on your stupid voicemail?"

"I came right over."

"I'll be out of here in a minute."

"No hurry, Ma." Odd to carry on ordinary conversation while a human being lay dead in the next room. At the doorway he glimpsed the formless shape on the recliner in the den. Shrouded by a crocheted blanket, his father's body seemed paired with the TV's silent screen. Gabe could not remember the last time the set had been turned off.

Spooked, he lost his nerve and about-faced, going through the kitchen back to the side garden's patio.

Gabe landed in the still-wet swinging chair, too mortified to sway, too jumpy to sit still. He folded his hands in his lap and wished he had a drink, something stiff and adult. Maybe he was his father's son after all, though the deeper Patrick drank, the more guarded Gabe's own drinking had become. After all, Pat's booze-fueled recklessness had not only wiped out indispensable illusions about his parents' marriage, but had helped wreck the most sustained relationship of Gabe's life.

On that thought of Marty, his phone sounded. "I guess I'm really going through with it, Gabe. My scholarship is still solid, and even though the feds have frozen my father's business assets, I'm paying for the flight to Rome from my savings. I take off next week."

"I miss you, baby."

"I miss you, too. But I can't stay here. I get the feeling my folks want me out of this nasty scene, anyway. They're going to try to sell the Castle Pines house for the equity and get a place in Denver while they endure my father's trial."

"I want to see you. When do you leave?"

"In a couple days. I can't see you, Gabe. It would kill me to say goodbye."

"It would kill me *not* to say goodbye. I still love you. I never stopped loving you."

"I never stopped loving you."

"Then live with me, for God's sakes! I'm an expert on living on nothing. We'll be fine."

"I've got to get away. There's no other way I can finish my degree, and the scholarship only applies to senior year at the Italian campus." Marty's voice sounded hesitant now, as if he was forcing himself to give a rationale. It didn't make any sense.

"I don't know how to make this more clear. I don't want to lose you. I want to spend my life with you."

Marty was crying. He couldn't speak for a while, then blubbered out, "I love you so much. Goodbye."

Gabe looked up into the locust. His pathetic sixth grade birdhouse was gone, an absence as unaccountable as Marty's confounding goodbye. Had some summer storm finally knocked the birdhouse to pieces?

He didn't see it in the branches. He was disgusted, flabbergasted, caught off balance by Marty's ridiculous phoned-in goodbye. It was like watching helplessly as someone beat their own skull against a concrete wall, or a moth fluttered toward a candle's flame. Or tried to fly to Rome. If Marty's love had any of the power and urgency Gabe felt, he couldn't do this. He and Candy, both saying goodbye on the excuse of academic goals. That wasn't love, it couldn't be. Fuck it.

From the swinging chair, Gabe turned away to the patio's other vista, the tall corrugated metal wall of Patrick's workshop. The sun blazed stronger through thinning clouds, but the yard immediately went into shadow behind the pitched metal roof.

This was Patrick's domain, and it showed. A newer, ugly concrete driveway connected Pat's industrial-strength steel workshop to the alley. His workshop occupied the space where Elena's mother's legendary vegetable garden had flourished before Gabe was barely old enough to remember—tomatoes, basil, peppers, fat zucchini, and corn as high as the toxic air could produce.

Now that the old man was gone, the whole prefab monstrosity could be unscrewed, disassembled, and sent packing. They could even blast away the foundation, resurrecting Grandma's garden.

"You've been thinking about the grandma you never got to know." It was Uncle Tony, appearing from the kitchen door to hand Gabe a Bloody Mary in a jelly-jar glass. "I can always tell by the limpid cloud that settles over your brow." Tony raised his glass. "She was a wonderful lady, just like your mother. Terrible errands ahead, Gabe, for you and Elena. Whatever you need, I'm here to help with arrangements."

"Thanks." Gabe clinked glasses with Tony's. What was the etiquette for this moment? Should they be half-crocked when the mortician arrived? "Have you talked to Mom yet?"

"Just checked on her. Elena hoped the shower might revive her, but she's just spent. She was up most of the night. She said to tell you she's going to take a break, lie down for a minute." Swatting off rain droplets, Tony joined him on the swinging bench. "And how are you doing, Gabriel?"

"Most of the past year, I've fantasized about killing him. Guess now I won't be charged with murder after all."

"We've all wanted to kill off the old man at one time or another. But, Jesus, just remember how hard he worked to keep your bottomless belly full."

"He did. Yeah. Mom cooked and served, no matter how many of her casseroles he pretended to gag on. She also did all the cleaning up—after working her twelve-hour shifts at the clinic, then stopping by the supermarket to spend her paycheck. But by God, Pat Rafferty did contribute some money for some of our groceries. Yesirree."

"Just keep in mind that he helped provide for my and Elena's mother, too, when I was still in the service and trying to start my family. Before cancer knocked him around so bad, let's remember who Pat really was."

"An intolerant asshole? You always gave him too much credit."

"You never gave him enough." Tony sipped from the jelly glass with exaggerated fastidiousness. "In my experience, anyone who calls someone an asshole is usually an asshole, too."

Gabe tried to absorb the truth of that, straight up, from his godfather. He thought back to his and Patrick's best times, after his sophomore year in college when Gabe took a summer job with the maintenance company, working by Patrick's side at the refinery. Gabe painted the metal skins of tanks and scaffolds while Patrick soldered a labyrinth of catwalks and supply pipes between the oil reservoirs. Scraping rust off metal railings above the sludge pots, Gabe had daydreamed he would sail that shit-stream out of Butcher Creek for good. He fantasized would develop into a real scholar, author of a seminal text—while still in graduate school—*Existentialist Tendencies in Contemporary Eastern European Poetry*. But at summer's end, Gabe had taken unexpected pride in that summer's hard labor beside Patrick, proud of the unwashable primer stains on his arms he wore back to campus in the fall.

"I can't be one of those guys who whines about I never got to know my old man," he told Tony. "I really did, that summer. But like any given asshole, I stuck around, came home too often, and got to know him too well after that."

"Too bad you couldn't see what was in front of your nose. Pat provided this almost middle-class, almost comfortable existence." Tony pointed toward the workshop. "You despise it, but it's as magnificent as Dioclĕtian's Palace. And why did he need it? Because the moment you were born, with my mom—your grandma—still living here, Pat provided for a bedroom of your own. Ingenious, how he rigged one for you out of that little garage he used as a workshop back then. So, he went without his work space the whole time you were growing up."

"He more than made up for it."

"It wasn't just a vanity project. Pat always hoped he could make a go of the furniture work. When his health starting going to hell, he just got stuck. Give your dad his due, Gabe. You're his shining achievement. Of course you're better than he is, that was the whole plan! He had to endure the Army and crawl though sewage to get as far as he did, and look. He raised a scholar and a gentleman, an American success story!"

"Ah, Tony. No wonder you sell so much real estate. You believe your own hype. Even now, you gin up our sad little tale as a patriotic narrative when it's really just another tale of a homophobic racist furious his only son was a faggy little bookworm."

"Come on, Gabe. I thought he handled the gay thing pretty well."

"He just didn't really care enough to fight."

Whatever his godfather started to say was lost when his phone rang. Tony kept working on weekends, always hustling the next deal or smoothing over any given client's troubled waters. Tony took the call into the kitchen along with their empty glasses.

Gabe knew he couldn't keep stalling. He would have to go into that house. He would have to rouse his mother, and together they would have to call the funeral home. But looking through the sliding door into the kitchen and the dark den beyond, Gabe found himself heading into Diocletian's Palace.

Inside, Gabe inhaled the familiar smells of oil on concrete, lawnmower gasoline mixed with sour grass clippings, and old wood chips on the table saw. Gabe's kiddie tricycle, his Sting Ray, and his battered road bike—another discard of Karlo's—hung upside down in the high rafters, a chronological transportation museum cocooned in cobwebs.

Yet the palace had its intimate corner, under the solitary window, which allowed faint light over the worktable. With its stool, vise, and pegboard array of tools, this had been his father's command central. An old snapshot was taped under the pegboard, Pat and his mom flanking Gabe at his high school graduation, Elena under a rococo Maria Callas hairstyle, Pat with graying copper curls and mischief in his eyes.

On the worktable, from God knew where, Patrick had put an old purple ceramic bowl holding a few nails and screws, that Gabe had carefully inscribed in third grade: Happy Birthday Daddy! And beside it, tottering on one of its many uneven sides, was Gabe's historic birdhouse, now in the process of being patched. At Elena's request, no doubt, Patrick had been reinforcing the rooflines with neat little redwood soffits and eaves. Only one little piece remained to be added. The wood glue was open beside it. Gingerly, Gabe set the cap back on the tube, fighting the feeling he was tampering with evidence at a crime scene.

He sat on the stool, lowering his face against his forearms. What had caused his father to abandon this almost completed, final handyman job? What pain could have been that intense, that hopeless? And why did he have to suffer it during this little act of love, for Elena, for Gabe, on behalf of salvaging—no, renovating—this contemptible little birdhouse?

This evidence of arrested vitality seemed cruel, seemed the very reason, in retaliation, that humans had invented art and God. It was too late ever to repair, salvage, or improve his experience of his father, too late to salve the wounds, too late to soothe Patrick's final seismic rages and ravages with some generous half-truth, some act of love. Even Gabe's last concentrated time with Patrick, shuttling him to radiology, had been a bitten-tongue endurance test for him.

Maybe love had to be an endurance test sometimes, not necessarily easy or easily avoided. Love had to exist in the unworthy father; love had to persist in the inadequate son. Maybe it called for forgiveness, even if Patrick never evolved toward equity or even decency.

Oh-so-decent, humane and equitable, head full of existentialist Eastern European poetry, Gabe realized he had never evolved toward forgiveness. He'd never even tried.

He splashed his face in the basin and prepared himself for his father's remains and his mother's exhaustion. When he crossed the yard, he saw Tony roving the driveway, his ear still fused to his phone.

Gabe passed through the sliding door to the dining room, finding his mother standing in the doorway that led into the den. Hands on her hips, her back to Gabe, she seemed to be mustering the courage to approach Patrick's body.

Gabe coughed so as not to startle her, coming up behind. "Ma, did you get some rest?"

"Gabe." She pivoted, burying her face in his chest. She smelled of Ivory soap. So thin, lost in her formless housedress, her damp hair combed straight out, she seemed so reduced, so unready for the great tasks awaiting them. "Naw, I couldn't sleep. Didn't really want to. I'll get some sleep tonight."

"What can I do for you, Mama?"

"That's what he asked me. The minute he wanted the TV turned off, I knew. I called you."

"I'll stay here tonight."

"Yeah, that would be good. And I think we should call the priest. For Last Rites. What they call Prayer for the Sick now."

At first, Gabe thought his mother's mind had slipped a little, understandable for one who'd gone without good sleep for so long. Then, peering into in the dark room, Gabe studied the blankets and pillows covering the figure in the orange chair. The shriveled mass seemed to stir.

Ah. All along, Gabe's certainty had been a trick of mind, intuition masquerading as fact. His mom had been trying to tell him the end was almost here, and he was needed. Tony had hurried to support her and his godson. *Terrible errands ahead, Gabe.*

"Your father's been asking for you." Elena nodded toward the armchair. "You better go to him. I'll call Father Rafael."

When his mother left for the kitchen phone, Gabe slunk against the open door into the den. He felt paralyzed, unable to force himself to go in. Alone! Jesus, now the endurance test offered a make-up exam.

Part of him didn't give a damn whether he flunked the test or flunked his second chance. His ironclad stubbornness, his urge to withdraw from interaction with his father, to leave the ball tossed in midair—wasn't that Patrick alive in himself?

The very thing that had estranged Marty and hardened his hurt feelings was Gabe's attempt to avoid sharing the full pain of his father's vast flaws. Just as Patrick had cornered himself here, refusing the world, Gabe had refused to overcome his shame. He had numbed his heart and shoved his father into a closet. Who needed to do the forgiving around here?

Okay, he could shove himself away from the door. Okay, he did. Now, what the hell would he say?

Gabe stood over Patrick, who seemed to have withered to this sack of bones overnight, even his wonderful coppery-silver hair bleached white, dry, already yellowing like dead matter. He was not really an old man, just sixty. This illusory geriatric frailty was just another of cancer's victories.

Overwhelmed by pity, Gabe hovered as if he were the ghostly one. His father's skeletal being seemed anchored in solitude, monstrous, self-contained. As if assigned to the ring of hell where his twin transgressions were Willful Intolerance and Pride of Ignorance, Patrick had become the very image of his sins, friendless, incurious, cast off from life's fullness. Fleshless, sterile, drained of color, he was condemned to stare at his stranded self in the dead screen of the television, a merciless reflection.

The dense silence hung, and Gabe longed for the good old days when the TV blared. He knelt by the armrest, his hand over his father's. "Hey, Dad, it's me. Gabe."

Patrick almost smiled, but it dissolved in a painful swallow.

"Wanna ice cube, Daddy?"

Patrick shook his head. He withdrew his hand from under Gabe's to clasp his son's fingers.

"You know, looking back," Gabe blurted, "I'm glad we got to spend that time together going to the radiology clinic." Amazed at the half-truth, Gabe was just as amazed at the strength of his voice. "Been meaning to tell you I'm sorry."

"For what?"

"Staying away. Not letting you know the people in my life. For being such an asshole."

This time Patrick really did smile. His hand went to Gabe's hair, which he tried to rough with his fingers, and then seemed to push his head faintly forward and down. As Gabe rested his head on his father's knee, Patrick pressed it there.

"I just been waiting for you," his father struggled to mumble. "I can't do any more for you or your mama, Gabe. I wanted to, but I can't. Can't do a damn thing for her anymore. But you're here now."

Gabe called for his mother to come, then buried his face against Patrick's leg. *Forgive me, Father, bless me*, he whispered as the hand that held him grew heavy, then cold.

PART II

Chapter Nine

Half In Love

Gabe's time in Paris was self-funded, a vacation summer week grafted on to a security systems industry conference in Barcelona. His plan was to explore Paris—spend his days wandering the streets and the museums, nights in the cafés and bars, maybe finding a friend among fellow travelers or amiable natives, then head south on the night train. South to Barcelona via a stopover in Arles, since he was on a Van Gogh kick, reading the doomed artist's letters to his brother, *Dear Theo*, each night in his cramped, peeling, sweaty room in the Marais quarter.

So, using his vacation time outside the Barcelona expense account, he was on the cheap. Great as the assignment might sound, he felt like a lackey. Though Todd Ramirez's wife, Zeena, his section boss, had championed him for the Barcelona conference, he was sure SecureTek approved him for Europe only because all his superiors were too busy making money and expanding the North American airport security biz to waste a week overseas. But they knew SecureTek Systems, Inc., needed a presence at the conference, so they sent their most expendable staffer.

His expendability earned him his first chance to see Europe and let him breathe free for a while. Evenings at the Grand Hotel Saint-Saëns—in a squeezed room not a quarter-note as grand as it sounded—he'd crawl under his window onto the fire escape and listen to the families in all the adjacent buildings argue at dinnertime. From the incomprehensible squabbles all around, it sounded as if every marriage in Paris was about to terminate in screams and shattered glass.

Gabe's hesitant explorations of bars hadn't yielded any new

friends. The sketchy taverns in the Marais seemed to specialize in shaven-headed, thuggish-looking guys who acted like mincing queens. The beauties in a Halles club catwalked like a nightly convention of male models, a self-possessed, insolent mass. When a few cute guys did try to pick him up, Gabe scared them off the minute he twanged, "parlez-vous Anglais?"

Because the love affairs with Adam and Marty—like vacations from himself—had both ended abruptly, without any clear cause Gabe could understand, and because he didn't really like bars or the cheery mendacity of hookup self-advertisements, and because his experience of promiscuity was a little exciting and a lot grim, Gabe wondered if the gay lifetime ahead was nothing but a big drag. Alone in Paris, he felt sick and tired of being gay, though he knew that was absurd, like being sick of eating or breathing.

But even in solitude, he was happy. Or thought he was. Each day of his introduction to Paris, he marched along according to the *Guide Michelin* in middlebrow, Middle American dumbbell enjoyment until, toward the end of the week, he finished the four- and three-star attractions and delved into the twos at the Musée Cluny. He wasn't into medieval textiles but was drawn to the museum's site, built over Roman baths. Around other gays, there would've been no end of stupid jokes about ancient bathhouse antics. Alone, Gabe just stared into dry, fleshless stonework. Studying the barren pit, he felt the first weariness with his *Guide Michelin* tour, and especially his own company. He looked forward to catching the night train south to Arles the following evening.

Gabe wandered from the baths to the famous tapestries, an entire room devoted to *The Lady and the Unicorn*'s six huge panels. As he read the *Michelin*ese, "each panel an expression of the five senses" in a woven forest of solitary trees, Gabe couldn't have been less ready or more charmed when a familiar voice called his name. Encircled by the medieval narrative, Candy Holmes was alone, looking relaxed and chic, her simple blond bob now grown out and tied in a ponytail. Laughing, her eyes went wide, then narrowed in mock suspicion. "Hey, are you really *my* Gabe? The real Gabe Rafferty?"

"I am." Brazen, they kept checking each other out. He took her hand, and they laughed, astonished at the unlikelihood of such a random meeting thousands of miles from South High Street. "I am forever yours, my damsel."

"Oh? Now I'm your damsel?" Her smile became sly, even more crooked and slanted than usual, and she squeezed his hand with a guy's crushing firmness. "Wish I'd known, Gabe," she said, letting his hand drop, "back in the olden days at Conrad's when I was half in love with you. As it turned out, I wasn't Ben's damsel, either."

"Huh. I thought it was poor Ben who wasn't *your* knight in shining armor." He glanced at the tapestries. "I knew you were nuts about French lit, but I just never would've guessed you were intrigued by medieval tapestries."

"I took that medieval lit class for my degree, and loved it, but now I'm just revisiting my lost enthusiasms. What are you doing in Paris?"

"I'm still working for SecureTek. They sent me over for a conference."

"SecureTek was supposed to be temporary! Just till you got rich and paid your bills."

"Guess what? After almost a year, I'm still not rich. But guess what? I pay my bills and have furniture now. You should check our old crash pad. It's almost civilized. I don't cross over to campus too much, except to shoot baskets with Todd Ramirez or swim laps at the pool. Our paths don't cross much anymore, do they?" The last Gabe knew, after her own graduation in June, Candy would see off the sorority sisters she'd mothered, shut down the house, and stay in Dallas for the summer to work for her father's company as a front office receptionist. "I sure hope you didn't lose your enthusiasms."

"Not really, but I'm not going to be on campus at all anymore, Gabe. I'm moving on to California this fall."

"Too bad! From now on, we'll only see each other by chance, then, in Paris?"

"I hope not. Like you and Ben, I decided to move on to something more practical. I got in touch with my sophomore communications professor, who's teaching at UC Davis. I got accepted there, with a public relations emphasis."

"Haven't you always been in public relations? Like your alumni hostess days, then as a kind of emissary from the straight world to virginal gay boys?"

"Well, one gay boy. No matter how hopeless it was, for a long while I was infatuated."

"With me? Come on. You always had much more intriguing fish to fry."

She smiled that wild, wonky grin that always slayed him. Then she stretched up to buss Gabe's cheek. "I never cared for fish."

❖

But within an hour they were wolfing down a Tunisian vendor's tuna sandwiches, Candy bringing Gabe up to date perched on the river wall between booksellers' stalls and the Seine. Her father, who'd so blithely funded her BA in literature without strings while she strung it along for seven years, now seemed to be deeper in the thrall of her stepmother. She persuaded Mr. Holmes that if he funded Candy for grad school, it would have to be in a career beyond academia. It was either that or return to Dallas and work in the family's business full-time at entry level.

"It sounds so much like Ben's predicament," Gabe said, "minus the evil stepmother."

"Ironic, isn't it? When I was so rough on Ben about it. Now that I've been back in Dallas for two months, I've had plenty of time to gnash my teeth and perform acts of contrition."

Candy was the only daughter among a small platoon of older, willful brothers. She'd always hinted her inconvenient gender was a nuisance to the family incubator supply company, which had incubated her brothers' careers in medicine, law, finance, and warfare. Her gender expelled her from this manly progression, as if the family's swanky subdivision had covenants against the grand ambitions of daughters.

"My dad actually refereed an argument between my stepmother and me a few weeks ago. Then he took her side. 'What else is a literature student going to do, anyway, except get married? And soon, I hope.' Can you believe that, here in the twenty-first century? But I'm proud of my degree, and I've got to say you inspired me, Gabe. Ben, too. Y'all's love of literature was so palpable, so intense. Even before I met you two, I was already getting wary of people who were studying business or real estate just to make a buck."

"You've got to admit, though, all three of us have ended up having to face the reality of making money."

"Don't say that, Gabe, please. Sounds like my dad's sermon."

Gabe noticed a new vulnerability in Candy. She did not seem so free or full of cheerful willfulness. Her dark eyes didn't quite meet his so boldly as before.

Gabe knew how deceptive those eyes could be. With lids at half-mast, she might seem to be seeking some idle pleasure, but she was probably going inward, lost in her alert, appreciative mind. Wolfing down the sandwich and gazing at the Seine, Candy changed the subject and got them back to BS'ing with their old, competitive energy, swigging from a shared bottle of vin ordinaire. She held forth about the importance of the tapestries and the intricacies of medieval chivalric amours, the surprising sensuality of middle ages art.

"I have a more basic issue," Gabe said. "How can there be six tapestries when there are only five senses?"

"Ah. Ah, ah!" Candy began, smiling at the chance for pedantry. "My theory? The sixth has our lady under a forest sign reading '*À Mon Seul Désir*.' Couldn't it be that the sixth sense is the self itself, Gabe? Our very souls finding the will to rein in the other five?"

"Ah. Ah. Ah!" he cried, hopping off the wall to bow before her as she licked her tuna-sticky fingers. "How can I argue with that, my lady? When I have struggled all my life, without success, to rein in even one sensuous impulse?"

"Oh please, Gabe. You were once the last virgin on campus." She accepted his hand, then slipped from the wall into his steadying embrace. They wandered, arm in arm, down the quay to Shakespeare & Company to find a yellowing, decades-old Bantam paperback of Hemingway's Paris memoir *A Moveable Feast* on a crowded shelf outside the shop. Candy flipped right away to a passage where Hemingway goes without lunch, then reveals it to Sylvia Beach, who founded the bookshop itself. "I have to confess," Candy said, smoothing down the page, "that I've been reading this, a little every night, while I'm here. Just like every other pretentious American in Paris."

"Okay, I'll admit I reread it on the plane, but only when the Disney flicks failed to hold my full attention. But a lot of it bugs the hell out me. His style's so precious. I mean, Hemingway is supposed to be so plain-spoken, so objective, but he's really the world champion bullshit artist. Like this very passage. He's all, *oh Sylvia, don't worry, I have plenty to eat, don't worry about me*, blah, blah, and we're supposed to be dying of pity for poor Ernest, who can't afford lunch because he hasn't sold a single short story. He always wants it both ways. Mr. Macho. Mr. Vulnerable."

"It's not possible to be macho and vulnerable at the same time? Where would romantic love be without our macho-but-vulnerable heroes?"

"Maybe where romantic love should be," Gabe said, "in the suicide crematorium. Beside Hemingway's precious ashes."

"So, along with poor Ernest, you want to incinerate romantic love? What did it ever do?"

"Nothing. Nothing at all. It just retarded about six centuries of human development. No big deal."

"Maybe sometime we can talk more about how Marty broke your heart?"

"Where would we start? Could we include Adam, too?" If it's possible to bite your lip and laugh at the same time, that's what Gabe did. He plucked the paperback from her hands and tucked it back on the shelf in front of Sylvia Beach's old bookstore.

Wandering among the hordes of watercolorists daring to paint even more big-eyed urchins pissing into the Seine, Gabe led Candy down a stairway to the river walk. Late summer sunlight angled across the water. Below this critical, postcard mass of central Paris—Notre Dame, Hotel de Ville, Pont Neuf—the sightseeing boats breezed by, wakes slicing liquid sunlight.

Candy was walking slightly ahead, her light, gauzy dress almost transparent in the dramatic light, her footfalls quick and sure. Gabe lurched to catch her hand again. As he pointed to the dock ahead where some kids played, light hair glimmering, Gabe couldn't resist faking a Hemingway quote: *"Sometimes, when I am feeling very precious, and Gertrude is being such a bitch, I like to come down here to the quay, and borrow a cigarette—a very neat, very perfect, but completely free cigarette—from the fishermen and their children.*"

"*But...but then, when the weather is very bad,"* Candy said, her face set and serious, *"and the river grows very turgid, and my stomach grumbles, I like to head over to the very good hotel where Scott and*

Zelda insisted on taking several rooms. Zelda, of course, was not feeling very well."

"And Scott's dick," Gabe added, swinging her hand, *"well, Scott's dick was shapely enough but very, very small. It began, then, to rain."*

Candy cackled. "Scott's dick began to rain?"

He shrugged and reminded her he wasn't as steeped, anymore, in the copy editor's life. "Now that I'm a corporate zombie, I've completely forgotten about pronouns and their antecedents, if I ever knew. So, dicks begin to rain."

"Sometimes, though," she said, "they don't rain enough."

At a riverside café, Candy and Gabe each ordered a decent glass of white wine, a splurge to celebrate their reconnection. She finally admitted to her *raison de* being here in Paris. "It's supposed to be a grand tour fling before my wedding. Labor Day weekend, okay? Don't look so shocked. I'm here with my fiancé. Though Buddy and I were high school sweethearts, this new phase all happened fast. We just collided again, thrown together in our fathers' country club scene, and it was like our decade apart didn't matter. Our base in Paris is a dinky room in a one-star hotel, just ahead, near the Petit Palais. Sometimes, though, I wonder if Buddy's dick has forgotten how to rain."

"But how could that be? I mean, look at you, Candy. You could turn a gay boy straight."

"Didn't work with you, you son of a bitch." She smiled. "I seem to have another magic power. My dark woods breed an evil enchantment. I make the unicorn's horn go limp. Apparently, I kill passion before it can flower."

"What's wrong with this guy?"

"What's wrong with me?"

I looked at her up and down, hard and brazen, appraising. "Nothing!"

"You're staring at my breasts like a straight boy."

"They're so soft and sweet. What man wouldn't get lost in them? I mean *enchantment*, if you will, without the evil."

Candy laughed. "*If you will.*" Then she frowned. "But I don't think Buddy would agree."

"What about your master's, then?"

"Oh, Buddy's coming out to Davis with me. Studying pharmacology. Their program's top ranked."

Gabe's impoverished Butcher Creek psyche could not stop puzzling over Candy's class of affluent people—just like Ben's—and their assumed prerogatives, as if everyone had such a wealth of choices, such a surplus of them they could just screw up and start a new sequence of privilege. Yet he couldn't puzzle with any concentration, not with the Seine pouring that golden light, captive in their goblets. He finally noticed the simple diamond ring around Candy's finger, gleaming in the sun.

He was, after all, really here, elevated from the Mile High to the City of Love in the company of an old friend who happened to be a gorgeous woman. He wanted to freeze this moment, seize it the way kids catch fireflies in glass jars and exult in the fleeting radiance. He felt fully adult, discussing Candy's love life and imagining himself a real man, for once, cosmopolitan, competent, desired, and sturdy. But he also careened too closely into full empathy, so intimate with man trouble himself, just another queer enjoying a woman's confidences and mirroring them back. That was the bald truth, but who the hell wanted to be bald or truthful in Paris? So he deflected the subject.

"You know Milan Kundera's theory of kitsch," he said, sipping wine, then gesturing with the goblet toward the river, ever the suave continental. "How it's really just the self regarding itself. The self treasuring itself having the emotions rather than really directly feeling them. Like the preciousness that crops up, say, in Hemingway's Paris memoir."

"I thought kitsch was just cute shit that's gone sour. Like, say, those kids-pissing-in-the-Seine watercolors."

"Okay. But what I wanted to say is that this moment, sipping wine with you by the pissy, golden Seine, feels so real, so direct."

"Isn't it pathetic, though, for us lit types to be so mannered, so distant from experience that we even need to spell it out? 'Real'? 'Direct'? I'd rather just have the fucking feeling, Gabe. Like a trailer park girl feels about her latest crush."

"But aren't you romanticizing her?"

"Okay. But what I wouldn't give to be that trailer park chick. Or the lady with the unicorn!"

"Oh yeah, that's direct experience. A freakin' fairy tale!"

"I'm not expecting Davis to be any fairy tale. I'll settle for a little direct experience, though. Even though Buddy and his friends who've studied pharmacy and toxicology in Texas might actually be too real for me. They can sound like sharks sometimes, focused on big profits. You'd think it never crossed their minds their work might save people from deadly conditions."

Gabe could not help think of Candy's risky infatuation with Conrad back on South High, ready to joke that he was another boyfriend into pharmaceuticals, but didn't say it. Instead, he wondered if Buddy recognized how Candy's moral viewpoint had emerged and matured since their high school romance.

Despite his improbable presence along this Parisian riverside and the surreal luck of the encounter with Candy, Gabe couldn't shake the sensation that this impulsive magic was as true and direct as it got. This slaphappy moment felt uncomplicated, existing just to be absorbed and enjoyed. He had become the trailer-park girl.

He walked Candy back to her hotel, which faced the Seine. The fading evening still seemed drenched in a gilded glow. At the doors into the modest, modern place, she gripped his arm. "Let me recite the verse that follows, Gabe, in the sixth tapestry. Under that overarching title, *À Mon Seul Désir*:

According to my desire alone
by my will alone
love desires only beauty of soul
to calm passion."

Inside the open foyer, a tall, disheveled, handsome young man applauded. "Bravo, mademoiselle. My sentiments exactly. Let love beat all passion into submission, that's what I say."

Buddy had been drinking in the hotel bar, waiting at the window for Candy to return. His shirttails half dangling and half tucked into cords, his long brown hair aiming in five directions, he looked like an overgrown preppy on a long bender. Candy accepted his hug, more ambush than embrace, and deflected his kiss Parisian-style, glanced off the cheek.

"Where the hell have you been, darling?" he asked with the slight Dallas drawl Candy had lost. "I've been worried sick."

"You don't look sick. You look kind of drunk."

"You look like you found a new boyfriend. Already!" He flashed a wild, white smile and extended his hand to Gabe. "You know, you two look great together. I could see you guys strolling up from the river bank, backlit in the evening sun, pretty as a picture postcard." Affable, earnest, and tipsy as hell, he studied Gabe, then blurted, "Why don't *you* marry her?"

❖

The next day, Gabe stored his luggage at the Grand Hotel Saint-Saëns until he could catch the midnight train. Candy was free in the late afternoon and invited Gabe along for dinner with her and Buddy that evening. So Gabe polished off a few two-star attractions he's missed near the Saint-Saëns, then wandered across the river, back to the Musée Cluny to regard it again in light of what Candy had taught him. He found a new appreciation for its medieval façades, the "refined communal longing" he'd been blind to before, as well as new admiration for Candy's easy academic curiosity and commentary.

In the nearby Luxembourg Gardens, Candy met Gabe alone beside a playground jammed with kids, crazy with monkeyshines. Even the parents seemed euphoric, exulting in yet another perfect late summer afternoon. The two friends kissed the Parisian way and laughed at themselves.

Gabe wore his best clothes, set aside for the Barcelona conference keynote, his only good slacks and a silk button-down, because he suspected Candy would again array herself brilliantly. He was right. She wore her ponytail collected under a tiny scarf, Ray-Bans, bright red lipstick, a light, frilly blouse that exposed her shoulders and showed off a pearl pendant on a gold chain and the cleavage it dropped into, and some kind of crazy, tight pedal pushers. The dads on playground benches stared at her, their cartoon eyes glued in helpless heterosexual automaticity. Somehow Candy looked both sophisticated and deeply American, and in a matching paradox, both schoolgirlish and seductive.

"So, where's Buddy?" Gabe asked, casual. But as often in Paris over the past week, his heart felt loopy as a chimp on the jungle gym.

"He'll join us for dinner later."

"So…" He stepped back, eyeing her head to toe with deliberation. "All this is for little ol' me, Candy?"

"*All this*? Look at you, Gabe. You even combed your hair." She took a tissue from her purse and swiped her lipstick off his cheek, then pinched his silk sleeve. "All for me, darlin'?"

"We gotta stop flirting. I thought we wrote the memo a long time ago. I'm a queer."

"So stop the goddamn flirting, then."

Gabe was lost in the moment, bedazzled, swept away in emotions he didn't understand and couldn't even name. Sex, he thought he finally understood. Love, not so much, and he wondered if he was not at least half in love with Candy. Maybe he'd always been.

They found a table at an outdoor café among old men playing chess. With the jubilant playground nearby, it was like a setup, Nature declaring "check" on two young adults clueless as to their next move, one crucial choice that would ease their transit between childhood and dotage. They ordered beers, big ones, and belted them back in the lingering heat.

"Look, I like Buddy," Gabe said. "He's funny, he's good lookin'. But what's his problem? You're a raving beauty, brilliant, and somewhat morally evolved for a dang girl. Why doesn't he just grab you, toss you over his shoulder, and book the Flying Elvises?"

"*Honeymoon in Vegas*?" Candy produced the sideways smile he wanted. "But isn't there another old Nicolas-Cage-in-Vegas flick where his alcoholism ruins everything? Anyway, it's not all Buddy's fault. We fought all the time in high school. It's been rocky from the very start, wild, yin and yang."

"Yin and yang? Come on. It's more preppy meets preppy."

"I thought Buddy was the real thing. And if I was wrong, that doesn't mean I was an idiot. It means I'm human."

Gabe felt like a prick, reducing her flailing engagement to some affluent straight people's realm of mating. His compensatory stereotypes were her stinging heartaches. "I'm sorry," he said. "I thought my love life was the only one that went like this."

"Yeah, what about you?" She laughed, small and cackling. "Did you and Marty make up, even a little?"

"He's off to Italy again. We did keep in touch but never got back together. It was as if he was willing to forgo something wonderful because his pride was hurt. Or some damn other thing I never understood. So, that's how it's gone. Fun and love, then sudden pain and agony."

"I think the real course of love is a lot like that a lot of the time, Gabe."

"Really? Or did I anger the gods without knowing why? Am I under a curse I can't break until I answer some riddle? Trouble is, I can't come to life until I solve the riddle. But I don't even know the question."

"I don't either, Oedipus. But I know the answer." Candy pointed to the kids on the monkey bars and nodded toward the old men slumped at their chessboards. "We come in helpless and prone, and we go out the same way. I think we're supposed to make the most of the time in between."

They waited for Buddy to join them for dinner at Gabe's favorite cheap Indochinese place, but he didn't show up at the appointed hour. Over appetizers, Candy explained how her father had been hounding her.

"On top of the poor investment I've been since undergrad days, now I'm back to being an embarrassment to the family, a disgrace far on the spinster side of twenty-five. It's so selfish of me, isn't it? Sometimes I feel like I'm getting married just so my stock goes up in my father's eyes. I just don't know where I'm going with Buddy." She idly pinched *une potsticker* with her chopsticks. "I've been afraid our engagement might not survive this trip. Maybe I should have listened to my family when they mocked my obsession with chivalric love codes."

Gabe thought her family's mockery was crass and wanted to defend love codes in all their manifestations. He disliked bottom-line corporate obsessions and how his job at SecureTek devoured more and more of his time and mental roaming room, to the point where in the past few months he hadn't read much, certainly not medieval love poetry. Instead he studied cost analysis specs for metal detectors in regional airports so he could appear conversant with aviation managers' bottom lines.

"Don't listen to your family," he said to Candy. "Close in on your dream. Get your master's, but not in public relations. Hack your way deep into the weeds of medieval literature. Seriously, don't let anybody stop you. If anybody even implies that chivalric love codes aren't the most important damn thing on this planet, you send 'em to me, okay?" He put up his dukes. "I'll fend 'em off with these."

Candy smiled and squeezed his upraised wrist. "Thanks. That's very chivalric of you. I like that in a man, Gabe. Passion."

"What I like," Buddy said, materializing at the table in preppy costume—polo shirt, chinos, and boat shoes—"are the exotic drinks they have at these Chinese places."

Candy flashed a sly grin. "Whiskey on the rocks?"

Buddy slipped into the booth beside her and kissed her cheek. "My sentiments exactly." He signaled a waiter before he shook Gabe's hand. "Great to see you again, Greg."

Despite his preppy couture, Buddy looked even more disheveled and careless. His hair drooped in oily bangs, and dark whiskers peppered his strong jaw. He'd been drinking, on the edge of slurring his words. Still, as he and Candy joshed and chatted, Gabe noticed something manic and preoccupied in his darting gazes, as if Buddy expected a very exciting fourth person to join them any minute.

As a trio, they continued the making-a-living theme through dinner. With great effort, Gabe succeeded in not lording his true-blue proletarian credentials reverse-status style over his affluent companions. He didn't even whisper a Marxist thesis or suggest some socialist sidebar. Instead, he retreated into Margaret Mead mode, cloaking himself in the guise of anthropology, studying the fascinating mores of that elusive tribe, the American Upper Middle Class, taking mental notes and keeping his mouth shut.

Buddy was the oldest son of a renowned Dallas lawyer who'd been indispensable to Candy's father in his incubator supplier empire's legal liabilities. Gabe took it in, giving no hint how bemused he was at the mating rituals, great expectations, and cozy family connections of their class, flabbergasted by the anachronistic, arranged-marriage feeling of it all. Their engagement seemed more fitting as a tale sewn into a museum tapestry than unraveling in the new millennium amidst moo shu and lo mien. Weren't they each too smart, too alert to the Arrangement, he thought, to let it snare them in a lifelong mismatch?

Buddy was "taking a break" after finishing his undergraduate work in pharmacology. He'd been able to extend his "gap year" into three or four. After which the clan's plan had been to "cap it all" with a glorious marriage of two of suburban Dallas's glittering professional families.

Gabe studied Candy while Buddy eased back the last of the whiskey and elaborated upon the grand illusion of the families' scheme. Even though there was charm in Buddy's self-mockery, he sensed that it hurt Candy. Their marriage plans seemed reduced to a set story, traded around over cooling noodles. Meanwhile, Buddy free-associated about an itinerary that did not specifically seem to include her, subjects and pronouns deleted: "Still not sure which *gare* to take out of Paris for the rest of the grand tour, not sure what direction, maybe Brittany, maybe Geneva, maybe even Berlin."

Around there, starting his second whiskey, Buddy inquired politely after Gabe's meager affairs in Europe. When he mentioned the Barcelona airport security conference, Buddy practically jumped out of his seat, as if whom or what he'd been waiting for had finally arrived.

"Spain! Yeah, that's it! God, Greg, sorry, Gabe, I really ought to catch that night train south with you, man. Pamplona, the running of the bulls. Jesus, that's just about to start up down there. We'd have a blast and a half."

"I won't be able to visit Pamplona, though, Buddy."

"Huh." Candy eyed Gabe sidelong. "Pamplona is a new one." She shrugged. "The first I've heard of it."

"I'll be stuck in Barcelona," Gabe said, "working."

"It's cool." Buddy drummed the table. "I was jazzed by the inspiration. I can, you know, head down there on my own in the next couple days. Catch a breather in Pamplona. From what I hear, the whole town's one big party."

So Candy and Gabe weren't the only ones filtering their experience of Europe through Hemingway. Buddy's chosen poison must have been *The Sun Also Rises*, a slight tale of alcoholic young upper-middle-class dolts and dastards drinking, bullshitting, and bull running in Spain. The narrator never mentions his balls had been shot off. An ingenious literary maneuver, because as long as the shot-off balls were never mentioned, they were all the reader could think about. *Sometimes, the dick didn't start to rain.*

After dessert and more drinks, Gabe mentioned having to catch his train, and Candy, to his surprise, proposed she and Buddy see him off at the Gare Lyon. But Buddy begged off, claiming he had promised to join "that Quebec guy who works the desk at the hotel for a nightcap." So Candy came with Gabe to the train station by herself.

Together they prowled the tracks to locate the sleeper car he'd reserved, but he now felt uncoupled from his goal-by-rail. Just because he had a reservation, did he have to leave Candy stranded in the company of her dissolute fiancé? It was as if sheer forward momentum—and, okay, a stupid work conference in Spain—propelled him irrationally into the dark distance. Gabe halted with one foot on the car's step as Candy reached for his hand. "I'm so glad we had a chance to reconnect," she said. "Now, we have to stay in touch forever, okay?"

"Okay. And if Buddy really does come down to Spain, why don't you come with him and join me in Barcelona?"

"Buddy always has these excitable plans. Usually, they come to nothing. But if it does happen, Gabe, I might be seeing you really soon."

"Yeah. 'In touch forever,' right?"

"Sure, Gabe."

"*Sure, Tatie.*"

"*We will have wine...*" she said, trying to avoid cracking up as she tried to recall the passage of Hemingwayese. "*And speak...and speak the true sentences.*"

"*Sure. And go to Spain and drink the true wine.*"

They kissed, peck to peck, cheek to cheek, then Gabe climbed the steel steps alone.

❖

Gabe lay sleepless in the top bunk of the train compartment, staring out the window, listening as most of the length of France clackered under the star-scattered, moonless dark.

Before the midnight train left the station, a brisk but friendly young mother had helped him adjust the bedding after she put her two boys to bed in the opposite bunk. She'd even tucked Gabe in, laughing as she and her husband stood side by side peering at the gawky, elongated American whose feet poked from the end of the bunk. Though he was almost their age, Gabe felt like one of their kids, the special one who needed all the help he could get. Then the husband took the young mother in his arms and kissed her deep and unembarrassed, then wished her *bon nuit* and *bon voyage* and *au revoir* before he hopped off the just-moving train.

Soon the young mother was snoring softly under him while the two kids muttered through deep dreams. Instead of dreaming, Gabe's mind replayed every moment of the surprise reunion with Candy. Despite his self-conscious enjoyment of those travelogue moments along the Seine with her, he knew they'd been the opposite of Kundera's kitsch. Rare, fleeting, they'd held life's most golden luxury, the company of a soul mate.

Soul mate! He'd always despised the term as some bogus, secular impulse to bless mere human bonds in the shimmer of the sacred. But maybe that's what he'd always had with Candy without fully appreciating their instant ability to jump into the other's references and dive into spontaneous parody or role play. They could join their separate lives as readers into a mutual exploration, embarking into the wonders of a vast, ongoing cultural adventure.

He'd once stayed overnight at her sorority house, when a dinner shift was to be followed by a parent-daughter brunch the next morning. Finding Gabe waking up on the sun porch daybed, a gaggle of sorority sisters held him captive and teased him: "We're all wondering, by the way. Candy's spent so many nights away from the house. Are you really her new man? Maybe her secret fiancé? Or at least a friend with privileges?"

Trying to smile, he told them, "No, I'm pretty much her friend with dining room duties."

"That's too bad," the boldest girl said. "Because we were all just saying you and Candy seem made for each other."

The night train rattled Gabe farther and farther from Candy, and despite the gentle noises of the little family arrayed around him, he felt ever more alone.

Nearing Arles, past dawn, the young mother gathered her boys, combed hair, buttoned shirts, cinched belts, and jokingly mimed doing the same for Gabe. He laughed and helped with the luggage as they all hurried out. The kids jumped into the arms of a gray-haired man, *Grandpapa!* Gabe waved them goodbye, feeling stupidly attached to the family and already missing them though they hadn't spoken a word in a common language. Someday, Gabe hoped, somehow, when he took a journey, there would always be someone he loved to see him off and welcome him home.

After the family disappeared into Grandpapa's Renault and the train hissed and groaned toward Marseilles, he realized he was alone at the small station except for the stationmaster, who played solitaire while his coffee brewed. Banners drooped on the lampposts, *Festival Cinema de l'Amour*, and the sun rose behind dusty trees, already promising stifling, breezeless heat.

Gabe's simple plan to stay in Arles and wander among Van Gogh's streetscapes and landscapes was thwarted as soon as he explored the small city's center, looking for an inexpensive hotel. A festival of romantic films was in progress at the Roman amphitheater and nearby venues, apparently a hot ticket for every footloose couple in France, since all the hotels were booked solid. Even the backpacker places were full up, every bunk.

So he spent the long, hot morning as if sealed in Plexiglas, aimless among the Roman sites, narrow side streets, and sun-wracked squares. With high noon, more and more couples appeared, hand in hand everywhere, studying the film schedule at cafés or dipping toes into fountains, laughing as if they were starring in their own kitschy movie.

In the stark shadows of crooked streets, Gabe dwelled on poor Van Gogh. He reread the Arles sections of *Dear Theo* in a sidewalk café crowded with more damn couples belting back beers and smooching. Here in Arles, Vincent's love life had been reduced to the occasional prostitute, and not much of that, since he often couldn't afford to buy bread. His mental troubles climaxed in Arles. He mentioned strange violent fights at brothels and failed to mention bouts in mental asylums, all the while assuring Theo, his benefactor, that his mind, at least, was just fine. In a funk, Gabe felt closer to Vincent than to the amorous festival goers all around him. He shut out their joyous noise and hunched into the paperback, marking passages that underscored the horror of Vincent's aloneness in Arles.

In defeat, he headed back to the station to retrieve his luggage and check the schedule for his next move. Maybe he could do something spontaneous. Aix and Avignon were nearby and probably not in the throes of a summer love-fest. God, maybe he could do something truly wild and head straight back to Paris and tell Candy about being half in love, being soul mates, and the dread of solitude. But the only scheduled train to anywhere within the next several hours was the express to Barcelona via Montpelier. Gabe felt doomed, his only conceivable fate to arrive in Spain for his conference one day early. A whole damn day early for work, not art; for work, not *l'amour.*

As he bought the ticket, a high-speed train screamed northbound through the little station without even slowing down, rattling the rafters as it hurled toward the City of Love, the City of Light.

❖

Gabe's Barcelona was dark. He toured the sunny Mediterranean city of wide, bright boulevards on his own two feet through his own two eyes. But his dark orbit eclipsed Barcelona's dazzling light.

SecureTek's travel agent had booked a guesthouse within the Gothic Quarter. Every time he came and went to the conference at a much more modern and grandiose hotel on sundrenched Las Ramblas, he had to wander through the quarter's dark, sudden-curving, false-start, dead-end stone passageways so narrow two people could barely walk abreast. Even the August sun could not penetrate the zone of dour façades and cobbled paths. Gabe learned the Gothic maze had been designed in medieval times to thwart any pirates who came ashore in hopes of sacking the city, to fool them into believing the luminous port was really a labyrinth of eternal night.

His first night there, Gabe reluctantly stopped by a queer bar out of sheer fatigue with his own company. A sweet, very young guy followed him back to his guesthouse just after midnight. Luckily, he seemed to know the Gothic Quarter by heart, so Gabe ended up following him. Though he felt fortunate to be desired, he suspected it was for the wrong reason—just being the big, healthy American guy who looked so hunky to this thin, effete European. It was a misplaced fantasy, an involuntary walk-on part, a cameo in a stranger's porno. At the guesthouse door, Gabe shook the sweet kid's hand and bid him *gracias, pero no gracias, buenas noches* like the fastidious virgin in an old-school romantic comedy.

He wouldn't remain fastidious for long, though.

By day, Gabe endured unendurable conference workshops like *A Cost-Effective Methodology for Self-Contained Magnetized Detection.* Now he knew why SecureTek's senior members didn't jump at the chance at an all-expenses-paid workweek in Spain. The days were long, stretching past dinner into evening sessions, all of it completely without humor or any human spark. He networked with global counterparts and gathered reams of dubious multilingual business plans, realizing he had become like any other schmo who chased a paycheck day in and day out for a job he didn't give a damn about. Zeena kept contacting him from Denver at odd hours, checking on his attendance, his mastery of jargon-crazed concepts, and exhorting him to attend every wares fair and social event "brandishing a SecureTek name tag and a firm handshake."

By late evening, though, he hurried to join the spectacle on Las Ramblas, the vast, busy, quirky pedestrian zone bisecting Barcelona's center. He hardly had time to join laughing onlookers ringing a quartet of Argentinean sketch comedians, an alleged talking monkey, or a fire-breathing angel in what he hoped were fireproof rhinestone-studded wings when a tall, broad-shouldered, dark-haired beauty slithered in beside him. "You must be from the States," he said, smiling. "I am too. I can tell by the way you laugh."

So began Gabe's affair with the Aging Model. He led Gabe to drinks in his favorite brick courtyard café just off Las Ramblas, where Gabe learned the Aging Model was the scion of Pittsburgh's renowned one-hour chemical dry cleaners. Would Gabe always gyrate in the centrifugal force of the American Upper Middle Class, orbiting entrepreneurial Earth no matter how he dreamed of floating into Marxist deep space? At least the Aging Model—AM for short—earned an honest expat living posing for European magazines and catalogues, often as an American-style dad in vaguely American spreads that featured such vaguely American activities as Outdoor Grilling of the Hot Dog Veal Sausages, Sunday Driving of the Tiny Opel to the Bierhalle by the Gravel Beach, or Hilarious Weekend Road Biking in Tuscany in Tight Yellow Spandex.

Gabe slept with AM every subsequent night in Barcelona, snug in his apartment, happy to curl into his warm, shapely, aging naked form until four in the morning, when he would reach blindly for his boxers, button-down, and slacks to slip along the pitch-black, abandoned Las Ramblas to steal a few more hours' sleep at the guesthouse in the Gothic Quarter. He didn't really want to deal with AM over breakfast, hear him defending certain conservative American presidents or even, for the love of God, Generalissimo Franco's long-gone, forty-year tyrannical rule of Spain. Not when he was so undefended, waking up, groggy, to the a.m. reality that AM was a casual fascist. When Gabe tried to explain that he would've joined the Communists during the Spanish

Civil War back in the thirties, that people like AM would have been trying to kill him, AM just laughed.

Gabe didn't. But he knew the deal. A mercenary arrangement, a worn-out gay template, the great-looking older guy afraid of eternal exclusion from the scene and the okay-looking younger guy afraid of never being invited in. AM had False Sophistication; Gabe had Useless Knowledge. AM knew People; Gabe was Nobody. Or, more simply, AM Would Inherit One-Hour Chemical Dry Cleaners; Gabe Had One Decent Pair of Dry Clean Only Slacks.

When he couldn't stop AM from blurting his admiration for certain ultraconservative icons, Gabe would flee to his balcony, groaning, and gaze toward smoggy stars, muttering incoherent prayers to Eleanor Roosevelt, Dorothy Day, Cesar Chavez, Harvey Milk, Desmond Tutu, and Bruce Springsteen. He longed to tell Candy all about it, to quote AM's most thoughtless observations, to hear her laugh and savor the retaliatory power of her oblique, humane wit. As much as he enjoyed passionate nights with AM, his waking drivel deflated him.

It seemed so cruel that even if he ever renewed more intimacy with Candy, their relations would probably be the opposite of his with AM. She and Gabe would have boisterous, politically copacetic love without physical urgency. *A lifelong mismatch*—he grudgingly approved of the tragedy Hemingway portrayed between Lady Brett and Jake. When it came to Candy, his gonads did not respond with the passion of his heart and mind. Gabe was the trailer park girl with balls shot off.

AM did possess one fine quality that Gabe didn't have, besides beauty—clearheadedness about his sexuality and heterosexual institutions. In a weak moment after two in the morning, Gabe had confessed about his mix-up with Candy when he was still an undergraduate, stuck in the idea that he wanted to step in as Candy's savior and be the baby's surrogate father. He went on for no good reason, mentioning his studly relations with Jamie and his paternal fondness for Mary Anne and Jamie's little boy, Leif.

AM challenged Gabe. "Years later, a college graduate, you're still in love with being in love with girls and fantasizing about being a father?" AM slipped his hand under the sheets, caressing Gabe's bare bottom. "You can't pretend to have brown eyes when you were born with blue ones. And phony contact lenses just make you look like a fool. Gabe, if anyone knows you're gay, I know."

Gabe was glad it was dark so AM couldn't see him blush. He'd used the same analogy when he came out to his mother, and now it was being used to shame Gabe into coming out more fully to himself.

They carried on variations of the same conversation at the courtyard bar, evenings after Gabe's workshops and AM's photo shoots. Gabe didn't care if AM wasn't really that interested. He babbled on, using him as a free shrink. "Candy's completely different now, though. Less impulsive, a serious academic. Maybe I'm not so confused. I'm just realizing my true mate is somebody from the wrong gender."

"This girl's going to marry the pharmaceutical fiancé, you know. For his money, for the stability of his family's connection with her family. She doesn't really have much choice. That's how it works in their corner of the straight world. Try to understand, since you're half in love with being straight."

Gabe was infatuated with the idea of being Candy's man, her protector and hero now that Buddy had disappointed and hurt her, despite knowing his heterosexual fantasia of pursuit might mess up her feelings even worse than he'd already hurt her when they'd toyed around at the house on South High Street. "Maybe," Gabe told AM, "I'm just torturing myself."

"This conversation is torturing me. Look, isn't that the food editor of *Elle*?"

Gabe didn't know what *Elle* was or why he should bother to look, and that had to be a disappointment to AM. Maybe AM's vast vanity saw a future for this fling, though Gabe had no intention whatsoever of seeing AM after the moment he fled the conference. AM invited him for the weekend at Sitges, the beach resort just south, to spend the few days before Gabe flew back to the states. He implied if Gabe ever abandoned his ludicrous "career" in Denver, he could always cohabitate with a certain Aging Model in Barcelona.

Gabe left him hanging, knowing he was being a prick. Sitges, not Sitges, who gave a damn? Had he regressed to the attitude of his promiscuous summer, after his first love fiasco with Adam, rejecting lovers before they could dare to reject him? Meanwhile, AM was wondering whether to call and firm up his reservations, stock up on champagne and treats, and make sure they had a *cama matromonia* for their beach-town honeymoon.

Gabe was lost to fruitless calls of his own. Candy's mobile was "not in service at this time." He wondered if Buddy really had abandoned her for a lark in Pamplona while her stepmother had persuaded her father to cut her European funding off. Was she penniless now, unable to buy international service or even phone cards? He imagined Candy hungrily roving the quays, selling her gorgeous clothes at Parisian flea markets in one last desperate attempt to raise cash for one last Tunisian tuna sandwich.

Gabe evaded AM's overtures, explaining he "wouldn't really have a chance" to join him in Sitges, and strolled alone the Sagrada Familia cathedral. He sat in a hillside plaza opposite as the cranes suspended work for another day. The ghostly steeples captured the evening sun. There was something thrilling about being witness to a modern cathedral still under construction, to gaze like a Dark Ages peasant upon the communal marvel, how its wild, fantastic detailing seemed to defy—or maybe liberate—gravity itself. Yet he knew its core was raw and underfunded, a mere work in progress, a personality still testing its ultimate form.

A happy mob of young couples popped from the Metro station under the plaza, smooching, laughing, teasing. As they crossed the plaza, all at once the guys stretched their arms around their girls to pull them close, which looked choreographed, yet seemed completely natural in its flawless ease.

That was all it took. Gabe took the Metro back to his hotel, where he tossed his scattered clothes in his duffel, checked out, and headed for the train station. The best connection he could make was a local to the border, where he could transfer to an express. If all went well, he could be back in Paris before noon tomorrow.

The slow train prowled the Catalonian twilight, stopping at every station no matter how abandoned, Gabe's resolve growing as the local inched toward the French border. He was ever more sure Candy wanted him to rescue her. Maybe he wasn't arriving on a white steed. But galloping to her side on the night express via Lyon, he would be better than some fairy-tale dream lover. Fairy, maybe, but her true soul mate.

This was not Romantic. It was not a risky impulse or some drunken decision out of Hemingway. His plan felt as down-to-earth and deliberate as the train, which smelled of old peanut shells and spilled beer. His fellow passengers seemed morose and ill-tempered, their kids whiny and restless. There was nothing to see but dim, distant farmhouse lights. He couldn't concentrate on reading, so his ardor to reach Candy hardened, steely but completely unalloyed in determination. He was sure he was making the most important journey of his life, whatever waited at the other end.

When he reached the border, Gabe decided to try calling her Paris hotel. The chatty Quebecois reception clerk, Buddy's drinking buddy, confirmed that the *mademoiselle trés belle* had checked out, together with "her charming American fiancé." He and the mademoiselle had told him they were returning to Texas to prepare for their wedding. He said he would gladly forward any "inspirational message" to the happy couple and waited long on Gabe's silence before he disconnected the line.

Now he had to wait on the Spanish side of the border in a cavernous, empty station designed for processing much busier daytime crowds. It would be an hour before the local returned to Barcelona. He stared at his phone's directory. Should he try Candy's number again, see if the disconnection was a fluke?

Instead, he saw Marty's number. Marty was just five hundred kilometers away, spending the summer session in Florence, almost done with his master's coursework. Gabe bought a beer at the concession stand, sipping as he considered his next move. It wasn't too late to call. Did he dare?

He did. The voice he connected with was sprightly, inquiring, curious, so glad he called. Barcelona, imagine it, not that far! "Is there any chance you can visit us, Gabe? We'd love to show you Florence, the real Florence, not just the tourist sites."

Gabe got stuck on that first person plural pronoun. "No, but I'd love to," he finally blurted. "I'm only here for another couple days."

"You'll have to come back to Italy on your next vacation, for pleasure, not for work!" Marty called in Italian to someone in the room with him, then returned his attention to Gabe. "I just told Giovanni you were on the line. He knows all about you, Gabe, my wonderful Denver boyfriend." Giovanni was his young Early Renaissance professor, Marty explained. Their academic relations had evolved into love. Marty had moved into his apartment, a great blessing, since money was getting ever scarcer due to his father's legal battles. He was already accepted for the doctoral program at the satellite campus, wasn't that brilliant? "Giovanni is saying, tell him to come, he wants to show you his family home up near Vinci. As in Leonardo da, Gabe! It's beautiful up there, surrounded by a mountaintop orchard."

Gabe tried his best to oooh and ahhh and promise to put Florence on his vacation schedule before he wrangled his way out of the call. Hearing Marty's happiness through his familiar manic tones made Gabe more heartsick than imagining Candy's penury. Sad, he faked a sprightly "love ya" of his own and terminated the call.

It was well past midnight when the same little train chugged right back to Barcelona. He took the Metro straight to the plaza overlooking Sagrada Familia and claimed the same bench, using his luggage as a footstool. Dazed, numb, having gotten exactly nowhere, he wondered if he had really taken that aborted round trip to the border or just daydreamed. Two couples of that same happy mob were still necking on benches across from him.

In a bout of self-pity and paralyzing solitude, Gabe felt shut out from the glistening norms of the world, an exclusion so sharp it ached like nothing he'd ever felt. What had happened to his hard-won acceptance of his sexual identity, enjoying his rogue status, even those bouts of bad-boy promiscuity? The call to Marty had only reminded him of his apparent expendability as a partner—the same judgment handed down by Adam.

His brief reunion with Candy had knocked the legs out from under his equilibrium. How perverse that he, of all men, would dream about assuring her stability. Gabe had to face it. He and Candy would never travel on overnight trains, setting their kids into shelf bunks like precious cargo and taking turns reading them fairy tales until they dropped into dreams.

Disgracing himself at twenty-three, Gabe had been pranking himself with the same brilliant, lost damsel. But it was more than a gay boy's delusions of normative love. He'd blundered out of his class and rank, as he had with Marty—a working-class punk sneaking under the country club gates, Gabe the Obscure.

Above the unfinished cathedral spires, arrayed high into the ridges that ringed the city, residential lights glittered in the summer night like a firmament of scattered families. He'd heard that higher yet, in the dark spaces past the last house lights, up the steep escarpments, haunted woodlands cloaked the summits, life-threatening forests with rumors of bear, wolf, and nameless predators. Catalan legend held that in ancient days, those bosky ridges attracted spiritual seekers, mystics, lunatics, and fanatical solitaries to the crags and caves suspended in the sky.

Part of Gabe craved to join the holy fools, renouncing the tantalizing society below, a lone pilgrim making futile incursions against mating, property settlement, and generational inheritance. But not all of him. He traced imaginary routes toward the illuminated crescent of Catalonia's shoreline. Could he guess the direction of Dallas? He then turned toward what he gleaned was the way toward Florence. He yearned toward those opposite orientations, still half in love.

Chapter Ten

Postcards from Condi Rice

Gabe moved some mail around on his desk while Leif snarfled and shuffled. The toddler napped on the little bed that Mary Anne and Jamie had provided for Gabe's home office when they'd moved into a bungalow a few blocks south of campus.

Since starting at SecureTek, Gabe could just afford to keep the apartment without a roommate, so he had the luxury of turning Ben's old room into an office. He was proud of how he'd finished it off, with curtains for the glass doors to the balcony, frames for his favorite prints, a decent lamp, cheap teak bookshelves, and a semi-comfortable used armchair. So he had a great home office at last, but working long hours at SecureTek's help desk and traveling to meet new clients, he hardly needed it now. He no longer brought home copy to edit from *Planet Quarterly*, and with his grad work at the International School on hiatus, he no longer suffered over foreign policy. The surplus square footage was an extravagance he'd never known.

He was always happy to babysit Leif when Mary Anne and Jamie each had something scheduled or just needed a night off from parenting, but he'd never dreamed his home office would become Leif's de facto, periodic playroom, where he'd riffle through the plastic carton that served as his toy box, rearranging stuffed animals and tiny trucks. Wanton, restless, he'd abandon Mr. Potato Head in mid-transformation to take up a coloring book, then mutter to himself about his building blocks' ever-shifting architecture.

After all that heroic exertion, he'd collapse into a nap. So Gabe sorted through a week's accumulation of mail, most of it junk he flicked unopened into recycling, including stuff that really belonged at work but had somehow found him at home. This was the dread creature he had become, communicating the special features of SecureTek's airport metal detection equipment to aviation officials at midsized regional airports.

Since there wasn't much competition, he didn't have to devolve into that even more dread being, a salesman. Instead, he spent long days online, or on the phone, or at small terminals in Billings, Montana, or Bismarck, North Dakota, as a somewhat sentient, mobile instruction manual.

How could this be the fate of young Gabriel Rafferty, the boy who couldn't build a decent birdhouse, now explaining technology to bolo-tied airfield managers in Provo, Utah? Gabe, who'd never in his prior life been fascinated by airports or security scanners, now mastered a small, repetitive array of operations and facts and had learned how to soothe the psyches and expectations of officials at midsized airports, though he would sometimes have to endure snark from middle-aged, midlevel clients like, "Are you subbing for your dad?" or "Is SecureTek sending their junior varsity because we're a junior airport?"

"Hey! Anybody home?" It was Jamie, letting herself in after rapping on the front door. She halted in the office doorway, smiling to see Leif was fast asleep. Now she whispered, "He's such an angel when he's like that."

Gabe joined her in the doorway, then urged her through the living room and onto the balcony.

"You'd never know what a terror he can be at our place, Gabe. Somehow he manages to roam into every room simultaneously yelling and screaming while performing his noisy happy dance."

"Then I lucked out. We had fun playing, then he dropped off into sleepyland. Maybe we can get him settled into your car without waking him up."

"That'd be lovely, then I'll put him down and fix a straight bourbon. Just for me, though. I'm not letting him into the hard stuff just yet."

"Rough interview?"

"I got some juicy material, but the creep kept hitting on me while explaining he didn't hate the sinner, only the sin, whenever I tried to turn the subject back to his policies on gay rights."

Jamie had just come from a downtown hotel lounge, getting material for her feature on a pro-Christian freedom, anti-gay freedom activist passing through Denver. He'd won a place in the new conservative administration in Washington on the strength of his campaign in Colorado Springs in the early 90s to defeat an ordinance that would offer workplace protection for sexual minorities.

"He was just as smarmy as I expected an ex-used car salesman turned right wing celebrity to be. He didn't drink alcohol, having never gotten the memo that his beloved Jesus actually adored the fermented grape, so we talked over iced teas. That's why I'm so desperate to dip into the whiskey when I get home. But with the creep pawing my knee under the table and inviting me up to his room for—what? More iced tea? Photos of his wife and kids? Anyway, I got some great details. The exact way the hypocrite acted is going in my article. I think I might get a cover on this one."

"Did you actually go to his room?"

"Hell no, Gabe! I may be just another lipstick lesbian writing for an alternative weekly, but I'm still a lady."

"I can see why he hit on you in your special girl reporter gray suit and white blouse. And the way your hair's growing out, all tawny. You look great."

"Don't flirt, baby. We'll get all mixed up and entangled again."

"You'll always be the girl who robbed me of my purity. Well, my hetero purity."

"See? I taught you so much. But let's change the subject." She leaned through the glass door. "I'm gonna check on Leif."

When she came back to the balcony, smiling and miming Leif's sleepy face, she mentioned how much she liked what Gabe had done to the office. "These big bedrooms at Edna Victoria are great, aren't they? I always loved the way they open on to these long balconies."

"Yeah, when my mom finally sold the house in Butcher Creek and needed to vacate by closing, I offered that room to her."

"Just like any good gay son."

"She'd actually be a great roommate. For a while, anyway. Plus, she's a hell of a cook."

"Ahh! What happened with that plan?"

"My uncle Tony offered her his guesthouse, a swanky carriage house over his garage out in Cherry Hills. She loves it out there, especially now that Karlo's wife has produced her first great-nephew."

"Speaking of which, you need to keep in mind that Mary Anne and I intentionally bought our place because of that extra unit. You know, the one with a separate entrance and private bathroom? And office nook? Overlooking the garden? All spacious and quiet? That one."

"Perfect to rent to some perky undergraduate."

"Don't get me wrong, Gabe. You've done wonders with this place. It looks like a real grown-up man's apartment now, not a funky student flop. But someday…"

"Thanks, Jamie, but right now I think we better collect Leif while he's sound asleep and bring him down to your car before he knows what happened."

"I wonder what it's going to be like when we tell the poor kid his real origin story."

Gabe eased down the breezeway stairs with Leif's face plastered against his shoulder, his sleepy limbs swaying. "He'll be glad to know his dad wasn't just a turkey baster."

When he tried to settle him to the car seat, though, Leif startled awake and tugged at his wrist, crying out "Gay! Gay!" his latest, best try at sounding out Gabe's name.

"Sorry," Jamie said, getting into the driver's seat and turning back to Leif, "I've gotta steal you away from ol' Gay for now, sweetie."

Gabe waved and tried his best to smile though he felt queasy, as if he hadn't prepared himself to surrender Leif to his mommies once again.

Maybe Gabe began his postcard stunt because of Zeena's irritating, old-school cultivation of privacy. No matter how much closer Gabe became to Zeena, now his immediate supervisor at SecureTek, he'd learned no more from her about her earlier life. She'd had a compelling childhood but refused to discuss her Southern upbringing or her renowned family. With SecureTek's other divisions having Defense Department contracts, a little workplace discretion was understandable, but why so much secrecy among friends? In that vacuum, and just for laughs at first, Gabe was practically forced to invent the postcards from Condi Rice.

Zeena had founded SecureTek with other friends from the university's ascendant business school and now headed customer relations. Way into her forties, several years older than Todd, Zeena mixed girlishness with gravitas. And beauty—long, careless red-blond hair, fair skin, and soft freckles sprinkled over a permanent blush. She drove Gabe crazy with her close-mouthed, slightly upturned, Buddha-in-repose smile, which was the only response she'd give to any remotely personal question.

Gabe had once tried to ask about her family's past. He'd learned from Todd that Zeena sprang from a long line of liberal white Alabama aristocrats. Her parents were both lawyers who'd argued landmark civil rights cases back in the 1960s and 70s. Martin Luther King, Ralph Abernathy, and Jesse Jackson had all dined at her family's table in some expensive precinct of Birmingham. When Zeena's mother died, Andrew Young, then ambassador to the United Nations, flew to Alabama to serve as a pallbearer. Gabe mentioned that Todd told him Coretta Scott King attended Zeena's first piano recital and that teenage Condoleezza Rice had been her babysitter.

She'd smile that smile. "Why would he ever bother to mention that?"

❖

That September, Zeena and Todd were stranded in a remodel of their bungalow south of campus, just around the corner from Jamie and Mary Anne's new place farther down South High Street. Todd, who was about as handy as could be expected for a philosophy professor, spent Labor Day weekend ripping out their kitchen, causing a plumbing catastrophe that kept them without running water for the first weeks of the fall semester.

Meanwhile, Todd took on new duties as coordinator of the Department of Philosophy's new emphasis, Global Ethics. "So, by day, I'm fighting for the moral fate of the entire globe," Todd told Gabe. "Then I go home to battle grease traps and ghostly sewer lines."

"Sounds just like the moral condition of the entire globe to me."

"But not tonight. Let's get some exercise."

On a brilliant Monday evening just before sundown, Todd and Gabe shot a few hoops at the forgotten court. Squeezed between campus and a little park ringed by generic apartments, so sketchy that neither university nor city seemed to claim it, the court felt like a neglected UN protectorate. Before long, two frat boys challenged them to a half-court game, which attracted two Iranian grad students. When Nigerian friends Gabe knew from his undergraduate days in world literature jumped in, they broke into teams and expanded the game to a full court. Two ninth grade girls from the neighborhood happened by, both better than anybody. They kept score, playing hard, and only stopped when someone noticed it was too dark to tell where the hoops were.

Everybody shook hands and split. Todd and Gabe stood alone in the twilight. A lingering seam of red-purple over the Great Divide made Gabe yearn for he didn't know what. Maybe just the perfect day itself, or the too-brief game. He wanted to snatch the lost thing, whatever it was, and take it back from the day's sudden disappearance.

Panting, Todd smiled into the jagged horizon. "Red sky at night…" he muttered. "And I stink." He took his showers at the campus pool during the plumbing crisis, so Gabe jogged to his apartment alone, only to find Zeena had already let herself into his kitchen, smashing garlic under the flat side of the butcher knife.

"This is the most poorly equipped kitchen I've ever seen," she said by way of a greeting while she pulverized the cloves. "Though I sure appreciate your letting us use it." Her hair was wet, cascades of rusty ringlets. Using the knife as an accusatory pointer, she turned to Gabe. "But as far as utensils, I expect much more of a guy like you."

"Sorry. I missed that gay gene for kitchen widgets."

She smiled, pure Buddha. "You're all sweaty, Gabe."

He raised arms to sniff his saturated pits. "This is how you have to take me when you invade my apartment without notice. Now, I'm going to strip naked and head into my poorly equipped bathroom for a shower. Okay, Zee?"

"Please disrobe in a discreet manner, young man."

Gabe pulled off his T-shirt and used it to wipe his neck and chest. "Sure thing, Scarlett."

She laughed and turned back to the garlic. He did the gentlemanly thing and removed his shorts in the bathroom, where he discovered

Zeena had just used the shower. No big deal, considering the evening before he'd given her and Todd keys to his place and invited them to use the facilities, but he didn't really expect Zeena to take him up on it so soon. He inhaled the lingering female scent of her expensive shampoo, so unknown here since Candy split from Ben.

"Here's my proposal, Gabe," she told him as he eased beside her, feeling spiff and fit, decent in a button-down and clean khakis. It was sweet to have a pretty woman simmering marinara in his tiny kitchen. "How about I just cook here most nights this week? You and Todd will get the civilizing influence of a home-cooked meal, and I'll stop going crazy at our place."

Not a bad deal, Gabe thought, especially since Zeena was just now harvesting her garden and was famous for her cooking, while he hardly did more than nuke leftover Chinese takeout. She reached into a woven satchel for her phone and called Todd, telling him to detour to Gabe's place on the way from the pool showers, and then produced a fresh eggplant from the same satchel. A single sheet of paper slipped out, a photocopy clipped from the *Rocky Mountain News*. Gabe caught it and found Condoleezza Rice staring back at him, next to an article announcing her visit to the International School.

"What are you saving this for?" he asked.

"None of your business. Would you mind rinsing that eggplant?"

It was precisely his business, Gabe thought since he was attending that reception for Dr. Rice the following evening. "Are you going to the reception?"

"No. I wasn't invited."

"Any student or graduate of the International School can go."

"I'm not really a graduate, Gabe."

Zeena had dropped out of international studies to help start SecureTek almost two decades before Gabe's own shirttail relationship with the school. As he rinsed and sliced the eggplant, he realized Zeena would have begun at the International School about the same time as Condoleezza was a doctoral candidate, before Dr. Rice's rise at Stanford and eventually into the White House as National Security Advisor.

"Weren't you and Condi pals, then? As classmates?"

Zeena snatched the eggplant from his wet hands. "I haven't *quite* reached the age of Condi Rice, Gabe!"

"I didn't say you had. But you were at the International School together, right?" He leaned against the sink as a new idea kicked in. "Ah, so you don't approve, do you? You don't think Condi had any right..."

Zeena lopped the stem of a tomato with a swift jab of the knife. "To?"

"To join this new gang of thieves and liars in Washington."

"Condi Rice? She had every right, my pretties," Todd said, standing in the doorway. He held out a bottle of wine. "It's the duty of any ambitious opportunist to exploit the greatest opportunity. Global ethics be damned. No worries, though. In three and a half more years, this administration will be a short footnote to our proud and honorable history."

Todd was wrong, of course. The following day was September 11, 2001, so the reception for Condi Rice was canceled, and the Washington gang she'd joined would occupy much more than a footnote. Instead, they would spend the early years of the new century dictating chapter after chapter.

❖

Zeena stuck with her plan to cook at Gabe's place, so all that week the three of them watched TV news with plates in their laps, simultaneously absorbed and dumbstruck. Whenever Condi Rice would make remarks or stand beside President Bush during a news brief, Todd would sneer and hiss at the TV screen. "Look at her, trying to seem so cool and competent and composed. And that poufy hair, that flip curl that's always frozen in place. What does she do, lacquer it?"

"Honey, three thousand people have just been murdered," Zeena would plead. "Give the woman's hair a break."

"And why didn't she ever get her teeth fixed, that crazy gap? Her parents had plenty of money, you know."

"The Pentagon, darling," Zeena said, "is still smoldering."

"The weirdest thing is the silence in the sky," Gabe's uncle Tony said as they took a Sunday afternoon stroll along the Highline Canal

near his house in Cherry Hills. "We're under a regular flight path, and I didn't realize how used I'd gotten to the sight and sound of planes. Now, with whole fleets still grounded, it's eerie."

"I worry what's going to happen to Gabe's new job," Karlo said, trying to hide a snarky smile. "No more flights for a while to glittering cities in, like, North Dakota and Kansas. They say you can't keep a boy down on the farm once he's seen the bright lights of Fargo and Topeka."

"Gosh, I guess I won't be hopping on a puddle jumper to some godforsaken airfield for at least a week," Gabe said. "It's my sacrifice for my country."

Autumn hadn't officially started, but yellow and gold already flecked the green canopies of the old cottonwoods lining the canal. Gabe had joined Tony, Karlo, and his mother for a stroll after Sunday brunch.

Almost as weird as the empty sky was Gabe's having gotten up at sunrise to drive Elena to eight o'clock Mass at their parish in Butcher Creek, then driving her all the way back here so she and Tony could prepare brunch, complete with their Croatian specialty, prženica, which they rhapsodized about from their childhood memories but was really just French toast. Gabe had been taking his mother to hometown Mass sporadically since she'd sold the house—socializing at her old parish was the only thing she missed about Butcher Creek—and though he sat still and quiet beside her during Mass, Gabe wondered if this hard duty was too much even for a *good gay son* to bear. This morning he'd sat stupefied by the priest's homily, finding Catholic doctrine more bizarre than ever, the sermon stilted and negative about human potential.

The priest had managed to imply that the 9/11 attacks were only part of a global war against Christianity itself and offered no comfort to the pews full of older widows, defeated elderly men, and scattered, anxious children, all of them sinners barely deserving of Christ's love. Will you please just embrace them, you vested son of a bitch, Gabe muttered within himself, hoping to keep his disdain from devout Elena, and clang a scented benediction over all these gray, home-permed heads.

"I do, Karlo," his mother was saying now, "I love it down here. Especially all the beautiful yards and gardens, the views of the mountains. All the flowers and trees are so much healthier. And the air's so clean! Not a factory for miles. I always enjoyed visiting your family down here, but I never in a million years thought I'd live here someday. It just shows—you never know."

"Well, we love having you here, Aunt Elena." Karlo carried his baby in a front-loading papoose, like the one they'd used for baby Leif, and Gabe smiled at the way the tiny kid dangled there, his happy face all goo-goo over the glories of nature on a sunny Colorado Sunday. "Not to mention your recipe for prženica."

"Good vanilla extract is the secret, the kind I get from my Mexican friends at the clinic. They make it lots stronger in old Mexico than our cheap supermarket crap. You get what you pay for. Anyway, I feel kind of guilty, Karlo, not paying rent. I feel like a freeloader in your father's beautiful carriage house."

"Freeloader!" Tony cried. "You're my goddamn sister!"

"If it makes you feel better," Karlo said, "you can babysit when Ivan gets a little older, Auntie."

"Along with tending to that amazing vegetable garden you've put in, and those flower beds," Tony said, "and your cooking, you've already more than earned your way. Not that you need to earn anything. You deserve so much more, Elena, than what you've gotten in life."

"Ah, you gotta make the most of what you're given, you know?"

"I just don't..." Karlo said, as if searching for the diplomatic way to ask it. "It's like, you and Uncle Patrick never seemed..."

"Happy? Compatible?" Gabe looked from Karlo to Elena. "We've all wondered, Ma. Why the hell did you marry Dad in the first place?"

"Back then, Gabriel, he wasn't like how he ended up, okay?" She glanced off west as they strolled the snaking canal, now offering a view of the Rockies over a golf course. For Karlo's sake, she summarized the old tale of how she'd once hoped to become a nun but postponed it when her father fell ill. She had to devote herself to helping out the family. While Tony was off to college, Elena dropped out of tenth grade to work as a clerk in the family's grocery store in Pueblo, then stayed on to labor there long after her father died.

"I gave up on becoming a real sister by the time I was into my thirties. One of the last things my father told me was to marry a good Catholic guy and start a family, and that always haunted me, you know, the last wishes of the dying. Anyway, one time our cousin Aldo in the

Springs fixed me up on a blind date with Patrick. He was good lookin' back then, and he was nice to me. When he had leave from Fort Carson, he'd drive down to Pueblo and take me out to dinner and a movie. It was nice, like nothing I'd ever known. You don't know what you don't know."

"You sure don't, Ma," Gabe said. "Did you ever imagine he was such a racist?"

"No. Not really. Well, sometimes he would let some comment slip, but that was normal back then, down in Pueblo. A lot of guys I knew were like that. But that secret society he belonged to in the Army? And that white purity crap him and that guy Kenny talked about that one Thanksgiving? I never had any idea about that. Like some kind of giggly girl, I got all googly eyed about getting married. Suddenly I thought it was kind of my duty, you know." Elena stopped, gazing at the canal, then turned with a smile to coo at the baby. "A sacrament, right? *Matrimony*. Something holy."

The three men exchanged looks, astonishment mixed with horror. Gabe sensed Tony and Karlo were thinking the same thing—of the always palpable, unholy unhappiness of that holy union in Butcher Creek. Nobody said anything, and the sky was silent.

In the long wake of the terror attacks, Gabe's position at customer support for SecureTek became profoundly more important. The federal government pressured every foreign airport that served US airlines to conform to intensified standards. SecureTek's domestic experience became crucial in upgrading air security across a planet where almost every provincial or regional airport needed upgrades.

For the boy from Butcher Creek who'd once yearned to travel the world, life became a nonstop series of global business trips. Any given week he could find himself flying anywhere from Calgary to Cape Town, taking questions about, say, methodology for magnetized detection from sour, sighing aviation officials in stuffy conference rooms.

In New York in November, at a JFK cocktail lounge, Gabe heard rumors that Condi Rice was passing through with a whirlwind delegation to Europe, "inviting" France, Germany, and Spain to increase their military support of America's recent invasion of Afghanistan. From the lounge, all he could detect were distant clusters of dark-suited men hustling into a concourse. He'd had a few after-dinner beers, killing time until he caught a red-eye to Dublin. On the bar, someone had left behind a slightly wine-soaked postcard, a scenic shot of lower Manhattan, the twin towers of the World Trade Center prominent against a Jersey sunset.

In the cable news glow, Gabe dried it off with a cocktail napkin. Over and over the screen replayed the American Airlines crash into a nearby Queens neighborhood, playing in rotation with a video clip of American GIs massacred on a snowy Hindu Kush mountaintop. In the shifting light of that gruesome montage, he forced his hand to craft generic block letters and composed the first of his postcards to Zeena from Condoleezza Rice:

DEAREST ZEENA,

JUST LEARNED OUT OF THE BLUE THAT YOUR CORPORATION IS CRUCIALLY INVOLVED IN THE WAR ON TERROR! CONGRATULATIONS AND MUCH GRATITUDE FOR YOUR PATRIOTISM & DEDICATION. SORRY I'VE OFTEN BEEN SO OUT OF TOUCH SINCE OUR DENVER DAYS, BUT I'VE NEVER FORGOTTEN OUR SHARED VISION (UNILATERAL ACTION AS GLOBAL EMERGENCY REQUIRES PLUS NO COMPROMISE WITH FOREIGNERS), NOT TO MENTION YOUR ENDLESSLY HELPFUL GROOMING TIPS! I OFTEN THINK OF OUR IDEALISTIC DAYS TOGETHER IN COLORADO AND STRIVE TO HOLD OUR DREAMS FAST NO MATTER HOW OFTEN I'M PRESSURED TO DISTORT THEM.

I PROMISE TO BE A MUCH MORE FAITHFUL CORRESPONDENT.

LUV,
Condi

Gabe wrote her name in a loopy cursive, but resisted the impulse to dot the "i" with a heart. Then, after he finished off the beer and addressed the card to Zeena's home address, he went ahead and added the little heart anyway.

❖

Gabe fought the unbearable wind, walking to Zeena and Todd's on a bitter December night, the kind when Denverites incanted their mantra it was "too cold to snow" while dry wind glazed old ice against curbs. Stars burned holes in a savage, moonless sky, and when he tried to glimpse Orion, his eyes teared in the lacerating squalls.

That soft September tenth twilight, that pick-up basketball followed by a warm evening scented with eggplant sautéed in garlic fresh from Zeena's garden, seemed as remote and unreal as a museum diorama of Mesopotamia.

Zeena bussed his cheek, then flinched, laughing from the icy grip of his hands. Gabe laughed back, for no other reason than he still had a foot in the door of Zeena and Todd's warm life. Their new kitchen was pungent with basil and coconut tossed into peanut sauce, a concoction she called Indonesian Stir Fry.

"We've missed you at the office," Zeena said, leading Gabe toward the granite-topped island that had just appeared in their kitchen like a new landform. "How was your flight?"

"Okay. Things are mighty tense, though. We were detained on the tarmac when I left from JFK. Bomb threat, I guess. National Guard gunmen were hovering around the gates. Battalions of 'em."

"It's weird, huh?" Todd asked. "It's like the States has become some militarized paranoid parody of itself. Darkness made visible."

"Still, when I fly now," Zeena said, "I feel so divided. I hate the heavy-handed security, but I sure appreciate sight of big brutes with rifles."

"Because they're American brutes?" Todd asked, smiling.

"Precisely," Zeena said, checking the oven.

Gabe spotted the postcard, held on the refrigerator door by the magnet he'd given them as a joke gift: *Admit Nothing, Blame Everyone, Nurture Grievances*. He stared at the sunny scene of pre-9/11 lower

Manhattan with fake curiosity and pointed at the postcard. "Oh, did another friend travel through New York recently?"

"Well," Zeena said, with a sly half-smile, "not exactly a friend."

❖

The year 2002 passed as a crazed blur. With so many complicated SecureTek jaunts overseas, Gabe's personal life seemed on hold. He hardly thought of the postcard hoax until the next fall, changing planes unexpectedly in Thailand. The first homebound leg of the flight was rerouted from Jakarta due to a nightclub suicide bomber in Bali who killed and maimed hundreds of foreign revelers and locals. Gabe had just spent weeks in Indonesia hopping from island to island, taking orders and calming the nerves of security officials at regional airports all around the archipelago. He'd even gone partying with an Aussie flight attendant—a handsome person of much interest—in that very nightclub in Bali.

Now he was idling at a Bangkok airport news kiosk while he waited for the airline to find a new connection through L.A. Though the Bali bombing was already in hysterical cycles on the cable channels, the story had broken too late for the city's English language daily. *The Bangkok Post*'s front page featured none other than Condoleezza Rice, smiling amid Thai officials as she arrived in Bangkok to brief the kingdom's prime minister "on America's plans for Southeast Asian security."

Gabe bought an oversize postcard of a golden monkey god gargoyle climbing a golden stupa, amazingly like the Wicked Witch's winged chimps in *The Wizard of Oz*. He had it written, stamped, and sent before his flight was announced:

DEAREST ZEENA,

I KNOW, I KNOW, I'M NOT A FAITHFUL CORRESPONDENT AT ALL. BUT OF ALL PEOPLE, I KNOW THAT YOU'LL FORGIVE ME FOR FALLING OUT OF TOUCH AGAIN. I'M SURE THIS YEAR HAS BEEN JUST AS INSANE AT SECURETEK AS IT HAS BEEN AT NATIONAL SECURITY. ANYWAY, THAILAND HAS

BEEN SO COMPLIANT, THEIR MANNERS AND THE "ROYAL" TREATMENT SO ENTHRALLING THAT I WISH I COULD STAY FOR MORE THAN ONE QUICK, CRAZY DAY. REMEMBER HOW WE ALWAYS USED TO SAY, "IF YOU WANT TO KNOCK SOME SENSE INTO SOUTHEAST ASIA, CARRY A BIG STICK BUT SPEAK SOFTLY IN THAI"? WELL, IT'S TRUE, AND I THINK WE'VE JUST CLINCHED EVERYTHING WE NEED FROM THE ENTIRE REGION, WITH VIETNAM, LAOS, AND CAMBODIA OVERCOMING SOME SILLY MISGIVINGS (!) ABOUT U.S. INTERFERENCE THANKS TO THAILAND'S CHARM OFFENSIVE. (AND TO US STICKING TO OUR GUNS, OF COURSE!) PROMISE MORE SOON AS I GET A CHANCE.

LUV,
Condi

The best part was, Gabe realized as he dropped the card in a mailbox, that no one at SecureTek need ever know that he'd been rerouted to Bangkok at the same time as Dr. Rice.

❖

"Have you ever been to Thailand, Mr. Gabe?"

Gabe stared at his neighbor, Tan, native of Chiang Rai province and scholar at the theology school. Did he really want to lie to a Buddhist holy man? He'd hardly unpacked from his Asian trip when Tan knocked to ask if he could use Gabe's cell to call and reactivate his disconnected land line. Somewhere in Gabe's carry-on still lurked *The Bangkok Post.*

"I once changed planes in Bangkok," he said. "That's it." He really didn't know why the little coincidence of Tan's question flummoxed him. The university was full of foreigners from everywhere. So what if Tan happened to be Thai?

"Ah. The north is very lovely. Not like Bangkok."

Gabe nodded, watching as Tan lifted his cell to his ear and then wagged it in his direction.

"Your phone is dead, Mr. Gabe. No buzz noise."

Gabe poked and probed the buttons to no avail, so he removed the battery. When he replaced it, his phone produced a sound like a buzzing roomful of voices, then gave way to a faint dial tone.

"Ah, now it works," he proclaimed after Gabe passed the phone to him. "You genius, Mr. Gabe."

❖

Soon after that, Gabe forgot about his brief, sporadic life as a Condi Rice impersonator. So, when Todd joined Zeena and Gabe for a Friday afternoon happy hour weeks later, he was blindsided when Todd mentioned the monkey-god postcard: "Come on, Zee, don't you think it's weird, too?"

She sipped her wine, looking away. "It's just a stupid practical joke."

"But you thought the first one was Gabe's doing."

"I haven't decided what I think."

"Is there any chance it's really Condi?" Gabe dared to ask, staring into his beer. "Maybe you had more of a relationship at the International School than you remember."

Zeena caught his eye and smiled, the full Buddha.

"Or maybe," Todd said, "Condoleezza herself is misremembering. She's mixed Zeena up with some fellow fascist from grad school." He explained the card's theme of American hegemony for Gabe's benefit. "These could be priceless, you know, if they're real. Communiqués in this weird sorority girl, world domination shorthand. Never meant to be seen outside the inner circle."

Zeena sighed. "So confidential they're written on a postcard?"

One weekend, Tan joined Gabe as he crossed campus on his way to a symposium, "*Terror: Is It Good for Business*?"

"It's ironic," Gabe told him. "Even though I was barely enrolled, I've officially had to drop out of my program in international relations because I was too busy flying internationally."

"Maybe this is your real education, Mr. Gabe." He went out of his way to kick through the fallen leaves with childlike glee. "To witness the suffering of the entire planet."

"I don't see suffering, though, Tan. I see sterile hotels. I see airports. I see harried local aviation officials, terrified of American regulations."

"Isn't that suffering?"

Though Tan normally wore Western clothes, sometimes he would wander between the apartment house and the theology school in his bright orange monk robes, one shoulder and lower legs exposed. He never complained and only marveled at the arid Colorado air. "*Prashna*," he would exclaim, days when the wind chased away the smog, "diamond-sparkling." As the winter progressed, he exulted in sharp, angular shadows from the near-constant sunshine, regarding the short cool days and long freezing nights as if they were miraculous. "In Thailand," he told Gabe, "we find the cold alluring. Precious."

Tan found technology alluring, too, vowing to build a website for his temple and school when he returned to Chiang Rai. But phones weren't his forte. He somehow disabled his service a few times, requiring more calls from Gabe's cell. Wanting to be hospitable, Gabe hid his apprehension. Ever since Tan had fiddled with his cheap mobile, Gabe endured clicking static as a prelude to any call.

Once he switched to a cell phone, Tan added a headset, enthralled by the clarity of international calls. Just before the New Year, Gabe opened his door to find Tan deep in loud conversation in the hallway, dressed in suit and tie for a community lecture he was about to give, yakking into his headset: "You will travel soon, too. You will encounter fresh ruins. Just prepare yourself, renew yourself, my friend. As your genius Emerson said of travel, *do not carry ruins to ruins*."

In the first days of 2003, Gabe stood, fresh from Tel Aviv, frozen in mid-step, drop-jawed among fellow travelers passing through Rome's Leonardo Da Vinci Airport. He'd hoped to get in touch with Marty in Florence, but events kept overtaking any such plans to conduct what he once fondly called his life. Overhead, raw news stained every cable news screen. Unknown scores of victims, more than a hundred. Five or six martyrs' brigades grabbed credit for a double suicide massacre. A Tel Aviv immigrant quarter was incinerated, then, minutes later, those helping to carry the injured got blasted by a second vested bomber. A blood-drenched African kid screaming in Hebrew, "We thought it was a missile!" The old central bus station in ruins.

Ruins. Once Tan had asked Gabe, out of the blue, if he agreed that the Americans ought to forgive those "idiot Saudi fanatics who flew into the Twin Towers."

"It didn't cross my mind."

"Yes, as a first step, we forgive the terrorists?"

"I don't know. Tan, I'm not that spiritually evolved."

Now, changing planes in Rome for a London connection to Reykjavik, Gabe watched live shots of three Tel Aviv teenagers attempting use a shattered billboard advertising the movie *The Quiet American* as a stretcher. Over Brandon Fraser's giant, bland face lay a lifeless-looking little girl with blood-smeared stumps where her legs ought to be.

Gabe felt less spiritually evolved than ever. Amid Italian names blaring from the airport loudspeakers, the shriek of Israeli ambulances in televised live coverage, and an old woman crossing herself at first glimpse of the televised carnage, he just could not project himself into compassionate empathy for the bombers. He had seen no more of Tel Aviv than the fluorescent general aviation offices, which could have been in Pittsburgh or Tulsa, but in the international concourse, he had noshed at a pizza shop. The vendor made jolly small talk about her granddaughter at college in Fort Collins, Colorado. Had that grandma commuted home via the old central bus station, her expressive life force extinguished in a split second?

So, Tan considered forgiving the guys who could even conceive of such slaughter? Gabe couldn't see how forgiveness was his to give. He was feeling weary of himself, his lost connections to the humanities and global studies. He was useful, he supposed. Well-compensated, certainly, but his pretentions about a humane future seemed ever more vain and distant. As a flying Dutchman corporate wage slave, what was his forgiveness worth and who would ask for it?

After three brews with a trio of American soldiers en route to an undisclosed location in the Persian Gulf, Gabe had just enough time to slip into a newsstand across from the gate for London.

His beer-buzzed head kept replaying the faces of those three danger-bound soldiers. The two boys half-heartedly improvised bravado, only to recoil into jumpy apprehension. The girl soldier had remained grimly realistic. "We just got a job to do, that's the way I see it. But I just don't get how we're supposed to use guns to stop some fanatic's bullshit. Some violent fuck who thinks he's hearing directly from Allah."

Just as Gabe hoped, the news shop had postcards from all over Italy. He chose a scene of Naples, home to the NATO Southern Command, and in those careful block letters carved Condi's next note to Zeena on the spot.

Back in Denver, in early February, Gabe ducked into Zeena and Todd's after a Saturday stroll around snowbound Harvard Gulch Park. Though he was welcomed with coffee and hugs, the tension between Todd and Zeena crackled around their little bungalow. Zeena seemed to be in the midst of shifting her home office files, while Todd fretted over real estate fliers and mortgage forms at the dining room table.

"I'm glad you're here, Gabe," Zeena said, "because maybe you can talk some sense into Todd. You know better than anyone how things have gone into overdrive at SecureTek. We're constantly hosting officials from Washington and overseas now. And I just can't invite them to this cramped little shack."

"Shack, she says," Todd said, pulling at his forelocks and imploring Gabe with wild eyes. "The shack we just spent thousands of gallons of our own sweat and blood to renovate from end to end."

"Blood that will translate into thousands and thousands of dollars of sweat equity when we sell it," Zeena said. "And it's going to sell fast, Todd, thanks to your beautiful work. Nothing's going to be lost."

"Whoever buys it is going to scrape it off to build another mini-mansion over its grave. And you know it, Zeena."

"I know nothing of the kind. But I certainly can't control what the next owners do, can I?" She picked up a flyer off the table. "But I do know that if we don't move fast on this new place on South Columbine, we're going to be screwed out of the best deal per square foot we're ever going to see. We've got to put in our offer by Monday morning."

"The trouble, Gabe," Todd said, "is that when they scraped off the last old farm-style cottage on that block, they scraped off the old lady's magnificent garden, too."

Up until then, Gabe hadn't really noticed the scale of the transformation going on all around the university as the economy anticipated an Iraq war boom. Speculators either popped second or third stories onto tiny old 1930s houses or bulldozed them to squeeze bland, stucco suburban monstrosities into city lots. But as one who hardly slept in his own apartment now, Gabe had no dogs in their fight and decided to sit this one out. He wasn't eager to fulfill that pleasant gay stereotype, the Friend of the Couple as Gender-Neutral Peacemaker. It was clear, anyway, that no matter how Todd might appeal to sentiment, Zeena was going to prevail. Sure as Bush and Cheney manipulated the country into invading Iraq, Zeena would be serving wine and cheese to Chinese clients in her new, spacious great room. In fact, she'd sign the contract on that Coming Soon mini-mansion on South Columbine the same day Baghdad fell to the Coalition of the Willing.

When Zeena was out of earshot, Gabe muttered to Todd, "Can you guys really afford it?"

Todd continued to tug at his hair. "Yeah, we can leverage this whole deal if we sell this place. You know, Zeena's making bigger money. But there are intangible things, Gabe, which we can't afford to lose at all. Zeena and I never even talked about acquiring a big house and hosting Pentagon flunkies. And considering her upbringing—well, her folks must be spinning in their urns."

"I can hear you just fine," Zeena called from the kitchen, where she fixed a fresh pot of coffee. "So, they'd be ashamed I've become a success?"

"With all due respect," Todd called back, "they might have some questions about the ethical qualifications of your clients."

"With all due respect," Zeena yelled over the scream of boiling water, "those clients are my bread and butter. And yours, too, dear. Increasingly."

Todd glanced at Gabe, his face a mask of wit's end incredulity. This tension at home paralleled Todd's crisis on campus, where his Global Ethics program had been cut from the spring offerings. Arts and Sciences claimed too many humanities enrollments were low. Even Philosophy itself was on the ropes, with talk of reducing it from a department to an "ethics emphasis" within the business school.

Zeena delivered the coffeepot, caressing Todd's distressed hair as she poured him a refill. "Honestly, Todd. Reflect for just a minute on my folks' real fate. They squandered an old Alabama fortune until they died penniless. Of course, they were noble and brilliant and committed to fighting injustice and poverty, but they did leave their only living daughter facing poverty herself."

Zeena excused herself, saying she needed to spend the afternoon getting caught up at SecureTek.

"That's the most she's ever said about her parents in my presence," Gabe told Todd when they were alone at the table.

"I haven't heard much more, believe me. And speaking of ongoing mysteries, there's this," Todd said, producing a postcard from under a stack of mortgage documents. "Another one."

Thanks to Italian efficiency, Gabe's Naples postcard had just arrived. "Another what?"

"I'm completely puzzled now," Todd said. "The sorority tone has morphed into something utterly new. Deterministic. I almost miss the old, chummy Condi. And I sure wish Zeena would fess up to her relationship with her."

Todd passed Gabe the card, Naples sprawling lovely around its crescent harbor, seeming far from Vesuvius. On the back, he reread Condi's message from the day of the Tel Aviv bombings, in Da Vinci Airport in January:

DEAREST ZEENA,

I DON'T MEAN TO BE TERSE BUT SUDDENLY I SEE THE ENEMY SO CLEARLY IT FRIGHTENS ME.

I WRITE FROM NAPLES, WHERE OUR MEETING WITH THE SOUTHERN COMMAND WAS DISRUPTED IN A NEW ROUND OF MIDDLE EAST SAVAGERY. I PRAY FOR RESPITE, NOW, AND THE SOLACE OF FRIENDS' FACES. THE KIND OF FRIEND, LIKE YOU, DEAR ZEENA, WHO ALONE CAN UNDERSTAND. A GREAT ERRAND AWAITS ME, THOUGH, AN ERRAND IN A

DESERT WILDERNESS. IT ALONE WILL DECIDE OUR FATE AS A NATION UNDER GOD AND HIS MANIFEST DESTINY. SO ONCE AGAIN I MUST POSTPONE ANY DENVER REUNION. UNFORTUNATELY, WE'VE GOT A JOB TO DO, AND VERY SOON WE MUST LEARN HOW TO FIGHT FANATICS WITH GUNS AT THE VERY CONFLUENCE OF THE TIGRIS AND EUPHRATES, OTHERWISE ONCE KNOWN AS EDEN.

LUV,
Condi

❖

Over time, of course, Gabe had to take ever more care and craft to keep the postcard hoax believable. He was surprised and pleased Todd had ceased to suspect him, and Todd's pressure on Zeena to recall her "relationship" with Dr. Rice seemed, at times, almost to crack the ice of her aloofness. Gabe realized anything linking his travels to Condi's, or any more coincidences of place, were out of the question. After all, Zeena was acutely aware of his itineraries.

So the cards became even more sporadic and unexpected. He would buy postcards of nearby sites while passing through any given destination—generic Rockies scenes while in Vancouver, the Hunter Valley vineyards while passing though Sydney—only to save them for months on end until a news item alerted him to Dr. Rice's real-world travels.

Then, thanks to burgeoning relationships with other international business travelers, he would compose a new message in Condi's hand and enlist a traveling co-conspirator to mail it. With an authentic postmark, the card would arrive with a stamped date when Zeena knew Gabe was working at the office in Denver or traveling on a different continent. More and more, Condi would mention her hopes for a reunion with her beloved grad school friend, Zeena. As Bush's attack on Iraq morphed into a grinding debacle, though, Condi's duties seemed to cast her farther and farther from her university days in Denver.

A year into the Iraq War, Gabe's improvised life as an air security sensor geek was scheduled to wind down. The USA had imposed its airport security standards worldwide until all that remained was Andalusia, a Spanish region as mysterious and elusive as Zeena herself. His last scheduled trip was to Seville's San Pablo Airport. On a warm afternoon in early March 2004, Gabe stood with Todd in front of their new house on South Columbine, telling him his plans. He would take some vacation time on the front end of his Spanish assignment and celebrate the end of his travels by really traveling. He would land in the capital, see the paintings in the Prado, feast on paella, practice his schoolboy español, then take the high-speed train to Seville.

"You're going to an airport by train?" Todd asked, his voice raised over the sudden snarl of a table saw. "Isn't that kind of heretical?"

"Yes, thank God. I'm going to love seeing more of a country than an airport conference room. Scenery going by out the window. Bulls, windmills, maybe Don Quixote himself."

"Speaking of impossible dreams, Zeena and I actually have a move-in date. Soon as we make up our minds about the tiles, and they hoist those fake rafters over the great room, we can move our paltry possessions into this manor house."

Gabe stared at his reflection in the manor house's enormous front windows, his elongated frame squeezed, child-sized, into one lower corner like a movie's extreme long shot announcing some dunce's doom. Vast stucco expanses stretched along the dinky lot. Like a hippo hunched on a lily pad, the mini-mansion seemed comically out of place among its tiny clapboard neighbors. Almost the entire yard, including the gardens cultivated over a century by the inhabitants of the scraped-off cottage, vanished under the square footage. Despite its acres of glass, the whole effect was massiveness and bulk, Mussolini Moderne. If this was her dream house, Gabe didn't dare to presume what it said about Zeena.

Behind its three stories of square footage, across a brick patio, a three-car garage squatted on the old lady's vanished vegetable garden. Down the street, a bulldozer grazed on the scattered boards of a fresh scrape-off.

Gabe and Todd had to step into the street to make room for the men installing a humongous dangling porch chandelier. It glinted in the sharp March light, into a sky so wind-washed, so pure indigo Gabe muttered, "*Prashna*."

Zeena appeared with a box of tile samples, imploring Todd. "Come on, darling. No more time for hedging. We've got to decide. The slate or the marble?"

"What's *prashna*?" Todd asked.

"Tan says it's 'diamond-sparking air.' Like it is today."

"Well, Tan's mistaken." Zeena rifled through the tiles without looking up. "In Sanskrit? In the sacred dialogues? *Prashna* just means 'question.'" She produced a square of gray slate, holding it next to Todd's face. "Oh, Todd!" She laughed. "Let's go for this. It matches your pretty eyes."

"Gabe," Todd implored, sighing as he took the tile and used it to shield his eyes from the sunlight, "this will be the first spring since Zeena and I got married we won't be putting in a garden."

❖

Gabe was sipping coffee from a paper cup at 7:39 on March 11, 2004, as the high-speed train to Seville left Madrid's Atocha station slowly, easing out from under the terminal's shed roof and into the explosion of daylight over the rail yards. It was slow enough that when nine backpack bombs aboard the commuter train behind them on Track 2 detonated, black dust splattered against the last car of Gabe's train, leaving a stain like outstretched fingers.

While Atocha blasted into triage and screams, scattered limbs, and pleas in all the languages of its international patrons, their train high-sped south without stopping. The whole way, the intercom blurted Spanish announcements much too garbled and rapid for Gabe to comprehend. Passengers faced backward, clustered around the windows as Madrid's outskirts retreated and the intercom kept squawking over suburbs blurring by. Anxious travelers punched their phones while fragments of information burst seat to seat in raised voices.

Helplessly transported farther and farther once again from the chance to lend arms to the effort to lift the wounded and find the limbs and carry the dead, Gabe wondered when the train would turn back to Madrid.

It didn't. The train didn't stop until the officials met it in Toledo. All passengers were sequestered aboard while the conductors and porters gathered in arm-waving consultations on the platform outside.

Nearby, a vendor watched cable news, standing, her back to her display of maps and postcards.

That night, by the light of the eternal news cycle, Gabe composed his last postcard from Condi Rice:

DEAREST ZEENA,

I AM AT WAR NOW WITH ALL DECEPTION, ALL DISGUISED LOCALITIES AND FALSE DISCLOSURE. MY ASSIGNMENTS ABROAD SEEM TO BRING STRANGERS EVER CLOSER TO DANGER. EACH TIME I MOVE ON, UNACCOUNTABLY, I'M SAFELY REMOVED WHILE HORROR INCINERATES IN MY WAKE.

AFTER TODAY'S ATROCITIES, I CANNOT LIFT MY MIND FROM THE BASEMENT OF THAT CHURCH IN BIRMINGHAM IN '63. FOUR YOUNG GIRLS BLOWN AWAY IN HATRED'S INDIFFERENCE TO THE BEAUTY AND INTEGRITY OF THE INDIVIDUAL. INDIFFERENCE NOT ONLY THE SOUL, BUT TO THE MIRACLE OF EACH PHYSICAL BEING, THE WONDER IN EACH PAIR OF ARMS AND LEGS, THE INTERNAL ORGANS, THE MIRACULOUS BRAIN. THE CAPILLARIES, THE VERY HEART. ONE OF THOSE LITTLE GIRLS WAS MY CHILDHOOD PLAYMATE, ZEENA. REMEMBER?

IT WAS AT YOUR PARENTS' TABLE THAT I HEARD DR. KING'S PRONOUNCEMENT ON THE CHURCH MASSACRE. THE FUTILITY OF ANSWERING VIOLENCE WITH VIOLENCE. MY DARLING FRIEND, I DON'T KNOW WHY GOD CHOSE ME FOR THESE MISSIONS OVERSEAS. IN TRUTH, I HARDLY KNOW WHAT CITY I'M IN TONIGHT, AND I DON'T KNOW WHERE I'M GOING TOMORROW. BUT I PRAY TO BE BACK SOON, WITH YOU, IN COLORADO.

LOVE,
CONDOLEEZZA

❖

"So we analyze the numbers," Tan told Gabe. "Bali one day, one month, one year after 9/11. Madrid nine hundred eleven days after 9/11. There is a design, a shape to this, but we can't step back to work the formula because we remain lost in its unaccountable arithmetic." Walking to a reception at Zeena and Todd's, Gabe found Tan in a Western jacket and tie, standing against a temporary chain-link fence on campus. It surrounded the space where that forgotten, open-air, freeport basketball court used to be.

Across from the university's remodeled, expanded recreation center and squeezed by the new law school, the basketball court had been obliterated to make way for the new School of Global Markets. Like so many sites on campus and the surrounding neighborhood, including the just-vanished Philosophy Department, the demolished court looked bare and small as it awaited new construction. Dozer tracks clawed the April mud.

Could Gabe calculate the arithmetic since those red-purple clouds got subtracted with September 10, 2001, that lost evening of diamond-sparkling air? What had become of those high-jumping frat boys? Gone to war-booming global markets, he bet, every one. "What does *prashna* really mean, Tan?"

He laughed. "One must be 'spiritually evolving' even to ask, Mr. Gabe." It turned out Tan was on his way to the reception, too, and mentioned that he'd been invited through contacts he'd made at the International School. "Now, we should go. We certainly can't keep her waiting."

As they crossed University Boulevard, an informal entourage of dressed-up students and older adults from the International School formed around them. Laughing and chatting in the spring's first warm evening, the group followed as Tan and Gabe strolled to South Columbine Street. Under golden buds drizzling on the willows, they passed through a blockade of immense black SUVs, their strobe lights flashing each to each down the narrow street.

As Tan and Gabe approached the pillars of Todd and Zeena's immense portico, Gabe saw one of their own SecureTek airport detectors had been installed under the hanging chandelier. Though Tan had to surrender a silver ankle bracelet, Gabe made it through without setting anything off. Security guards gathered around the detector, muscles straining their dark suits, and kept watch at the entry to the great room, their right ears wired.

Zeena caught Gabe's eye and smiled, then indicated the flip-curled, poufy-haired woman in a tightly tailored suit who stood with her back to them. Tan leaned toward the woman, whispering and indicating she ought to turn around and meet the young gentleman from SecureTek.

"In all our operations overseas," Zeena said as her erstwhile babysitter turned to face him, "whether he knows it or not, Gabe Rafferty has been explosively instrumental."

Chapter Eleven

Ask the Marriage Expert

Gabe didn't belong in this old Sacramento tavern. The guys playing pool nearby must have noticed his open laptop, then heard his order of vodka and tonic with a lemon, please, and wondered what the hell such an airy fairy was doing in their hangout.

So did Gabe. It wasn't an auspicious start to his first business trip for his new position, back with *Planet Quarterly*. He'd finally resigned from SecureTek after witnessing how the company's profits escalated with the increasingly catastrophic Iraq War. Zeena had become embedded with more and more unsavory projects, including lucrative contracts for new US embassy compounds shooting up in Middle East capitals.

Like the war, the university itself continued to expand. As the endowments grew more generous, narrow but massive new buildings squeezed any available space between century-old brick and stone pseudo-Gothic departments. Neo-pseudo-Gothic towers for the law and business schools loomed where a service alley was obliterated, their gilded parapets and grand entries hidden behind a parking structure. Wealthy benefactors expected their names carved in stonework over columnar entries, such as the Herbert and Eleanora Schotter School of Global Markets, as well as the Harold R. Keyes Doorway, and even the Ida Marie Ramsbottom Garden Bench.

But one benefactor, rumored to be an International School graduate and state department official who'd later grown rich as a Washington lobbyist for global markets, preferred anonymity in funding a funky campus entity that had no garden bench or columnar entry, *The Planet Quarterly*. On condition that the journal "boldly publish the best of global literature and nonfiction without commercial or political constraints," the benefactor set up a trust to endow the magazine in perpetuity. The editor, overwhelmed by the sudden windfall of capacity and prospects, reached out to Gabe to see if he had any interest in returning, this time as assistant editor for a much more respectable salary. Though it was still a substantial pay cut from his position at SecureTek, Gabe didn't have to think about it. He notified Zeena of his resignation the following morning.

The Planet Quarterly funded his flight to Sacramento and his fee for the Association of Academic Journals annual conference. After years of circling the planet in business drag of slacks and tie, Gabe yearned to travel in T-shirts, shorts, and flip-flops like every other guy his age. But he'd decided to respect his colleagues by trying to make a decent impression in button-down, travel khakis, and well-tamed hair.

This was what looking respectable got him. The lumpen working-class guys in the bar kept stealing glances at him, signaling to each other. As they intended, he could overhear their comments: *Fucken faggot with a laptop. Fucken orders a vodka tonic.* They shot balls across the pool table like artillery. They glared at Gabe.

Was it that obvious he really was queer? Though he could easily out-working-class any of these punks, it was all about perception. He'd invaded their sovereign territory, an old-school tribalism that didn't fit with his first impression of mellow, easygoing Sacramento years ago, when he first came here for Candy and Ben's wedding. This sad sack little neighborhood tavern was all male without being the least bit gay. Though looking barely drinking age, the guys bitched about their wives and insulted women's private parts with every known obscenity. What was the deal with straight boys and their contempt for the lady bits they craved?

One guy prowled near Gabe's red vinyl booth with a beer in one hand and a pool cue in the other. Skinny and tightly grimacing, he wore an XXX large team jersey, looking like a boy waddling around in one of his mother's housedresses. Gabe looked up from his laptop with a half-smile and asked the guy, "How ya doin'?"

Stone cold, the kid ignored him and hustled back to the pool table to report his brave foray to his comrades. *Fucken faggot asked me how I was doing, can you believe it?*

Gabe figured he'd cut his losses, take a few more sips of the strong well vodka and get the hell out. He'd call Ben back and ask if there was another neighborhood joint to wait for him, maybe a coffeehouse? As Gabe reached for his phone, a hulking figure hovered over the booth, a dark shape blocking the dim side lamp. The hulk thrust his arm across the booth straight at Gabe.

"Great to see ya." It was Ben, shaking his hand. As he sat, shuffling across the booth into the light, Gabe checked out his office suit. It gave Ben the plush appearance of being a full-grown adult, all dressed up for the onset of middle age.

After Ben clasped Gabe's arm in greeting, Gabe observed the pool players' disgust over his friend's shoulder and caught their comment: *Now there's* two *fucken fags*.

Ben settled in, his back to the boys, oblivious. "I've never been inside this place yet, Gabe."

"Isn't this a couple blocks from your house? I figured it might be your and Candy's favorite watering hole."

"We never have a chance to go anywhere anymore, except to drop off or pick up the girls from preschool." He glanced around the dark wooden bar and smiled at the ancient jukebox. "It's kind of an old-fashioned dive, huh? Cool."

"It's not one bit cool."

"What do you mean?" Ben asked. "I love places like this. These guys are authentic, you know? This is real."

"You only think that because you grew up in suburbia." Gabe never quite understood Ben's visions of authenticity. What if the authentic object of his approval still sucked? "If you'd grown up around these clowns, you wouldn't romanticize them."

"It's like, when these guys wear their Kings tank tops, they're not trying to be cute or ironic or whatever. They're totally passionate about their home team."

"So, they're passionate about corporate athletes from all over the continent putting on a local jersey? To play a kids' game for money?"

"Gabe." Ben smiled, looking wistful. "I've missed your bullshit."

"My bullshit?" Gabe smiled back, then tried to down his drink in bigger gulps. "I've spent my life trying to avoid being back in this reality. I might as well be back in Butcher Creek."

"I'm just glad our street still has this bar. I thought this neighborhood was going to be old and funky, but it's turned out be old and trendy."

Ben ordered a drink before Gabe could talk him out of it, so they caught up right there in the smelly booth, a stab wound in the stiff red vinyl between them.

After that chance meeting in Paris, Candy did enroll at UC Davis, but not with Buddy. They'd had a fight about Buddy's drinking and decided to end the engagement when they returned to Dallas. Her advisor helped her land a paid internship as a legislative aide to a prominent, progressive state senator. After graduating with her master's in communication, it became a permanent position in speechwriting and media outreach. The capitol was only a short drive from Davis over the causeway, and before long Candy ran into Ben at a downtown happy hour.

Candy had been so steadily satirical of Ben's foibles, and their breakup had been so total that Gabe was astonished when he found one of those multi-sheet, tissue-papered, embossed wedding invitations in his mailbox at Edna Victoria.

"Every day's a complete surprise," Ben said. "Ever since the girls were born. Babyhood, toddlerhood, and now preschool…" He sighed. "With Candy and the girls, the whole house is so female. I keep learning about girly toys and accessories and, like, processes I never knew existed."

Gabe smiled at Ben's puzzlement. That abashed gaze of his that hadn't changed in more than a decade, since they were freshman roommates, as if any logic and precision on this chaotic planet would forever be a tantalizing, impossible promise. "Processes?" Gabe asked. "Icky girl stuff?"

"Icky and sticky."

While Ben took off to fetch his girls home from preschool, Gabe unpacked in the enormous third-story attic room. One corner was a random mess of kids' toys strewn across the plank floor with puzzles and picture books scattered across built-in shelves. The opposite corner held a defunct TV and stacks of obsolete electronics, stereo speakers, receivers, even a cassette tape deck. Here and there cardboard boxes were stacked in jumbles against the low side walls, neatly taped and labeled as if for a move, or never unpacked. The single guest bed was the only furnishing in an alcove that overlooked the backyard.

Gabe studied the view, a yellowing lawn surrounding two ancient elms whose intertwined canopies spread almost the size of the fenced yard and topped the height of the roof's peak. Had they been pruned and cared for, the trees would have been magnificent like many on this block of century-old houses near the capitol. But Ben and Candy's elms were thirsty, full of dead branches and long-amputated limbs. Squeezed between an overgrown hydrangea and the back fence was a sturdy metal swing set over a bare depression where many little feet had dug into the earth.

After knocking and coming to Gabe's side at the window to buss his cheek, Candy followed his gaze. "Aren't those old swings great?" she said. Still dressed for work in matching jacket and skirt, she held an armful of sheets and bedding. It jolted Gabe to see Ben and Candy dressed so professionally when he was more used to their Colorado student selves in T-shirts and shorts, or wandering around the apartment in even less than that. "It reminds me of the swing set at my grandmother's, which was already an antique when I played on it. We're lucky this came with the place, and the girls love it."

"Yeah. Makes me want to get down and swing myself."

"Be my guest. I do it every chance I get, which isn't often. I hope this room is all right, Gabe," she said as she started making the little bed. "I think your feet are going to dangle over the end of the mattress."

"It beats some sterile hotel. I've had my fill of those."

"I've been looking forward to your visit since the minute you called. I would've killed you if you didn't stay with us."

"Now, that's my kind of hospitality, mortal threats and everything." He caught the bottom sheet's edge and helped her fit it. "I'm hoping to spend some free time with you and Ben."

"Good. We haven't had any house guests in, like, forever—as you can tell by the condition of this attic. The girls won't drive you crazy up here, either."

As if beckoned, two little girls pounded up the last attic steps, mock-yelling about something faux-scary, but got shy, caught short by the sight of Gabe helping their mother make the bed. They stopped tussling. The littler one, Maggie, hid behind Chelsea, who just stared with her big dark eyes. Candy laughed. "Come on, girls. Say hello to our old friend Gabe."

"I promise I won't upset your toy collection," he told them. "Or your hi-fi equipment."

"Oh, don't worry about that stuff," Candy said, pointing at the toy corner. "That's just the spillover from the other five hundred toys they have in their own room. The trouble with all this extra space is that you tend to spread stuff instead of managing it."

"Managing?" Ben appeared at the attic threshold, changed to baggy gym shorts and a floppy, wrinkled T-shirt that looked fished out of a laundry basket. "We talking about the household budget?"

"No, Ben," Candy said without humor. "I don't discuss budgets with friends."

"Too bad. I thought maybe Gabe had some management ideas." Ben caught Chelsea's upheld hands while Maggie clutched his bare leg. He shuffled to make progress toward Candy, who leaned out to kiss him, then each of the girls, as she finished fixing the bedsheets.

"God, I hope you didn't expect me to manage your budget," Gabe said. "That would be a tragic mistake."

"Daddy, Gabe said God!"

"That's funny, huh, sweetie pie, since God doesn't exist."

"At T Street Tots they say don't take um name in vain."

"Um name? What's that?" Ben still held Chelsea's hands up, and she began to dance, marionette-like, while Maggie raised her hands, too, ecstatic, chanting, "Um name! Um name!"

Candy glanced at Gabe with a half-smile and an expression that seemed to include him in a mutual understanding he did not yet understand.

❖

During dinner at a neighborhood Italian place, Gabe came to understand the intensity of pressures on Candy and Ben. He flinched to recall how, at twenty-one, he'd seriously fantasized about raising Candy's child, which could only have grown out of his pure innocence of childrearing's reality, its loud, authentic icky and stickiness. Caring for Leif at random times had only given him the smallest taste of the challenges.

Tonight's dinner out was full of continual interruption and enormous tolerance of the little crises involving getting food into children's mouths. Chelsea and Maggie seemed to be pretty good girls, content with kiddie meals while the adults shared a giant bowl of pasta—until Chelsea wanted to try it, too, then Maggie decided she needed some as well. At some point, Ben and Candy became consumed with spooning pasta on little plates of half-eaten wieners until Chelsea declared the pesto sauce was snotty and gross while Maggie managed to goop most of her serving in her lap.

In between tending to the girls, the three adults had tried to bring each other up to date on their career developments, but facts and stories stayed fragmentary as the girls' giddy upheavals derailed trains of thought. Candy's position as a top aide for the influential state senator was her career dream come true, but she was underpaid and the job was too demanding of her time out of office hours.

Ben's position with a regional accounting firm was rising, with decent but not stellar income and gobsmacking stacks of work that rivaled Candy's for being more than a nonexistent God could ever demand of a mere human, let alone humans with two children. Gabe imagined their lives consisted of nonstop stress, existence-as-continuous-coping he'd experienced only during college finals, or during final edits on a new issue of *Planet Quarterly*. For Ben and Candy, the pressure cooker's mad rattle never ended.

In the distracting free-for-all at the restaurant table, one topic would surface, then get lost, then get mentioned again, as if they were all reluctant to dive into it but recognized its inevitability. With the girls preoccupied with crayons and coloring pads provided by their waiter, Candy asked about Zeena and Todd's divorce. "I didn't know her that well, but I sure liked Todd. I hope it hasn't been too bad for them."

"The marriage changed so much when SecureTek started to completely dominate Zeena's life. It just didn't work anymore. Todd was a dedicated academic, and when the university cut away the philosophy department, he found himself marooned, teaching global ethics in the business school."

"Wait a minute! They cut away philosophy? What kind of university doesn't teach philosophy? My father still has contacts on the board of trustees, Gabe. I should sweet-talk him into starting some kind of action. Restoring philosophy, for starters."

"I think it's too late, Candy. It killed me to see the look on Todd's face when the ax came down."

"When I took Ethics 101 from him, I just couldn't believe how intense, how alive his classes were. The way he tied the topics to the current news cycle, then to classic literature, then to a personal incident with a car mechanic or something—it was unforgettable."

"But these esoteric academic departments don't attract a lot of majors or prestigious publications," Ben said. "The small classes can be unsustainable. The university has to make money, or it doesn't have a future."

"Does it have to come down to money? I thought philosophy had inherent value," Candy said. "I can't imagine how devastated Todd must be. His whole department reduced to a subcategory of the business school."

"Then he'd come home," Gabe said, "to have dinner with guest security and weaponry officials at the new mini-mansion he hated. It's their marriage that wasn't sustainable."

"It's fairly common, I guess, that old-couples-grow-apart cliché." Candy sighed. "But I sure didn't understand it. I was a giddy schoolgirl mooning over my dream marriage. I actually thought it would be a static state of happiness ever after, like a fairy tale. I had no appreciation of how married people could change so much they might not even be recognizable to each other by the bitter end."

"I think the divorce was actually good for Zeena," Gabe said, "so she could devote herself completely to SecureTek's profits without any of Todd's moral qualms about the Mideast wars. He always stood up for noble causes while she was getting more and more enmeshed in casus belli."

"God, she sounds awful."

"Yeah. I had to get away from Zeena. And SecureTek, too." Gabe had come to wonder if Zeena had placed herself on the opposite pole from Mary Anne's profound faith or his mother's simpler one—not just a nonbeliever, like Gabe, but a complete moral zero, blithe in her self-interest. "I felt I was being manipulated in ways I didn't understand, an unwitting lackey. Her dumbshit accomplice in fanning the flames of terror to hype up defense profits. She even capitalized on her childhood connection with Condi Rice. So, I got a small taste at work of what Todd had to live with at home. After the 9/11 attacks and all the security contracts, the old Zeena was disappearing into an ethical black hole."

"Oh Jesus!" Candy cried. "Poor Todd."

"My teacher says never to say Jesus um vain," Chelsea advised, "Mommy."

"Jesus was a wise young rabbi," Ben put in, "who saw what a mess human society was in."

"Daddy, are you going back in the cave when we get home?" Chelsea asked, apropos of nothing. Gabe could remember no mention of spelunking and was glad for the distraction her question produced, because he didn't want to discuss Todd and Zeena's divorce anymore. As the couple became increasingly estranged, they'd turned separately to Gabe to sound him out on strategies, culpability, and prospects for salvation, expecting the one single gay guy in their orbit to be their marriage expert.

In fact, Gabe had never advised anything. He just listened to both of them, which made his role even more sought after. Todd and Zeena believed he was wise and impartial when in fact he was just numbly paraphrasing what each desperate character unloaded on him.

On the short stroll back to the house, Candy and Gabe chatted while the girls danced and swooped ahead around Ben, using their father as a giant, ambulatory playground. "I won't blame you if you check into that sterile hotel room," Candy said, "for the rest of your conference."

"No way. Anyhow, I'll be working the conference both days while you two get to enjoy the weekend."

"Ha! We both brought work home, and the girls don't seem to recognize that weekends around the madhouse should be any less insane than the weekdays." She gestured ahead, where Ben had taken Maggie on his shoulders while Chelsea screamed in an ecstasy of feigned pursuit, eluding the two-headed monster chasing her.

"Ben really seems to be having fun with the girls."

"He is, but most nights are not like tonight. In fact, it's almost never like this anymore. For the girls, having Ben's attention right now is like Christmas morning, and just as rare. I think he's more relaxed and open to them because you're here, and they sense it. It's a holiday from our usual tense reality."

"Come on. It's obvious they enjoy each other, and it's got nothin' to do with me."

"Believe me, Gabe," Candy said, "just having you stay with us is a welcome change from our perilous norm."

❖

It wasn't yet nine thirty when Gabe, teeth brushed and wide awake, went downstairs in pursuit of company and maybe sharing a nightcap—which he planned to provide from a plastic bottle of corporate California brandy he'd slipped into his duffel. Candy was reading the girls to sleep in soothing tones, smiling at Gabe as he passed, one arm around each of her snuggling daughters, the very picture of contented domesticity. Gabe waved and passed down the long hallway toward the wedge of light from Ben's office.

"Remember when we used to sip cheap brandy and bullshit about Dostoyevsky until three in the morning?" Gabe produced the little plastic bottle with a smile.

"Yeah! Hit me with a shot." Ben finished off a swallow of water from a plastic glass crazy with Disney characters, then held it out. Gabe sat on an overturned plastic crate beside Ben's computer chair. His home office looked exactly as if he'd transplanted his bedroom at Edna Victoria, a chaos of books on boards held by concrete blocks. "I don't remember one thing from Dostoyevsky except Raskolnikov killing that old lady for laughs. But I've memorized every minute of *The Little Mermaid*."

Gabe glanced at the computer screen, pulsing with columns of numbers. "Homework on Friday night?"

"I'm just killing time with some state budget data. Fiscal data gets updated the end of next month. Just trying to get prepared."

"Are you helping out Candy with her senator?"

"God no!" Ben looked in mock horror. "I just try to keep up with general budget data. For laughs."

"I think I'd rather kill an old lady." Gabe hoped for a laugh, but Ben was already explaining the intricacies of CalTrans maintenance expenditures in Yolo County for the previous quarter, and since Gabe could not find a way to change the subject, he drank ever deeper of the rotgut that originated, for all he knew, in the heavily indebted brandy fields of Yolo County.

❖

Gabe walked back to Ben and Candy's from the downtown hotel's conference rooms after the keynote Saturday night dinner. A former poet laureate's witty paean to literary magazines had been the best part of the day.

He was tired now. Hurrying from session to session, Gabe had been amused by his fellow dowdy academic editorial staffers from all over North America playing dress-up and enjoying overpriced hotel bar cocktails just like real professionals. The day had been long and most of the workshops bloated with jargon and cooked-up controversies. If tomorrow's sessions weren't more focused on practical improvements, the whole weekend would have to be written off as a waste of time, though he had managed some useful schmoozing with other editors and publishers, and gladly collected compliments and contacts when he manned the *Planet Quarterly* booth during breaks.

Heading upstairs, Gabe found a repeat of last night's routine, Candy reading the girls to sleep and Ben in his office lit only by the numbers on the computer screen. He headed up to the attic to retrieve the corporate brandy and share the last of it with Ben, hoping it would knock him out for the sleep he needed to face the long day Sunday. To his surprise, Candy followed close behind on the attic stairs, already in a pajama top and gray sweatpants, her long hair loosely tied in a ponytail.

She modeled for Gabe's benefit, vogueing in the great open expanse between the bed and the excess toys. "Saturday night fashions in married-with-kids land, Gabe," she told him, curtsying. "Count your freakin' blessings, boy."

"I think it's kinda sweet, all this domesticity. I have my own Saturday nights in sweatpants, but they're much more pathetic when you're alone."

"Who says I'm not alone, now that the girls have fallen asleep? Anyway, I just wanted to check in, Gabe. Do you have everything you need? Enough blankets?"

He nodded, thanking her, but it seemed like a pretext, since more blankets were the last things he needed on a warm May Sacramento night already on the verge of the city's summer inferno. Candy roved closer to his alcove then joined him, sitting on the bed. "I'll bet you have lots of interesting Saturday nights."

"That would require a man of interest, and he's absent every night of the week. I mean, nonexistent."

"Come on, Gabe. I know how you are."

"Okay, I'm kind of dating two guys right now. And I do mean dating—movies, coffees, walks in Washington Park. But the one I really like isn't at all physically attractive to me. And the one who's hot is kind of a prick. It's the usual standoff. I don't see any future with either one."

"Well, you see my future all around us. I suppose you've noticed we're married to this crazy mortgage now, this insanely oversized white elephant."

He had noticed the antique plumbing, the odd-shaped country kitchen with its funky, decades-old appliances and rust-stained metal cabinets. Brown wall-to-wall carpet was worn through in places and seemed to underlie everything but the kitchen's checkered linoleum. A shaky back porch led outside on even shakier back steps. "It's charming."

"Nice try. It's a dump, a pathetic money pit." She sat on the bed and launched into a long exposition of how they'd ended up mortgaged to the rickety old place. Ben's father had encouraged them to buy into the gentrifying neighborhood as a co-investment, and Ben, to raise fast cash, invested in a tantalizing fund for Central Valley tech start-ups on margin. It went bust in a sudden tech stock crash and Ben had to borrow even more money from his father to pay back the less than worthless margin options. "That's why Ben's become obsessed with our budget. We're in deep debt to his father, who is not a forgiving type. As well as owing our half of the mortgage to the bank, which is not forgiving at all."

Gabe recalled the crude punks in the corner tavern yesterday and, walking here tonight, some of the houseless citizens he'd passed shambling with shopping carts into a neighborhood park that surrounded a lake. He wondered how fast the neighborhood really was gentrifying just as he thought of Ben's Yolo County spreadsheets from last night.

Though calm, Candy clearly was unnerved enough to violate her own rule about discussing budgets with friends. He felt almost as if he were back in Denver alone with Zeena, in direct aim of confidences about Todd he didn't want to receive. "I was just about to offer old Ben a snifter or maybe a Disney glassful of our favorite cheap brandy," Gabe said, holding up the little half-empty bottle. "Why don't you join us?"

"Thanks, but no. I'm sorry for dumping all this on you. Sometimes I just crave another adult to talk to. I mean, one who's really capable of listening."

"I'm all ears."

"I feel overwhelmed by motherhood. Of course, I love my girls beyond imagining. I just feel stretched to my limits, not challenged or fulfilled, an inadequate working mom and wife. I've never really had passions, Gabe, except when I started studying literature for my bachelor's. But that was personal, you know, my love of the stories, my love of the poetry, not something I wanted to parlay into a doctorate and an academic career. And now, if I dare to crack open a novel, I'm asleep in ten minutes. No matter how wonderful the writing is, my face is mashed, drooling, in its open pages. I do enjoy my work, I admire my senator and his politics, and I'm damn good at what I do! But politics aren't really my passion, either. I don't have any big ambitions, and though I've got degrees now, I'm really not so different that that pathetic, lost creature who wandered up from Conrad's basement and knocked over your door."

"You were lost, maybe, but never pathetic. I was crazy about you." Gabe realized what he'd always felt for Candy, including that muddled moment in Paris, wasn't so complicated. It was tenderness. Though he'd confused its depth with attraction, it had really been about connection, a yearning for her presence, her beauty, and her wit. "And come on, we've both changed a lot. We've got careers. We've grown up."

"Yeah, I've grown into a perfect exemplar of the Sacramento hausfrau at thirty-five. Isn't it obvious I've made a terrible mistake? I would've been better off with Buddy, just another country club wifey-poo with a charming drunk for a husband. No, I broke up with Ben for a reason, back on South High, and it was a good reason. When he caved to his father's demands, when he was so blindly willing to give up his passion for some illusion of security, I knew. Oh, I knew. But I didn't listen to myself. It's not like I had a deep bench of suitors at Davis, and when I ran into Ben again, the old hormones kicked in, and before you could say two drinks for the price of one, I was acting like a brainless floozy. I got pregnant with Chelsea, and no way was I gonna have another abortion. So, here I am." She leaned to kiss Gabe on the cheek.

"You're ganging up on yourself." He kissed her back. "The old Ben would've been easy to fall for, right? Where's that beautiful guy randomly quoting Tolstoy on a hike to Devil's Thumb Pass? The wind catching his wild hair overlooking the Great Divide? The passion in his voice, the joy in his eyes? Where is that guy?"

"He's lost, to me at least. And to himself, too. Look, Gabe, don't pity me. I've got great work, and I adore my girls with insane, overwhelming obsession. I've drunk the Mommy Kool-Aid in great two-for-one draughts, and I'm addicted. I'll always have my girls. But you do need to take what little time you have with Ben. He doesn't really have friends anymore. He'd love to share a Disney glassful, and I know he loves having another grown-up to talk with, too."

Gabe and Candy parted ways on the second floor, where she blew him another kiss good night and ducked into the master bedroom. He found Ben in the same position down the hall, the office completely dark except for the bright screen, his face lit from below, campfire demonic. Ben accepted the brandy, distracted by whatever budget he was engrossed in, then abruptly turned all his attention on Gabe. "So, do you ever worry about the national debt?"

Gabe gave a shocked laugh. "I'm not losing any sleep over it."

"I am. Seriously, I think it's the greatest crisis we face."

What the hell? "Ben, we've both been living with massive national debt for our entire lives. We always hear it's such a big deal, but it never goes away and yet never seems to have any impact."

"Oh, it's coming. Like that meteor that destroyed the dinosaurs." Before Gabe could do anything to stop the onslaught, Ben was flipping data bank to data bank, demonstrating the massive size of the debt and multipliers that produced even greater debt years out. Ben obviously knew his way through the facts and links by heart and easily navigated a vast array of numbers. Gabe got the impression that this exploration was Ben's hobby, here alone in the dark, and maybe his escape from the girls and their demands.

But it went farther. Ben became more engrossed, his brow crinkled in the screen glow, more ardent and hard edged. He showed Gabe links to California and Colorado state and county data, then on to other seemingly random states, all of it available so briskly and organized it seemed rehearsed. Ben was trying to establish that along with the unimaginable national debt, a substratum of additional state and local debt raised the national amount of red ink to tsunami stage, poised to drown us all before we knew what hit us.

"At this stage, we will never be able to repay this all that we owe. Debt will sweep away our assets, and our wealth will completely disappear. All commerce will cease, including agriculture, energy, sanitation, and safe water systems."

His eyes adjusting to the dark, Gabe noticed a whiteboard scrawled with hasty equations, and, leaning against the bare walls, flip pads open to similar calculations.

"I think I'm finding the true formula to prove this," Ben said. "There's a point where the economy will freeze up. In the simplest terms, the market exchanges that keep the monetary supply replenished will simply cease."

"And if you're right, what are you going to do? Notify the Federal Reserve, what?"

Ben looked at him in honest astonishment. "There won't be any chance for that, Gabe." It was as if his formulas would cause, not prevent, the coming catastrophe.

In the isolation and darkness, this hooey took on a spooky reality. Gabe wondered if it was all a mental transfer of Ben's anxieties about his own household debt to the grandiosity and abstraction of nationwide calamity, somehow soothing in its very hopelessness. But there was more. Ben told him he had connections to a whole network of similar debt-heads and began to surf through message boards, hundreds of anonymous comrades trading around the same anxieties and stark spreadsheets.

"And recently we've been linked by some interested political organizations," he added, flipping through several provisional-looking websites, some with winking Stars and Stripes, some with crude references to patriots, the oppression of white people, and the dangers of the Dark Tide. Surging ever out from spreadsheets, Ben's obsessive but reasonable budgetary tsunami dribbled into open sewage, white supremacist fantasias of unstoppable, oceanic forces.

"Ben, doesn't it worry you, all these extremist web pages?"

"Sure it does. But with the whole establishment media conspiring to silence the full extent of the debt, sometimes we have to find allies on the fringes."

A Confederate battle flag flickered across a website, jumpy with a question in a banner: *Why Is Racial Purity a Crime?* Ben shook his head. "Pathetic, huh? But at least they've got the right ideas on excessive public spending."

❖

The conference ended late afternoon Sunday. Gabe had planned to spend the evening with Candy and Ben then catch his plane Monday morning. He was beginning to realize, though, that Candy and Ben did not spend their evenings with each other. Ben had deteriorated from a math-adept phenomenon to a numerical Casaubon, lost in some impenetrable Key to Mysteries. Had he married Candy to his spiritual decay?

When Gabe walked back from the hotel, Candy was supervising the girls at the backyard swing set. "I don't know how he can juggle numbers all day at work, then stare at those spreadsheets every evening, sometimes till past midnight," Candy told him, her voice lowered. "Now he's even spending most of Sunday in his office, playing with county budgets in Kansas or Texas. Most weekday evenings, he still showers and plays with the girls for a little while before he hunkers down in his dark cave for the duration. But I can see the day coming when he forgets to clean himself. Or spend a minute with his daughters."

Those daughters were squealing and giggling as Gabe and Candy took turns pushing them skyward. The sun dazzled, dappling Chelsea and Maggie as they swung in opposing arcs in the shade of the giant elm, their light brown hair flying to catch gold highlights from the late-afternoon sunshine, then swaying back into shadow. Gabe could not comprehend why Ben would rather obsess over computerized columns of data than enjoy his exuberant family in the last of the tolerable late-spring sunshine. He could not think of a single reassuring comment.

"It's not like I'm completely oblivious to budget data myself," Candy went on. "Our office gets data from the state constantly. I mean, I'm right there in the guts of the capitol every day, where we might actually be working on a bill to help struggling farm workers in one of those Central Valley counties Ben is trolling, or funding a forest preserve, or adding staff to preschool programs. The state can't really run up too much of a debt before we have to start cutting, since states can't print money. I'm sorry to belabor the obvious, Gabe, but I just know firsthand our budget's not a dark mystery. But he thinks I'm a lackey, duped by some false matrix."

"Baby, come on. I don't think you're a lackey." Ben had arrived from his cave, unannounced and unseen behind them. He looked stern, steely-eyed. When Ben retreated into this self-contained mode, Gabe always feared he could behave like a gangster with three turns of the wrong switch.

Candy turned, startled but covering it up by reaching for Ben's arm to pull him closer. "The girls would love a fatherly shove."

Ben ignored Candy's request. "Not a lackey, no. I think you're trapped in a hopeless system."

Gabe got busy pushing the girls himself. The girls cheered, demanding ever higher launches into the blue sky.

"You're right, Candy." Ben went on. "It's not a dark mystery. It's a simple matter of our drowning in red ink. The tax-and-spend mentality at the capitol has got to stop."

Candy hesitated as if listening to her better angels. But more urgent angels must have won out. "Tell me, then. What the hell else are we supposed to do with taxes? Not spend? Tax-and-not-spend?"

"It would be a start." Moving out of the elms' shadow into the sunlight, Ben's face seemed even more pale. The outdoorsy spark that once lighted his masculine good looks seemed drained away by all his time alone in the dark. There was little trace of Gabe's Colorado hiking buddy or the ski partner who attacked expert slopes with beautiful, swooping turns while Gabe, tentative, traversed mogul to mogul, jealous of Ben's unstinting glee. Now Ben's dark eyes bored into Candy. "But I'm sure it's already too late."

"Too late for what, Ben?" Candy's question sounded strained, as if she were trying to imitate normal conversational give and take.

"All of this. One day soon we're going to turn on the lights, and nothing's going to switch on. Same with the water tap and the stove. Cars will run only until the last drop of gas is used up. Which will be a blessing, because without any traffic cops paid to enforce the traffic laws or working signals, it'll be kind of dangerous out there." He smiled, wistful with appreciation of his own understatement. "It's not going to be crazy, not like a bad Hollywood version of the apocalypse, just a slow and final collapse."

"Glad to hear that," Candy said in that same flat way. "I think I'll take the girls inside."

"No, Mommy!"

"Planes aren't going to fall out of the sky or anything. But once they land, they'll stay on the ground, since there won't be any more air traffic controllers." He smiled again. "Not paid ones, anyway."

At some point, the girls' swings had gone still. They dangled their legs in a jittery rhythm. Ben and Candy each held the chains, calm, looking at the top of each daughter's head. "Daddy, is T Street Tots going to stop, too?" Chelsea asked.

"No, honey," Candy rushed to answer. "Daddy's just talking about a silly movie."

"Can I see it?" Chelsea asked.

"Me, too!"

"Oh, you'll see it, girls," Ben said. "Someday soon."

"Girls, we need to go inside for our snack," Candy said. "Apple juice and animal crackers."

"Juice boxes?" Chelsea squirmed out of her seat, followed by Maggie, helped by Gabe's guiding hand. "Juice boxes, Mommy?" Chelsea repeated, doing a little dance, swinging her hips in a wide swivel so that she bopped right into Maggie as she exited the swing.

"Yes, if you want. Juice boxes."

Maggie was crying now from the irritation of Chelsea's swivel. Candy scooped her up and kissed her head with dramatic smooching noises while expertly taking Chelsea by the hand. All at once, Gabe was alone with Ben, face-to-face with him with the swing set between them. Ben continued to stand, as if entranced, staring ahead, his hand still on the swing's chains.

Gabe felt a twinge of apprehension, wondering for a moment if Ben had gone catatonic. "Hey, I was thinking of taking a jog before it got dark," he said, inventing the thought on the spot to break the spell. "You wanna join me?"

Ben stayed still for a moment, still staring without seeming to focus on anything. Then he snapped out of it. "Thanks, but I've got to get back to my calculations."

❖

Gabe ran a route that skirted that park with the lake, busy on Sunday with teenagers smoking on the shore and young parents strolling the paved surround with strollers. This late-afternoon jog seemed inevitable now though he hadn't planned it, imagining in his deluded state that Ben and Candy might have a backyard cookout or maybe even a visit to a pizza place for Sunday dinner. Now he wondered if the couple ever had a home meal together anymore, feeling relieved to have escaped the big house and inhaling gratitude for the fresh, cooling air.

He crossed Capitol Park, where tourists, homeless guys, and joggers alternated among the abundant May flower beds, and glanced as he passed at the capitol itself, sensing the anguish that Candy must feel constantly, working to spend state funds more equitably to provide public opportunities while Ben mired himself in the end of all taxation and all expenditures—all of civilization—from his dark cave, tangled in a gauzy stitching of scary figures.

Gabe pounded his way down the deserted outdoor mall, then past the conference hotel and toward the river. Crossing under the interstate, he found himself in Old Sacramento, bustling along the waterfront on this perfect Sunday. He finally stopped, steadying his breathing. With the restored pioneer storefronts behind him and the plank walks groaning with visitors, it was easy to envision the rough, rambunctious 1849 river port hosting Gold Rush hordes of global dreamers.

God, look at the state they built! They didn't shrink from the challenge and hole up in dark rooms. What could have shrunken Ben's hunger for art and nature, his massive capacities to such calculating, constricted fixation? Was the tug of convention and financial affluence that powerful?

Now Gabe had no choice but to jog back to that house, back to Ben's stubborn obsession and Candy's stifled dead end. Was this where adulthood had marooned everybody? Zeena and Todd were kaput. His own beautiful chances at connection had come to nothing. Only Jamie and Mary Anne seemed happy for the long haul.

In the morning, all three adults would hustle out at the same time, Ben and Candy dressed to the nines for their office jobs, Gabe duly representing *Planet Quarterly* in the same khakis and button-down he wore on the inbound flight. Before he slipped into the airporter, he'd shake Ben's hand and thank him for the hospitality and kiss each of the girl's heads before they were whisked away in Ben's big luxury sedan. Before she would hustle across the lake park toward the capitol, Candy would hug Gabe and whisper, *I really need to consult you, my marriage expert. Maybe you can think of what I can do to recover my life with Ben? Or have I already lost that?*

Now, overlooking the river in his jogging shorts, Gabe meant to quench his thirst at a water fountain and laughed in shock when it didn't work. A few yards away, the next one worked just fine, shooting a blessed arc of cold, pure H20 fresh from the Sierra Nevada. He took in one last eyeful, too, of the open sky over the Sacramento River and the public promenade. Between the levees, barges and pleasure craft plied the dappled water, the golden sunlight flickering across their bows. The old-fashioned drawbridge rose gracefully, no groaning or complaints of age, to let through a barge stacked high with some golden, bundled crop. The day's final light poured between the canopies of the trees lining the public space, just-released graduates laughing and dancing along the river's western shore.

Chapter Twelve

The Archbishop Comes for Gabriel

"Is this your little boy?"

Gabe looked up from the translated poem. Its translator stood in his office doorway at the *Planet Quarterly*, gesturing toward Leif.

"He's my friends' kid," Gabe said, waving in his visitor. "I watch him a couple days a week."

"He looks exactly like you, man."

"Yeah, it's a curse being three foot, ten inches tall."

Army Master Sergeant Jacob Kovac smiled. "The brown, wavy hair." Brazen, he stared at Gabe's face. "The blue eyes."

"Yep." Gabe smiled. "We were both born that way, Leif and I. But I thought we were going talk about these poems, Jake."

More and more prone to daddy-seeking, Leif stared and stared at the handsome soldier, peering from his cardboard box construction project in the corner of Gabe's office. Jake approached Leif's cardboard pile, stooped beside him, and extended a hand to shake. Leif offered his, laughing. Jake said, "This kid's a champ, Gabe."

"He is, but I can't take any credit. I just watch him here Tuesdays and Thursdays, when one of his moms is taking a morning class at the theology school."

Jake nodded. Crouching near the wall, he helped Leif steady a cardboard steeple-like shape on the pile. "Quite an ambitious venture."

"It's a church!" Leif clarified, and Gabe had to admit it was starting to look like one. Never mind that he'd brought three spiffy new picture books, a watercolor set plus paper pad, and the entire Completely Updated Mr. and Mrs. Potato Head Family Fun Kit to amuse the kid.

No, a torn cardboard box had absorbed Leif all the past Thursday and this Tuesday. The kid slotted the steeple into its place. "A church, see? Just like my mommy's!"

"And what do you think of my project, Gabe?" Jake asked, looking up. "Any hope?"

"These translations?" Gabe put on his best editorial poker face. "Hard to judge, since I can't read Serbian. Or Croatian."

"They're one language, of course," Jake said, now dangling his car keys, complete with a rabbit's foot, to dazzle Leif even more. "Like I told ya. Two alphabets, Cyrillic and Roman, but the same vocabulary. Since the Yugoslav wars, after Serbia and Croatia split off, they like to pretend they have separate languages, too. It's bullshit." He touched his lips. "Dang. Pardon my French, Leif."

Gabe glanced at the stack of papers below the translations Jake had submitted to *Planet Quarterly*—sheets of blue ink in European handwriting, some in the Roman alphabet, but wild with odd accent marks, tails, and inverted carets, others in Cyrillic script, as if culled from holy texts in some Eastern Orthodox monastery. Kept in secret during the war, the poems had been bequeathed to Sergeant Kovac during the last days of his deployment in the Bosnian Serbian sector.

"Carving up Bosnia into Catholic, Muslim, and Orthodox sectors was the purest donkey shit," Jake had explained a week before over beers at the Stadium Inn, where he'd passed the packet to Gabe. "Before the war, most folks were non-religious anyway. Maybe a few old village ladies still went to Mass or mosque. Bosnians were united, speaking one language, until a few Serb separatist thugs started killing people over their one, true, Christian Orthodox nation. And most of the thugs didn't really give a damn about it. It was a power grab in God's name."

To Gabe, the sergeant looked like any Denver dude who revved Jet Skis at Chatfield Reservoir, worshipped the Broncos, and partied at Shotgun Willie's. He seemed no more likely as a translator of smuggled Serbian war poems than Gabe did as anybody's father. But when Gabe studied the cache of poems Jake had painstakingly translated with the help of his immigrant parents, he realized the sergeant had the soul of a poet. Sharp, clean, and idiomatic, Jake's translated stanzas sounded like the most natural, accessible contemporary verse.

During that exploratory beer session, Gabe had asked him to name his favorite poets. Jake didn't hesitate: "Elizabeth Bishop. Rita Dove. Joseph Brodsky. Delmore Schwartz."

"Delmore Schwartz?"

"Yep. Delmore fucking Schwartz."

"Nice. You know, my grandmother knew Croatian, but she was gone by the time I was a toddler. My mom just knew a few expressions. She used to tease me with one when I was getting taller—bad grass grows fast."

"*Loša trava brzo raste.*"

"Yep."

Gabe swiveled his office chair to face Jake, who was still on the floor, tick-tocking the rabbit-foot charm before Leif's delighted face. "What you've brought to light with these translations makes me wish I knew Serbian. Or Croatian. Or Serbo-Croatian."

"All-righty then? You're going to publish them?"

"Hell yes. I just need to run your versions by my translation guy out in Berkeley."

Jake shut his eyes, then sighed deeply, as Leif extended his arms. Jake rose, extending his reach to Leif so they locked index fingers. "Imagine. A scholar in Berkeley deciphering these messages from Bosnia."

"He'll just double-check. You've already done the deciphering. Got a secret decoder ring somewhere, Jake?"

"No. But I'm a lot like the wartime poet herself," Jake said, letting go of Leif. "My heart's broken in the same places."

❖

After Jake left, Gabe studied his beer-spotted notes from their conversations. He needed to shape them into an essay to introduce the poet and her poems in *Planet Quarterly*. Now that he was head editor of the journal—when the founder and editor retired a few months before, he'd asked Gabe to take his position—he enjoyed following his own direction, but at times, like now, he felt marooned, unsure which was the best route.

That broken-hearted Bosnian poet had survived the war but not the peace. Like so many young people in the prewar, unified, communist version of Yugoslavia, the poet had found love outside of her faith. A

Bosnian Croatian, she'd married a Bosnian Serb, something no more exceptional before the war, as Jake put it, than "some Catholic chick in Iowa marrying the Lutheran dude down the lane." The honeymoon ended when Serb extremists declared their hometown would be "purified" of non-Serbs. Sixty thousand Catholics and Muslims were "encouraged to relocate" elsewhere. Scores of bodies turned up at a local concentration camp. A thousand more citizens just disappeared.

Then the poet's husband, championed by Serb secessionists, became one of the renegade sector's wartime administrators. His wife's Catholicism, never more of an issue than her left-handedness, suddenly seemed menacing. Helpful aides encouraged her to convert to Serbian Orthodoxy. Rowdy Serb in-laws reminded her of Croatian atrocities against Serbs during World War II. "You people sent us to concentration camps to starve."

It was no use to remind them that she was born three decades after World War II ended. Now she was "you people." Her husband and in-laws were now "us." She became a prisoner of war in her own home.

In perilous isolation, she poured her distress into poems, often copying each draft in a Cyrillic version. "Many are like parables," Jake had told Gabe, "little tales of outcast farmyard animals in verse, conflicted friendships, or love affairs. Sometimes fantasies of an idyllic past, where disparate creatures joined together for protection and just plain good times. She kept these on top of the stack, ready if her husband or in-laws ever found the poem cache. She hoped they would judge them trite and harmless and miss the social analogies. Under those, she hid her free verse collection, critical observations on the ethnic cleansing of her city."

Surviving the war by her husband's ultimate mercy and her cunning claim to keep looking into Orthodox doctrine, she was one of few Croatian-Bosnians left in Banja Luka when Jake Kovac's unit was stationed outside the city. Jake was part of a postwar, UN-led delegation stabilizing the sector. The deputy governor's pretty young wife befriended him over ceremonial cognac. They discussed Bosnian literature, the teenage poet he'd met in Sarajevo, Adisa Bašić, and chatted about Jake's struggle to become fluent in Serbo-Croatian. The deputy's wife had cautioned him, with a wry smile, to refer to the language as Serbian, "at least while you are here in Banja Luka."

A few days later, the young wife, now in jeans, sandals, and a

Gandhi Be the Change T-shirt, visited the Americans' headquarters. She tracked down Jake and passed him a thick clasp envelope sealed with packing tape and tied with a red string: "Merely some poems in that hyphenated language we discussed, Sergeant Kovac. I want you to have them. Maybe you can practice your language skills?"

Jake offered her plum brandy. She accepted a small snifter and they spoke about the morbid summer heat and the hikes at the nearby Pools of Heaven that he must take before he went back to the States. Abruptly, she rose and kissed his cheek in parting. He would never see her again.

❖

The next Tuesday, Leif actually played with the Potato Head family in the corner of Gabe's office. Mr. and Mrs. and their potato-headed children marched stiffly into the cardboard church. It was Mr. Potato Head who served Mass and delivered a singsong sermon on the cruelty of mashing innocent tubers.

Early that morning, Gabe decided to contact the archbishop's education office with an inquiry about the Catholic Church's role during the Bosnian conflict. He needed some background for his introduction and realized he had always been puzzled. Back in the 90s, why had there been so little Vatican wartime intervention in—or even mention of—that four-year, slow-motion genocide? Why hadn't the Pope used his authority to protect Catholics, let alone other victims, from torture camps, expulsions, and sniper fire? Gabe figured the extremely conservative archbishop of the Rockies Diocese would be sensitive and defensive, so he crafted his email in neutral language, merely that of a journalist seeking facts. He added, by the way, that he himself, Gabriel Rafferty, was Catholic.

Now, as Leif quietly refined Father Mr. Potato Head's sermon, an email popped into Gabe's inbox from the Catholic archdiocese. It was from the archbishop himself:

Dear Gabriel,

Thank you for taking the time to inquire. First, I am most pleased to hear of your Catholic commitment, as every

Catholic journalist is another voice raised for our beliefs and teachings. We have been aware of Planet Quarterly *for some time, the accolades it has accumulated and the apparent prestige it has brought to Colorado, but never dreamed that its editor practiced the faith.*

Old terror twisted Gabe's guts. Mere fallen Catholic, he reddened in contrition and stopped reading the message halfway through. He needed to breathe before he tried to finish the rest.

Indeed, we have never found any evidence of our faith in the journal's slant and commentary. Its humanist selections are decidedly secular and often radical. I must ask, Gabriel, do you really believe what the Catholic church teaches about faith and morals? Unless you do, you must hold a very inadequate definition of what a Catholic is.

Jesus. This was the very archbishop of the Rocky Mountains! Not only aware of the quarterly, but critical of its slant. Out of forgotten, childlike shock and awe, Gabe marveled at his own automatic reversion to reverent wonder and fear. The very archbishop had composed this message, fresh minutes ago, and hit "Send" with his very own finger. A finger that probably wore some crazy jewel-encrusted ring.

So, he had been called out by the big man himself. Even if the archbishop was a blowhard, he was a mighty crafty blowhard with a potential direct line to the Almighty. Gabe considered, reddening even more, how in the last issue he'd headlined a searing expose of abuse and violence against transsexuals in Brazil, including a section on the Church's indifference. In some grand Catholic reckoning in the afterlife, might there be penalties for publishing radical humanist critiques?

For starters, an eternity in hell.

Gabe checked on Leif, still happily babbling his condemnation of potato genocide, and braved the rest of the message:

As a Catholic journalist, then, Gabriel, you must regularly read the Denver Catholic Gazette *and therefore must have been aware of my many commentaries during the Bosnian conflict. I deplored the loss of life on all sides. I am sure I don't need to remind you that, after the war, Catholic Relief Services was among the foremost agents of charity and succor to the victims.*

Being a Catholic is not simply being baptized a Catholic, but embracing what the Church believes and teaches, not sliced into quarters, but planet-wide.

Yours in Christ,
Archbishop Leroy Francis DePaul+

❖

"DePaul totally busted me," Gabe told Mary Anne. "He took my simple question about the church's response to Bosnia and turned it upside down. It was practically an attack on my integrity as an editor."

Most Thursdays, Gabe picked up Leif at Our Lady of Miracles KinderCare, a few blocks from the university. Mary Anne walked with Leif while on her way to theology class—which she hurried to squeeze in before managing her auxiliary Catholic charity—then handed him over to Gabe at his office. This gave them a few minutes to catch up. Today, there was too much to catch up on, so he walked Mary Anne all the way to her class. She was excited about her recent promotion to head the charity's Social Justice office, but Gabe was still freaked that the Actual Archbishop of the Entire Rocky Mountains had personally responded via email. "I can barely turn on my computer. DePaul's still in there, pulsing his electronic reprimand, shaking his damn crucifix in my inbox."

"So, delete him." Mary Anne bent down to wipe something crusty off Leif's nostril, then took his hand and continued walking. "You know, Gabe, you presented yourself as a Catholic, so he had no choice but to engage you as one. And *Planet Quarterly* is not exactly an organ of Catholic doctrine, is it?"

This was more evidence of why Mary Anne infuriated Gabe and why he loved her, how she used logic in the service of belief. She expected the church to be anti-woman and anti-gay—and never took it personally, forever haloed in equanimity about her idealistic vision of what the church really was, or could be.

"Okay, okay," Gabe said, taking Leif's free hand as they hurried down a leafy block. "I was a fraud. I shouldn't have played the Catholic card. But, Jesus, he not only questioned my faith, he totally blew smoke about the church ignoring Bosnia."

"The church couldn't do much, Gabe. During World War II, the pope backed the bad guys in Yugoslavia. The church championed the Croatian Catholic fascists who really did attack and massacre the Serbs. I read about this Croatian Franciscan monk who led the charge and personally herded Serbs into concentration camps. A Franciscan!"

"So even by the 1990s the church still had zero moral authority in the Bosnian civil war?"

"Less than zero. The pope had to stand by mute. And he was wise to keep the church's mouth shut. Otherwise, they'd come off like hypocrites from hell. Which they were."

"Man, what a ringing endorsement of the faith!"

"Oh, Gabe. The faith will always survive these men in robes and funny hats. Don't let 'em get to you. DePaul's a stinky blip on the screen of eternity." She bussed Gabe, bent to kiss her son, and hurried under an old stone archway into the theology school.

Another Tuesday came. Today Leif had two schoolmates from Miracles KinderCare, Jesus Garcia and Courtney Killigan, joining him in the corner. Moms Garcia and Killigan had an afternoon meeting with Lady of Miracles' priest—a Garcia son was about to marry a Killigan daughter. Gabe had been suckered into babysitting on the spot when he picked up Leif. "Okay, but I wanna go to the wedding!" he'd cried to the two mothers.

"How about we save you some cake and champagne?" cried Mother Garcia as she'd headed into the rectory, arm in arm with Mother Killigan.

Luckily, the kids weren't bad. Now the Potato Heads were in play with the watercolor set. Jesus painted a great blue lake. Courtney created a cardboard diving board. Leif supervised the Mr. Potato Head family's subsequent bellyflops, jackknifes, and Olympic swan dives into the paper lake.

They allowed Gabe enough peace and quiet to concentrate on emails from his Berkeley poetry-translation expert, who'd already vetted the poems through the Department of Slavic Literature. The expert green-lighted the Bosnian collection for *Planet Quarterly*, so all Gabe had to do was decide which poems to highlight in the print edition and which to post on the website as a teaser for next issue. He reread the first stanza of one of his favorites, dated as the poet's last effort:

OUR KIND OF PLACE

Since we are all Serbs—
since only Serbs survived—
this must be our kind of place.
In our makeshift markets
idle avarice dangles,
staring back from the eyes
of butchered hogs. In blood
puddles of once-tidy villages,
we face a gaunt Narcissus
"feeble from self-adoration,"
I tell my husband, who frowns.

Gabe stopped in mid-poem. Yeah. He might even borrow that phrase, *a gaunt Narcissus*. It could give a name to the whole poem cycle.

"How's it going in here, Gabe?" Sophie, now his assistant, was asking from the doorway. She laughed. "Your office looks like the world's smallest kindergarten today."

"Someday," Leif announced, "I'm going to the big school."

"Me, too," Jesus chimed in. "Soon as we finish Miracles."

"Imagine being so little," Gabe said, "that first graders seem like cool studs."

"Cool studs!" Courtney cried.

"This threesome is only for today, you understand. And when Mary Anne finishes her course I'm back to childless bliss every Tuesday and Thursday."

"Oh right, Gabe," Sophie said. "You actually love this. You'd arrange for Leif to stay with you always."

"Can I, Gabe?" Leif asked, dancing one of the Potato children on top of Courtney's head.

"Anyway, the other mommy wants you to call. Jamie. It's not urgent, she says, but she left her work number." Sophie passed Gabe the number, which led to the news that changed all arrangements.

❖

Though it was a Wednesday, Gabe stood at the doors of Miracles KinderCare, Jamie squeezing his hand. They stared at the entry intently, as if truly expecting a miracle, a last-minute commuted sentence from the archdiocese.

Down the avenue, security guards fended off news vans from local news affiliates, Fox, NBC, CBS, and ABC. A colleague at Jamie's alternative weekly had alerted her to the school's discovery of Leif's two-mommy parenthood as well as their quick decision to expel him, but word soon got out to the wider media. The guards made an effective cordon, and the reporters kept their distance from the school doors.

All the usual parents gathered at the doors, like any other workday, but without their chummy, laughing tales of kids' exploits. It remained quiet, whispery, just as the well-dressed and well-coiffed spokeswoman of Our Lady of Miracles Schools had implored: "Let's get through this with a minimum of fuss, people. Anything, anything we might say for good or ill is going to be grist for the media circus."

"Isn't that a mixed metaphor, Jamie?" Gabe muttered, leaning closer. "It pulverizes circuses into flour mills."

"Shut up, Gabe, please? I just want to pick up Leif and get out of here." She unsqueezed his hand and hugged his waist, stretching up to kiss his cheek. "And thanks again for coming with me."

Mary Anne had already missed enough work since she started the theology class, so flexible old Gabe was the go-to guy again, the semi-father-figure on hand to retrieve the little boy. Leif had been expelled from daycare because "of what was going on at home," according to Channel 9's teaser. After an emergency meeting with archdiocese officials, the school authorities had determined that "homosexual couples living together as a couple are in disaccord with Catholic teaching," and that all parents were expected to follow the church's beliefs. Church authorities had agreed to let the boy finish out the school day, collect his toys and drawings, and say goodbye to his teachers and friends. He would exit the school, as would every child, with a minimum of fuss and no contact whatsoever with the gristy media.

Finally there was action at the entry. A trio of teachers held back glass doors for five or six tykes who came flying out, careening on wings from some pageant rehearsal. Ushered by a very young, sad-eyed teacher, Courtney and Jesus showed up amid the giggling, swirling, sudden crowd of kids. Stopping at Jamie and Gabe's feet, the two stood bewildered-looking under matching caps that had leopard spots and cat ears. Each reached for a big person's hand.

The teacher held a paper bag crammed full of picture books and toys. Leif, without any costume flourishes, appeared beside Jesus with a bag full of drawings and art supplies. The kids didn't seem to understand what was happening. They didn't say goodbye. They didn't cry.

Jamie took the bag from the teacher and held it high to hide her face. Gabe scooped up Leif, paper bag and all, and called out goodbyes to Courtney and Jesus.

❖

GabeR@planetquarterly.edu
Thursday, October 2 11:48 AM
To: Archbishop DePaul
Subject: Thank You for Your Letter

Forgive me, Archbishop DePaul. It has been more than a week since my last correspondence.

Thanks for your kind words about our journal, Planet Quarterly. *I wish it really had the "prestigious" stature you imply, but we do gain in stature when a prestigious citizen reads us. Thanks, too, for setting me straight on your concern for those endangered in the Bosnian war. There is nothing like charity to heal another nasty war in another insignificant polity. Not to mention succor.*

I have studied your commentaries in the Gazette. *Church doctrine, literally and strictly enforced, surely has no greater champion than Archbishop Leroy Francis DePaul. Over and over, you urge Catholics to choose obedience to church rules, and indeed, complete surrender to archdiocesan authority. An authority more awesome than the mere temptations of human sympathy.*

I also read with interest today's Archbishop's Column, *supporting the expulsion of Leif O'Malley-Anderson from Our Lady of Miracles KinderCare. Your full-bore, spirited defense of our ancient, powerful global institution is nothing less than breathtaking. I never realized this boy and his mothers were such a menace to Catholicism. Faith, as you say, must be "unflinchingly taught and unstintingly practiced by all Miracles parents."*

Though I had concerns about your expulsion of this tiny menace, my heart blinded my unflinching Catholic judgment. Now I realize Christ's teachings on social justice and compassion must be unstintingly ignored.

LFDePaul+@CatholicGazette.org
Thursday, October 2 1:02 PM
To: Gabriel Rafferty
Subject: Re: Thank You for Your Letter

Dear Mr. Rafferty,

I have received your email. Mr. Rafferty, I must ask, are you truly involved in the life of your Catholic community?

Jesus did not give sermons about "social justice." He spoke of God's love and human relationships. We answer His call to serve our neighbor.

Yours in Christ,
LFDePaul+

PS. Can you tell me how you came to know the name of the child involved in the events at Our Lady of Miracles daycare facilities? We have striven to keep his identity, and that of his guardians, from public scrutiny. Mr. Rafferty, judging by the somewhat condescending tone of your letter, I hope that you are not considering exposing these unfortunate souls.

❖

"I picked up the phone when I got home from class," Mary Anne was telling Gabe, "and there wasn't any voice on the other line. Just big, slushy sobs and heaving gulps. It was Jesus. Jesus Garcia."

"He misses Leif a lot, poor little guy," Jamie said. "We've got to arrange a play date soon."

"And Leif?" Gabe said, turning to check his closed door down the hall where Leif was already, Gabe prayed, fast asleep. The day after of the expulsion, he'd stopped by Mary Anne and Jamie's after work, walking in the warm autumn evening to their house farther down South High. "How's he adjusting?"

"He's pretty resilient," Mary Anne said. "He's so sweet natured, I don't think he's capable of imagining what they really did."

"Which was just raw bigotry," Gabe said. "Against a tiny child!"

"Don't start," Mary Anne said, "not tonight. Please?"

"So, we lied. I'm not a Catholic, so it's not a sin," Jamie said, glancing at Mary Anne with a wary smile. "We told Leif we found a better preschool with better hours to match his mommies' schedules."

"Eventually, we're going to have to tell him some version of the truth." Mary Anne looked into her wine goblet, as if it were some helpful, sin-free serum. "Or this will come back to bite us, big time."

When her phone rang, Jamie listened intently. "Courtney, sweetie? Is that you?" She held the hand set close, so Gabe could hear the sobbing, and the hard, caught breathing when the little girl tried to respond. Now Jamie was crying, too, so Gabe took the phone himself and tried to coax Courtney to steady herself. "Leif's sleeping now, honey, okay?" he implored, joining the little family's tendency to tell soothing white lies. "It's all going to be just fine."

❖

GabeR@planetquarterly.edu
Friday, October 3 10:13 AM
To: Archbishop DePaul
Subject: Forgive Me

Forgive me, Archbishop DePaul, for I didn't realize it was I who was endangering the "unfortunate couple." They happen to be friends of mine. I would never dream of exposing them, of course, only supporting them through the crisis and pain caused by the archdiocese's haste to expel their boy from Miracles KinderCare.

And of course, you're right. I am a bad Catholic and a wrong guy in general. I thought the church was a cradle, a solace, and a refuge where we heed "His call to serve our neighbor."

Instead, you've helped me learn that it's a closed and unforgiving club. With a catch that's ingenious: the church forbids holy matrimony for loving couples, and then punishes their child because they're not joined in holy matrimony.

Some neighbors are more equal than others, then, in His judgment?

❖

LFDePaul+@CatholicGazette.org
Friday, October 3 2:19 PM
To: Gabriel Rafferty
Subject: Re: Forgive Me

Mr. Rafferty, do you close your eyes and your ears to central truths about the Church? You must, for how else can you express such patronizing anger?

Do you believe in the church's obligation and your obligation as a Catholic to protect those who cannot protect themselves? Or do you embrace the "modern" view that couples involved in a sexual relationship outside of marriage will not taint the integrity of the entire school community? This threatens the sanctified position of marriage and the family, which bless our futures through the production of new life.

The female couple agreed to abide by the church's rulings on these matters when they enrolled the child. When their violation of the agreement was uncovered, the school had no choice but to act to protect the other children and families from such deceit.

I implore you not to use your position at Planet Quarterly to amplify this painful circumstance, or to advocate for your friends. We continue to review your magazine with alarm. When does such a wide-cast, unbridled, secular perspective descend into degeneracy? There may be consequences you are unprepared for.

❖

MAOMalley@hotmail.com
Friday, Oct. 3 8:37 PM
To: GabeR@planetquarterly.edu
Subject: Re: FW: Re: Forgive Me

Oh, Christ, Gabe, did you really say that? The Church is a "cradle," all right. A cradle that once sheltered a fledgling faith, a beleaguered band of martyrs and holy fools. But now it's just a hostile ward of old men, striking out from intensive care. It's not worth your beautiful anguish. I love your cri de coeur on our behalf, sweet Gabriel, but it's futile.

Amazing about DePaul's hostility, even threats, at the end. These are the last gasp of a power that has lost the consent of its constituents.

I do admire you for hanging in there. Especially given your status as a long-collapsed Catholic. You obviously hit DePaul where it hurt, or he would have never engaged you in the first place. (Imagine the crackpots he hears from, daily!) I love you for caring so much, baby. But be careful.

Mary Anne

"Should we call the police, then?" his assistant Sophie was asking. "At least, the campus police?"

"Maybe, sure," Gabe said, standing over his ransacked desk. The top poem, "Our Kind of Place," was torn and cast to the floor. He bent to retrieve it, smoothing the page and thinking of its improbable journey to placid Denver from cleansed, agonized Banja Luka. Over untold time zones, every syllable hard-fought, hard-won by both poet and translator, now ripped and tossed to the floor. "Let me think about it. I've got to consider whom we've offended lately."

Sophie laughed. "No end of rejected freelancers and poets. Plus, Chevron for our Ecuador exposé. The entire Chinese Communist Party for our piece on that dissident filmmaker. I could go on."

"Don't. You're scaring me. I still can't believe anyone ever reads us. I never envisioned this inky old office as a target for secret agents."

"So I'm supposed to tell you, Mr. Literary Magazine World Magus," she said, withdrawing from Gabe's office, "what the pen is mightier than?"

The interlopers had rifled through Sophie's accounts payable ledger and her business checkbook. God knows what they studied on her—or his—computer files. The recycle bin was overturned, revealing a sushi takeaway menu, an empty ibuprofen bottle, and extra copies of a rejected poem cycle about Romanian orphans. Why the intruders' too-crude shuffling and blunder? Was he supposed to be intimidated?

He was. What if they tried this stunt in his apartment? Photos of long-lost, sometimes long-dead boyfriends, love notes, saved erotic emails, bad poems, mix tapes, forgotten stashes of pot. In long unvisited corners of the extra closet, tossed and lost condoms loaded with old-century DNA, bottles of lube and dried-up poppers. Certain old phone numbers, some still current, bewildered guys being grilled about a certain long-lost one night stand. Squinty blue eyes and brown, wavy hair. Back in the day? Kind of a prick? Think.

He imagined a crew of undercover monks dispatched from the archdiocese to expose all his sins. Exalting in every piece of evidence that proved Gabriel Rafferty had given in to every temptation of the flesh, over and over. And over. A collapsed Catholic as far from God as he remained from holy matrimony.

"*Sophie!* Can you hear me? Hey, don't call the campus cops, after all. Nothing's been taken, looks like. I'm just going to clean up this mess."

❖

GabeR@planetquarterly.edu
Monday, October 6 9:32 AM
To: Archbishop DePaul
Subject: Thanks Again

Dear Archbishop DePaul,

Thanks again for your efforts to enlighten me. It's a miracle that you still have any faith in my powers of comprehension. It is as if my mind resembles my desk, messy and, especially this morning, completely trashed.

I've tried to open my brain and heart to the Church's rulings on the holiness of Holy Matrimony. I do understand that the sacrament is designed for procreation of new little Catholics. I understand that homosexual couples cannot fulfill this production without fertilization from an opposite-sex donor.

What I can't understand, then, is why the church blesses with holy matrimony male-female couples who don't or can't procreate out of free choice, for medical reasons, or advanced age. And why is the church, so slow to expel sex-predator priests, so quick to expel one female couple's little boy? Just asking.

Sincerely,
Gabriel Rafferty

❖

LFDePaul+@CatholicGazette.org
Monday, October 6 11:47 AM
To: Gabriel Rafferty
Subject: Re: Thanks Again

Dear Mr. Rafferty,

I wish you would turn your attention to the full gospel and the complete teachings of the Church. I trust you are beginning to perceive what true power resides in our faith. The holy offices of our doctrine reach far into the most private and ordinary lives of the laity.

When I next I hear from you, Mr. Rafferty, I hope you can tell me your real relationship with the Church. I hope you know that everything you treasure, the Church treasures. But of the things you neglect, the worst is rejecting the heart and mind of Christ.

I promise prayers.

Sincerely yours in Christ,
LFDePaul+

❖

The afternoon was alive with earthly treasures. Ash trees shimmered their first autumn-purple tints. The locusts were already golden. Students sunbathed on plush green hillocks, pairs studying thick texts or just texting.

Before his next meeting with Jake, Gabe had lunch outside to enjoy the sunshine. Balancing Lebanese takeout and copies of the poems, he sat on a concrete curb beside the university's oldest structure, a redstone chapel from the 1880s. It anchored a series of modern reflecting pools, water cascading from one to the next down a gentle slope. The final pool trenched around the chapel, which appeared to be weightless, floating on a skin of reflective water.

Above the chapel, fresh mountain snow powdered Mount Evans. Smooth summits undulated like arches on a crown. Munching a falafel pita, Gabe burst with uncontainable adoration. He wanted to tell somebody, *I am so grateful for my life. I am so grateful for chickpeas, peppers, cucumber, wheat, and lo-cal ranch yogurt dressing.*

The unsaid phrase felt like a godless prayer. The chapel reminded passersby that the university was founded first as a seminary, once tethered to Methodist enthusiasm and idealism. The tether had severed long ago, though the theology school did its best to keep the faith, hunkered on the edge of the sprawling, secular campus now renowned for its schools of business, law, and cable television technology.

Like the university, Gabe had lost his faith at the end of childhood. Religious devotion was no more within his memory's grasp than a forgotten cradle would have fit one of these six-foot, bare-chested sophomores on the quad suffering Dostoyevsky or Adam Smith or html code. When anxious, though, Gabe missed the lost warmth of that cradle, the blanket comfort of Catholic certainties, the perfect Q and A of its closed system catechism.

At times, he longed for the faith's invisible world of immortality and benevolent possibility, the intimation of something more than chemicals and optical illusions in this deep blue Colorado sky. The promise that the Earth was more than mere rock and water, that little stone chapels really floated on water and Jesus had walked on the Sea of Galilee. The Bosnian poet wrestled with that longing in one of Jake's translations:

I glean what the Holy Ones mean
when they refer to reflected water,
how its tempting glimmer is illusion,

liquefying mirror of solid life on shore,
while everything solid ever transforms
like a leaf upchurned then submerged,
vein by vein, demolished. Yet water
seems to shimmer, a promise
stretched, transparent, a sheen,
not of what's reflected,
but of what's unseen.

It could be humiliating, being a mere human. Our eyes could not really verify which redstone brick was real, the cornerstone upright in our sights or the mirrored one beneath it, pooled, perfect in every captive notch and shadow.

"Not a bad life, Gabe!" Jake yelled, approaching from the direction of *Planet Quarterly*'s office. "I wouldn't mind brown-bagging it, myself, here in heaven."

"Am I late, Jake?" Gabe swiped his lips with a napkin. "Sorry."

"No worries. I'm early. Sophie told me this is where you usually have lunch." He sat down beside Gabe on the high concrete curb. "I wanted to get here before our meeting to ask Sophie something, I hope you don't mind. Basically, I wanted to know if you were…available."

"I am, Jake. Anytime you want to contact me. That's what I'm here for. Poetry in translation is practically our lifeblood. Well, next to investigative nonfiction that pisses everyone off."

"I meant personally. Sophie said you weren't dating anyone. She joked about you becoming a dried-up old spinster." Jake laughed nervously, charming in such a big bruiser. "I guess I'm asking if you'd like to go out for coffee sometime. Just get to know each other better."

Gabe inhaled his shock. He'd read Sergeant Kovac so wrong despite those queerish tendencies—his earnest, heartfelt translation, his appreciation of good poetry. Gabe's gaydar must have gone completely whack. Along with Jet Skis, Broncos worship, and Shotgun Willie's strippers, he'd imagined solely on the basis of his paternal ease with Leif that Jake must be also be married with the requisite 2.5 children. At last, he exhaled. "I'd love to."

"Good! Now, I'm dying to find out what Berkeley thought."

"Let's go over it right here. No need to abandon heaven."

Gabe wadded up his brown bag and splayed the poems across his lap. He told Jake the good news. There were hardly any questions about his translations, just scholarly quibbles. Gabe went over the "approved" final stanzas of "Our Kind of Place" with Jake:

Away from international eyes
we plow memory into furrows
still gutted with unidentified
organs—livers, maybe hearts.
The world's maw seems hungry to chew
the worst, those orthodox video bites:
    yes, watch as our boys opened fire
on first graders then gang-raped
    their mothers and buried their fathers alive
in trenched fields they claim we stole
from honest farmers.

Not even Serbia extends a hand
to us, as if we were her just-paroled
country cousin. World, you want irony?
Our towns endure the dumb, mud invasion
of our own country cousins—refugees—
clodhoppers who piss in dry fountains.

Since this sector was forged in our name
despite our defeat, only Serbs survived,
only Serbs remain, and Serb is all we are.

Our currency? Stolen cigarettes.
Our soldiers? Zit-faced executioners.
Our leader? A poet turned extortionist
who proclaims from his bulletproof car,
"we're completely cleansed at last."

Jake liked naming the cycle "A Gaunt Narcissus" but also suggested "Cleansed at Last." He sighed, leaning back, glancing at the students studying in the sun. "I could really love this life. Maybe I should look into getting my master's." Jake smiled at the sky. "What could be better than this?"

"Nothing," Gabe said. "Nothing." He stared at the chapel and considered how the men who laid that cornerstone matched their faith in God with a matchless faith in men and women whose sheer will raised this university, this metropolis out of the high prairie. "So, tell me, Jake. What on earth happened to your poet? Why'd she give you that packet? Where is she now?"

"Six years after the war officially ended, there were riots in Banja Luka, not that long ago. The few remaining Muslims had tried to rededicate their main mosque, savaged during the ethnic cleansing. The poet, as the deputy administrator's wife, lent her support to the project. But extremist thugs couldn't tolerate it and went on a rampage. 'We gave our blood to cleanse Banja Luka of these vermin!'

"The riot devastated her. I think she thought intolerance was all behind them now that the war was really over. That a new, unified, fledgling country could somehow steady on its haunches and rise to its feet. But the separatist thugs kicked it in the ass and bludgeoned it all over again. Only a week after the rampage at the mosque, she came to me with the poems." His face grim, Jake stared ahead, as if reluctant to say more. "Right after the poet met with me, she drove to that forest preserve, straight to the Pools of Heaven. She hiked down to the bank of a quiet reflecting pond, pulled her husband's pistol out of her backpack, and shot her brains out."

"I went to Mass with my mommies." Leif pointed out the little plastic window to the main chapel of Our Lady of Miracles. "I can still go into that church, Gabe."

"Of course you can, buddy. You're the main guy. The prince of the church."

"I am, huh!" Leif pronounced it with open wonder. He smiled down from the top of the slide. "I am!"

The moms were checking out new preschool options, so Gabe had taken Leif to the public park playground next to the church—not Gabe's first choice, but Leif insisted. He was in love with this slide.

It had a little plastic house perched on top that he loved even more than sliding down. Now, with no other kids waiting on the ladder, Leif claimed the house, tramping around as he poked his head out of each of its three windows.

Inspired by the sight of the steeple, Leif started up a solitary fantasy. He was some kind of high church holiness, maybe even the pope himself. From his perch, he hurried to each window to signal the sign of the cross with the side of his hand, Vatican-balcony style.

A mother on the bench across the way caught Leif's signal and returned the favor, blowing him a kiss. "Thanks, little priest!" she called. "I can use all the blessings I can get." To Gabe she said, "You've got such a cute little boy!"

Gabe smiled and kicked up the swing he sat in, calling, "Thanks!"

Leif quickly tired of his papal mumbo jumbo and slid down to join Gabe on the swings. He shoved off, kicking air, trying to match Gabe's sway. "So, am I your boy, Gabe?"

"Sure. You're a child of the universe, man."

"Will you become my daddy, someday?"

"Well, I'll be around. Okay?" He used his feet to brake his swing. "I want to watch you try to get as tall as me."

"I will!"

"Fat chance. You just try. I will always be the tallest. I am the god of tallness."

"I am the god of tallness!"

"That's pretty funny, coming from a dude on a swing whose legs can't even reach the ground."

"You just wait."

"I will, Leif. I will."

The bell rang in the church schoolyard next door, just behind the chain-link fence boundary with the playground. Gabe glanced at his watch. Christ. He'd forgotten to mind the time. Quick, he tried to distract Leif with a swinging contest. "You can't swing anywhere near as high as me."

"Well, give me a push!"

It was too late. Courtney and Jesus were already squealing at the link fence, crying out Leif's name in a happy chant. "Come and play with us!"

Leif hustled to the fence, legs sprinting in a roadrunner blur. Gabe hurried after, but the boy was already clinging to the fence, entangling his fingers with his friends' as all three whooped.

"Can I go in?" Leif asked. "Gabe, can I play with 'em?"

Gabe offered a tight, fake smile to Courtney and Jesus, then picked up Leif just as one of the teachers, the sad-eyed girl, approached with an alarmed arch in her brow. "We've got to go now, kids," Gabe explained. "His mommies are waiting for us."

Gabe couldn't watch as the sad-eyed teacher implored Courtney and Jesus to come away. Whether they stamped their feet or their eyes misted over, he didn't want to see. But Leif watched, looking backward, pressed against Gabe's shoulder, watched and watched as Courtney and Jesus were forced away from the fence. For the first time, Leif started bawling. He howled, a vast explosion of gasping tears.

"It happens, doesn't it?" the woman on the bench said, tsk-tsking in sympathy. "They just go off like somebody's taking aim at them."

Gabe nodded, jostling past while Leif cried and cried, his legs dangling. Gabe didn't look back, aiming straight down the avenue toward his office as fast as his god-of-tallness legs could stretch. But he imagined the scene he couldn't watch.

The kids of Miracles KinderCare would gather in the schoolyard for the afternoon games, forming a giggling cordon that would open wide to accept Courtney and Jesus. All the kids came from good Catholic homes, sin-free zones headed by a man and managed by a woman. Now all could enjoy their wholesome Catholic pre-school free of outside threats.

The school was purged of Leif and his kind. It was cleansed at last.

Chapter Thirteen

Au Bon Pain

It was one of those Google searches that begins with "noxious weeds" and ends in long-lost love.

Yeah, that one, the first on Gabe's flaky foray into carnal knowledge. In May, editing an article in his *Planet Quarterly* office, Gabe meant to verify a writer's casual reference to a noxious weed, the wrong-sounding "many-toed flax," when Google plunged him into a nearby universe.

Did you mean: marshy toadflax?

Screen after screen seeped into vast deltas devoted to marshy toadflax. In tight, single-spaced teasers pasted from websites, the search results index kept repeating one name, genetics expert Dr. Adam Schneider. So Gabe googled him and found his article in *Genetic Science Journal*, "Marshy Toadflax: Toxic Weed or Genetic Marvel?" was itself a renowned research marvel.

Adam's specialization in a poisonous marsh weed had led to a long career at Nebraska State University. He'd become so famous for studying this natural alternative to pesticides that websites linked to articles like "Nobel Buzz around Schneider: Marshy Toadflax to Bloom in Stockholm?" and "Youngest Ever Nobel Winner?"

Gabe burned away most of the time he'd meant to devote to fact-checking the article, lost in web links about Adam Schneider's illustrious career and present-day glory at NSU. He ended up at Adam's webpage. Cheery photos of graduate research teams posing on Greek-columned stairways or peering into microscopes featured a tall, short-haired, professorial man in the background, looking a little blurry and camera shy. Gabe could not really recall details of Adam's face from their time together as graduate students, and these pictures didn't help. Web photos from news stories lacked enough pixels, forming only a fuzzy blot in glasses and lab coat.

When he tried to remember Adam's appearance, Gabe dreamed back to his long, unruly brown hair, still damp after a shower. Freckles on smooth shoulders. Downy, sun-bleached hairs on tanned forearms. The gravelly voice that sometimes croaked, an authoritative but froggy bass. He could easily visualize how tightly Adam's Wrangler jeans hugged his butt and recall their first kiss, lusty, shameless, their lips stuck through last call on a bar's crowded dance floor. His fingers could even now retrace the raised letters—backwards, MADA—on Adam's cowboy belt as Gabe seized it, the pounding music suddenly silenced, lights up. Closing time.

But Adam's face? At first, it had seemed nondescript. Then, after he had fallen in love, Gabe realized it was breathtaking—sly smile, strong jaw, pale blue eyes. Their affair had been so intense, yet so brief and sequestered, less than a semester. Saturday nights at Gabe's first apartment in Denver alternated with weekends an hour north, in Fort Collins, where Adam had his "hovel," a converted garage behind his grandparents' house near the Colorado State campus.

Apart from briefly meeting a few of Adam's gay buddies, or once having dinner with his mentor, a cell biologist who was famously "unlocking the secret of immortality," Adam and Gabe kept only each other's company, often in bed, and no photos ever recorded those private moments. So, while Gabe had five pix of a Summit County bartender he dated for one ski weekend and several shots of a glacier hike with a law student he never saw again, he didn't have a single picture of the first love of his life.

Gabe copied the email address from an NSU website, then opened his inbox, distracted by a new message from the author whose new article he'd been editing:

> *Gabe—I have to thank you again. Got the advance from my publisher for the book, so I'm gonna take you out to lunch and on the spot, write you a check to pay you back in full.*
> *—Kyle*

After excerpts appeared in *Planet Quarterly* and *Harpers*, a major New York publisher bought Kyle Montoya's lyrical, haunted study of a Malaysian coral reef's life and death. Gabe thought Kyle's current article on the social and natural wastelands of northern Alberta sand-oil extraction pits was his best work so far, no matter its wobbly references to many-toed flax. He felt Kyle Montoya might join the company of poetic science writers like Lewis Thomas and Loren Eiseley, and maybe even bring reflected glory to the Denver quarterly of international literature that launched him.

Opening a New Message box, Gabe felt a pang of envy. Adam's early success had led to real acclaim in early midlife. And Kyle, not yet thirty, had won a lavish book contract. Gabe saw himself in contrast, sunken in a coral reef, a nobody choking on oxygen-deprived, murky water. He soon came up for air, though, and dared to compose an email to the great man in Nebraska.

A week later, just arriving at his *Planet Quarterly* office, Gabe faced his computer's big smeary eye with contempt. He hadn't received a response from Adam Schneider and began to imagine that his simple email—brief, totally disingenuous, hi, happened to find ya online by accident, do you even remember me?—had been buried amid torrents of Adam's email from toadflax fanboys, urgent requests, needling objections from competing research teams, press inquiries about upcoming prizes. Either that, or Adam the renowned geneticist didn't remember their affair among scores of others and decided to ignore the faintly embarrassing inquiry from a forgotten nobody in Denver.

But no. Finally, there it was:

Hi Gabe!

Good to hear from you after all these years. I have wonderful memories about meeting you at—what was that the name of that joint with the dance floor?—staring wolfishly at you, finally dancing, then going to your apartment. As I recall, we were up most of the night "talking and not talking" as

Joni Mitchell once put it. I also remember your visits to Fort Collins and going up the canyon.

The truth is, it killed me to have to say goodbye. I've also wondered what happened to you. Now I know! Editor of the Planet Quarterly, *which is becoming such a big deal (so my literary niece tells me).*

Sorry I took a while to get back to you. I was in DC, testifying at the National Science Foundation on boring policy matters. It's nice to be back in Nebraska. My folks are still in Fort Collins, so I pass through Denver on family visits.

Write again when you get a chance. I'm glad we reconnected. Take care—

Adam

P.S. I've got to say, Gabe, you were hot, hot, hot!

The truth is, it killed me to have to say goodbye. This astonished Gabe even more than the PS's claim of triple hotness. This from the guy who kissed him off with such anvil-dropping finality?

How weird, too, that the illustrious professor wrote in such a nice ta-hear-from-ya, nice ta-be-back-in-Nebraska chattiness. And even though he sometimes used it himself, and no matter how flattering it might be, that *hot* irritated him. At what point, exactly, had people stopped being cool and started being hot?

Anyway, as Gabe understood it, his own sexual clumsiness with Adam had obliterated all claims of hotness. So he decided to wait until the end of the workday to respond, playing it cool on the keyboard:

Adam,

I'm glad you wrote back. I have the same vague memories of our times together. Anyway, it may sound strange to congratulate you after all these years, but to me you were frozen in time as a student research assistant, and I'm so impressed with what you've made of your career, and what you've contributed intellectually and institutionally to science and science education.

Gabe paused before he hit Send. He disliked and distrusted his own stilted tone. It might sound smarmy or even sarcastic to someone who was so accustomed to praise and acclaim.

Worse, it left so much unsaid. All these years later, almost a decade deep into a new century, a new millennium, a geologic epoch, he was still stuck here, living and working on South High, pretending he barely recalled one of the most overwhelming loves he'd ever felt.

It was the same warm, May kind of day in the same place where he and Adam had made love above that boggy spot under the intense blue sky. Who knows how many many-toed flax or marshy toadflax they'd crushed under their eager young bodies? Gabe asked Jake Kovac to check out the scene of the crime with him, saying it was "a personal historical site." Jake had never explored that open space on former ranchland, so they took a Sunday joy ride to Poudre Canyon. On the hike along the side stream, Gabe told him the story of his first relationship. "So, why do you think he ended it so abruptly? Did I suddenly lose my triple hotness?"

"I wouldn't say triple," Jake said, laughing. "But you were a lot younger then."

"I realize I'm old and horrible now, but truth is, I wasn't so hot back then either, just a skinny overgrown kid scared to death of getting screwed. I thought I got the hang of it, considering the endless poundings I endured, but I must've been a drag for Adam."

"I'll bet it didn't have that much to do with sex. It could be that Adam was scared of feeling too much, feeling at a depth he wasn't ready for at that age."

Jake's speculation bounced against Gabe's own long-held speculation about his own sexual ineptitude and Adam's having found someone more attractive. It was too hard to absorb the perverse idea that he felt too much instead of too little, so Gabe fell silent as the trail followed the stream around a rocky escarpment. Around the bend, though, he gasped at the altered landscape.

The boggy flat below the old ranch dam and the higher glade where he and Adam had made love in that meadow had been stripped, scraped back to ochre sand, raw earth, and upended roots. The plank walkway over the bog was scattered over a deep gash of dried mud and tumbled rocks. “It’s unrecognizable! Jake, I swear, this was a beautiful little glade back then, an oasis in all this scrubland.”

Farther on, they could see what had happened. The spring runoff from the winter’s heavy snowfall must have burst the old earthen dam, cutting deep, muddy grooves in the stream bed, straightening its meandering course, flattening its gentle riffles, and tearing out its fringe of riparian life. “That glade’s a gulch! Man, I should have never dragged you up here.” The trail kept winding along the edge of the escarpment, unbothered by the ugly upheaval below. “Now I really do feel old and horrible. Talk about living long enough to witness epochs of geologic time.”

They stopped to survey the damage. “If you’re that decrepit at thirty-three, what does that make me, at almost forty?”

“I will always be seven years younger than you, Jake, but you will always be more hunky and handsome.”

Jake put his arm on Gabe’s shoulder and pulled him close. He indicated the wide, rough gap where the wall of rowdy runoff must have coursed through the dam. “Maybe nature’s trying to tell you something about your ongoing communication with Adam. There’s a poem in here, somewhere, Gabe, or maybe just a warning. Old dams breaking. Pent-up reservoirs obliterated.”

“Gorgeous meadows gored into oblivion, gorged-out willows and evergreens. Maybe this cheesy poem even has a moral. Stop writing to Adam.”

Pulling him even closer, Jake planted a kiss on Gabe’s cheek. “I’ve got to admit, I’m a little jealous.” He tried to frown, but broke into a smile. “Who knows where this is going, e-flirting with your first love?”

“I think we see it, splayed out before us. An unnatural disaster.” Gabe checked out the trail behind and ahead for any approaching hikers, but it remained all theirs. He pressed against Jake’s slightly higher height, pressing his lips to his, moving in to wrangle his tongue with his. He loved the way Jake pressed back, his solid body hard against him, a body that after six months of exploring, Gabe found ever new, ever compelling. "I don't think you have anything to worry about."

❖

Gabe,

I've been reading the last Planet Quarterly *to shreds. It's amazing. I liked the recovered Neruda poems. Along with the whacked Estonian "folk tale." Who knew the wolf was the good guy, and granny a Russian oil oligarch? But the piece on the industrial ruination of that valley in Indonesia, wow. (I think my family has stock in that company, yikes.) My niece says there's a meditation on nature, science & environment like this in every issue.*

You have a lot to be proud of, Gabe. You didn't study Comparative Literature for nothing!

Speaking of my niece, she's graduating from Colorado State, and we're having a big family party. I'll be flying in from another conference in DC. So it looks like I'll be passing through Denver soon.

Let's have lunch together—I'll plan a couple hours between my arrival at Denver airport and my sister picking me up. There's that café in the main terminal, up on the mezzanine, Au Bon Pain.

May was busy out the open window of Gabe's office, too many manic birds swirling in too many budding branches. Their birdsong wasn't really musical, just a maddening wall of random crackle. Why was this older Adam so chatty and considerate? The global genius must have found free time, while awaiting that call from Stockholm, to humor the obscure editor.

All that vintage Midwestern niceness irked Gabe. Why did Adam keep writing these newsy missives? Now he'd planned a Denver rendezvous. What did he really want? Was the great man so petty as to stoop to some humiliating photo op, some shutterbug in his entourage capturing the reunion, with a caption for the biology department newsletter: "Dr. Schneider—Never Too Busy to Lunch with a Common Peasant!"

Gabe scrolled back through the thread of emails. There it was: *The truth is, it killed me to have to say goodbye.*

It did, huh, you fucking son of a bitch? As Gabe firmed up their meeting plans at the airport, he planned to conceal any sense of how devastating Adam's rejection had been. No matter how illustrious, the professor was not his confessor, and the first love of his life didn't need to know how deep his dismissal had made him descend into all those reckless hookups. Or more precisely, that whole summer of sluthood.

After his long, strange breakup with Marty, Gabe had endured that protracted single spell punctuated by sporadic, less-than-compelling dates. Through his whole chapter as flying Dutchman lackey for SecureTek, Gabe was the officemate who had no photographs in his cubicle or office. One workplace Secret Santa jokester had given him a cheap frame with a Discount Photo generic family smiling inanely. "Put this on your desk and presto, you're not so pathetic." But even after years in supposed recovery from the loss, he wished Secret Santa had also brought a photo of Adam Schneider or Marty Montgomery to fill that discount frame.

Greeting Mary Anne and Jamie on his final day at Edna Victoria, seeing them in their scruffy gardening shorts and dirt-smeared, holey shirts, Gabe flashed back to the days with Candy and Ben slumming around the apartment in hardly more than underwear, and Friday evenings playing poker and sampling whiskey with Mary Anne and Jamie, who loved to live in cut-off jeans and T shirts on weekend nights. But for years now, he'd mostly seen them coming or going from work in their office finery, all dolled up as they dropped off or picked up Leif. They'd all grown up, or at least become older, while this apartment overlooking South High Street had remained his steadfast home in its long transformation from a student flop to semi-respectable domicile.

Mary Anne looked around at the boxed-up yet barely contained chaos of the place. "It's kind of sad, isn't it? I still have so much nostalgia for Edna Victoria and all the times we had here. I can't imagine what it's like for you, Gabe. You've probably lived here longer than any other human being in history. Hardly anybody else between these walls who started out as a student stayed to become a completely full-fledged adult."

"Am I? Thanks."

"And now, you're embarking on the next phase of your life. Live-in co-parent!"

"Am I? Thanks. And I'll be contributing my rent to your mortgage, not Stone Corner Properties," he said of the massive corporate property system that had taken over Edna Victoria. "I'm gonna miss her, though."

Jamie, who'd been chasing Leif, who'd been searching for his toy box in Gabe's office, now re-emerged to join Gabe and Mary Anne in the living room, Leif caught in her hand. "I think your toys are boxed away, kid."

"I want my GI Joe," Leif declared, not whining, just stating an obvious fact.

"He's been kinda queer for GI Joe," Gabe muttered, "ever since he met Jake."

"Speaking of macho guys," Jamie said, "that's one of the things we're going to love, Gabe, how you'll be right there, in our household, mentoring Leif in the manly arts."

"Yeah, like poetry and flowers!" Gabe said. One of the deciding factors for the move was the wonderful position of his separate quarters, bounded on three sides by the garden, a marvel that Mary Anne and Jamie had cultivated for several seasons now, spreading out between an old maple and a mature honey locust, bursting now in late spring with iris, lilac, bridal veil, basket of gold, and just-planted radiant-verging-on-gaudy petunia beds.

Speaking of beds, he'd bought a new one to match the new bedroom, a king-sized, plush top extravagance that would occupy a corner formed by two huge plate glass windows that overlooked their pond, with its rock garden edges and cascades through piled-up mountain boulders. This fed his fantasies of waking next to Jake, naked on a warm summer mornings. It took little effort to envision Jake's gorgeous muscular butt half covered by his new king-sized sheets, but now was not the time to surrender to lustful imaginings. There were boxes and furniture to be loaded for the four-block journey down South High.

"But you really are outdoorsy for a big fairy," Jamie said, "forever hiking and skiing and mountain biking, all the things that Mary Anne and I are kinda lazy about. We want Leif to get out there and play. He needs your influence. I'd never admit it, but we actually want him to be like you."

"So you admit I turned out okay for a public school kid, right? Is Mary Anne going to be open to my idea of sending Leif to the neighborhood school next fall? It's a really good one."

"See?" Mary Anne asked Jamie, smiling. "This is how it's going to be, having him in our very household, co-parenting."

"I'm with Gabe! Your Catholic preschool didn't exactly work out, Mother Teresa."

"I'm open to thinking about it," Mary Anne said. "If I can overcome my apprehensions about our precious boy mingling with those public school ragamuffins."

"Like me!" Gabe said. "Me! You know, the one you want Leif to turn out like."

"I will," Leif said, pausing his search for the toy box, pointing to himself with pride, "Except I'm gonna be taller."

"So, what are you gonna be," Jamie asked, "a yeti?"

"Oh, here comes the real muscle," Mary Anne said, turning to the open doorway. "No offense, Gabe."

"None taken, I like his muscles, too." Gabe extended his hand to Jake, leaning in for a quick smooch.

Carrying down the desk was a breeze compared to struggling it up, eleven years ago. Jake carried the down slope side, studying the glossy surface. "Your dad built this? He must have been an artist."

"Just a skillful carpenter," Gabe said, groaning forward down the stairs. "This was his best work."

"Naw," Jamie said, following with a box of kitchen stuff. "Gabe was."

Jake and Gabe got the desk into the van in painless harmony.

❖

No red carnation necessary at Au Bon Pain. I'll be in my usual off-duty drag, flannel shirt and jeans. Gabe, just don't expect me to look quite the way I did when I was twenty-seven, okay?

❖

Gabe kept expecting his own decrepitude to stare back at him in the morning mirror. Instead, for all his sins and godless evil, he still looked okay at thirty-three. To punctuate his okayness, he bought a new shirt. Form fitting, silky, black, it set off the blond strays in his thick brown hair. He didn't really know what he was trying to prove, and as he entered the airport he was aware of how ridiculous this vanity was—so déclassé, so faggoty.

Gabe was uncharacteristically early. He thought he'd hate being at the airport again, but it was strangely serene, late morning on a quiet Sunday. With no flight to catch, no clients waiting in some far time zone, his habitual air terminal tension vanished.

He could see the whole span of Au Bon Pain up on the mezzanine, almost empty except for a few older couples having that older-couple early lunch. He had no luggage or carry-on, obviously a fraud, an interloper, maybe a terrorist among the wholesome groupings of families journeying for graduations or weddings, the celebratory rituals of late spring. He relaxed in the airport's mood, hushed under the opaque light from the white fabric roof.

Up on the mezzanine, Gabe stopped in a restroom to check his hair and make sure his shirt was properly tucked to show off his waistline, then he headed toward the entry to Au Bon Pain. He saw a middle-aged, solitary man waiting there, looking avuncular, maybe, but not in a reassuring way.

Wait. Could it be him? Flannel shirt. Carry-on. Clean, crisp jeans. But little remnant whatsoever of the beautiful guy he'd fallen for. Somebody's nervous uncle, maybe.

"Wow. Gabe. You look just the same." Adam lowered his voice after the waiter seated them. "Hot, hot, hot!"

Again, that suspicious triple hotness. "And you, Adam, you—when did you get those ears? I don't remember those ears sticking out like that."

"I suppose my hair was longer then."

"It's cool. I like 'em." It was true. Gabe was a sucker for them, and had voted for Obama in the February primary partly on the basis of his sticking-out ears. He stared and stared without shame. Who the hell was this man? Who would want his face in a frame on anybody's desk? Prematurely wrinkled, his hair thinned out, wispy, not so much balding as a slow vanishing act. Where was that lush, sleepy tangle? The blue had drained out of his eyes. Adam was painfully thin, lacking muscle mass under the flannel's flopping folds. Behind rimless glasses, his face was drawn, hangdog. Truly, if they hadn't made arrangements in advance, Gabe wouldn't have noticed this geeky dude at all.

Gabe ordered a Bloody Mary, a double. Adam requested iced tea. They made chitchat about Adam's niece, the family doings of the weekend, and then he dropped the Big Question. "What do you remember, Gabe? About why we split up?"

Instinctively, Gabe thought of lying. *Split up? Whaddaya mean? I don't remember shit like that. Nothing touches me, man.* What was the big deal, beyond almost dying of abandonment, surviving only to disgrace himself in strangers' beds all across the city?

But some force tugged Gabe toward the truth, the capital T, true Truth. "You were five or six years older than I. You had gay friends, experiences, and I just felt so young and klutzy. I was inept, Adam," he stage-whispered, so the adjacent blue rinse and gray beard couple munching nearby would be spared a homo soap opera with their Early Bird Lunch Specials. "I was just plain bad in bed. What can I say? You got sick of my whining and sex drama and immaturity."

Adam laughed, his ragged, deep, bass howl the most convincing evidence that the stuck-out-ears, withered, flannel stranger across from him was really Adam Schneider. "I'm sorry," he said, squelching his laughter then matching Gabe's whispering tones. "Yes, you were inept. You were bad in bed, especially at first. But I loved that. It made me feel like the big man. Like I was the grand master and you were the novice." He leaned closer. "It was actually sexy, your squeamishness. I adored you, Gabe. I loved you so much, and I never stopped loving you. More than anybody. Ever."

He'd heard that line before on the patio in Butcher Creek, when Marty, crying into his phone, professed great love while he kissed off Gabe for good. He never wanted to hear it again, not least because it would inspire more impulsive, involuntary recollection that seesawed between being savagely pissed off and terminally confounded. Gabe stood up just as the waiter delivered the Bloody Mary and the iced tea. He grabbed the cocktail and didn't excuse himself.

He paced to the rail overlooking the mezzanine, his back to Adam, sipping as he watched travelers await security below. Gabe let the feelings roil. Flummoxed, angry, and mind fucked all at once. Adam's words blasted away The True History of His Heart, drafted over a decade, its chintzy binding exploded.

Under the airport's familiar white fabric roofline, with Au Bon Pain perched above the main concourse, Gabe felt he hovered in defiance of gravity, in motionless flight. He needed some silence. He needed to absorb those words. He watched the travelers come and go, join and separate, separate and join, families determined to freight themselves across the clouds to witness vows and honors.

In no hurry, he carried his drink back to the table. "Sorry. This is not so easy for me, Adam. Because I loved you, too. It's my crime, that I never told you that night on the capitol steps. But I did love you. I loved you like crazy."

"And that's why I wanted to meet you here. I know damn well why we split up. Why I split us up. I owe you a huge apology. I lied. I hurt you. I was terrified, and I took it out on you, left you in the lurch." Adam went on. "But I knew you would get over it, because you were sane and self-controlled. In your own way, very tough. Everything I wasn't. I never told you how tortured I was. My family put such stock in me, the oldest son, scion of the Schneider Empire. The whole time I fell for you, I was drinking like a freakin' trout. Didn't you notice, Gabe, the constant theme? Beer, whiskey, vodka? The bottles, the cans, the flasks?"

"We were students. Everybody drank like trout back then."

"Not like me. I lied. My team didn't really go to Massachusetts until the fall. I stayed in Fort Collins that summer, going in and out of detox. A friend of mine on the campus clinic staff admitted me without any family notification, but the clinic's program didn't work for me. My drinking actually got worse. My sister, in league with our grandparents, forced a family intervention. I was shipped off midsummer to a rehab center in California."

"But why didn't you contact me?" Gabe asked, calm, but amazed that he didn't shout it. "I could've supported you, joined you in California, helped you. You didn't have to suffer alone. Why didn't you give me the chance?"

"Oh. Oh, Gabe." Adam shook his head. "I couldn't have faced that. I could never have shown that side of myself to you. I wanted to isolate myself, then dedicate myself to the bottle until I died alone."

"But you weren't alone. All those friends!"

"You're thinking of those guys in the bars? They weren't friends, though I deliberately let you think they were. I wanted you to think I was cool and socially adept. You were the only gay guy I ever connected with, back then, as a fellow human being. Everybody else was a quick trick. I had no intention of getting close, no idea how to do that with another male, no desire to. I was terrified once I confessed I loved you, so I ran away. My family just wouldn't accept it. They would hate it as much as I hated myself."

"I had no idea. I must've been blind. I feel like I let you down, Adam, oblivious to your pain."

"No. The very thing I was drawn to was your innocence of my self-hatred. And your easy self-acceptance. You might've been clumsy in bed, Gabe, but you were graceful out of it. You were so self-contained, untroubled. Unclouded."

"Not so much. I was just inexperienced. Once I got past a messy attachment—to a dang girl—I just decided I would live as a gay man. I knew the problem wasn't within me. I didn't want to be gay, but since there was nothing I could do about it, there was no use torturing myself. There was nothing wrong with my sexuality. I knew it, I just knew. It was the straight world that needed to evolve, not me. So, I lived in the present with people who accepted me, and in the future I wanted, the future I knew would come, being gay wouldn't be objectionable, just another valid human condition."

"It took me years to find that future. If I ever really did," Adam said. He got out of rehab to join the team on Cape Cod, stayed sober while he earned his doctorate at Harvard, taught at Nebraska, and pursued the research that had led to his breakthrough. He met his current partner at an AA group affiliated with NSU.

Gabe could finally detect the younger man, tantalizing behind the scars of that long battle with the bottle. Gabe considered his own innocence of and freedom from that torment in his own life. Had his lucky avoidance of addiction and gay self-hatred led to another kind of defect of character, to his failures of insight and empathy? He shoved away his half-gulped Bloody Mary in self-disgust.

Other people's lives weren't shiny happy websites of achievement and glittering prizes. It was another defect, too, maybe a common American one, as well as his own personal failing, to suppose the glossy surface had more reality than the chaotic, churning magma underneath. In all Gabe's fantasizing and second-guessing about his alternative life with Adam, he had never once considered that Adam faced struggles of his own, struggles far more injurious than anything he himself had ever endured.

Gabe noticed Adam reacting with amusement to something just beyond their table, and turned to find Kyle Montoya standing behind him, a flight bag slung over his shoulder, a wide grin splashed across his face. Kyle put his hands on Gabe's shoulders and apologized to Adam for interrupting.

"I just got in from in New York, where I met with my publisher's editorial board." Kyle's smile turned to a one-note laugh. "I've always wanted to say those words! How cool is that?"

After bringing Gabe up to date on the book deal, Kyle moved aside to stand at the table's edge between both men. "Gabe," he said, "I meant to tell you before my trip. I was totally wrong about one important reference in my article. That whole motif about 'many-toed flax'? There's no such thing. It was freezing up there in the sub-Arctic tar sands, and I couldn't keep my pencil steady. Then I misinterpreted my notes when I got home."

"I figured it out during a Google search, Kyle. You may not realize it, but Adam here happens to be the global authority on marshy toadflax."

"You're Adam Schneider? Oh my God! Is this why you guys are meeting? Are you going to write for *Planet Quarterly*, too, Dr. Schneider?"

"Maybe…?" Adam looked at Gabe, half smiling. "But we'd have to collaborate, Kyle. I'm not much of a stylist. I'm not up to the quarterly's standards. I'm a grind."

"Some grind," Gabe said. "I can't believe it took me so long to catch up with you, Adam, when you're so famous."

"I'm only famous to the twelve or thirteen earthlings who care about marshy toadflax."

"Au contraire," Kyle said with a smile. "Seven billion earthlings are going to thank you for saving the planet from a slow, toxic death via pesticides. And a future of safe crop yields."

"I think you just pitched your next article," Gabe said.

"You got it!" Kyle caught Gabe's gaze, then Adam's. "Gabe is the best editor ever. He even loaned me a couple thousand bucks out of his own pocket so I could finish my research."

"Just a bonus I saved from my former job. Easy, tainted corporate money that was lying around."

"My wife thinks Gabe is a saint. She said the hell with Desmond Tutu and the Dalai Lama, give the Nobel Peace Prize to Gabe."

"What have I ever done for peace?"

"Man, you won't believe how much more peaceful it was around our house once you loaned me that money!" Kyle laughed. "You saved my life, Gabe. And maybe even my marriage." He turned to Adam, smiling. "Though my wife really is in love with Gabe. Thank God he's—" Kyle stopped, glancing at Adam, biting his lip. "Thank God I'm so damn irresistible."

As Kyle left, Adam turned to watch him walk away. "That kid really is pretty damn irresistible. Exuberant."

"Way too exuberant." Gabe knew the reunion was over, glasses pushed aside, watches studied. It was as if Kyle's interruption had broken a spell, as if that better future already waved its brash wand.

Adam's phone rang. His older sister and her daughter were heading upstairs on the escalator in the West Terminal. Was he ready?

They stood and strolled side by side but wordless to the walkway that connected East and West Terminals, a kind of wide catwalk above the main concourse below. Far across, Gabe could see two women in summery dresses waving, signaling claims on Adam's time and company. Adam shrugged, smiling, and Gabe moved into his outstretched arms. He pressed into Adam's fragility, into sympathy and sorrow for Adam's rock-bottom affliction, endured behind the scrim of dazzling achievement.

Pulling away, bound for opposite directions, the two men eased apart. Gabe turned to watch Adam walk, hoisting his carry-on and listing a bit, toward his sister and niece. The women seemed indistinct yet incandescent under the luminous teepee-on-the-prairie canvas overhead.

Now Gabe felt a true sense of lift, almost levitation, as he exited the East Terminal. Was he afloat, finally, into his own future, cut from the ballast of self-delusion, or as usual—surprise, surprise—just light in the loafers?

So, how he'd once described the narrative of his life was wrong. The detour had been the main route, all along, the opposite of "The Beast in the Jungle." He'd been down to almost zero in his human connections and had learned to expect nothing from others. But he climbed back from zero, never once repudiating, like his father, like Adam, his chances for connection. Nor had he drifted, passive, like Ben, into accommodating parental demands; nor, like his mother, like Candy, gotten trapped in an unsuitable suitor's clutch. Pressing forward, being willing to lose and gain connections maybe taught him to fear nothing, least of all the future. What had waited for him there wasn't his own fear, pouncing from beastly crouch. Instead, he'd gained a life so much more interesting and sweet than he ever expected it to be, abounding with experience, attachment, alive among great company, and occasionally, achievement.

Small achievement, but so what? Heading outside through a concrete tunnel, the sensation of floating intensified. The airport was so far out on the plains it seemed to occupy a different life zone than the city, a different atmosphere, blinding, shadeless, oxygen depleted. Numb everywhere, inhaling with deliberate gasps, Gabe really did feel aloft, tumbling through some Chagall dreamscape, airborne at the airport—the landlocked region's portal to the wide world from which, once untraveled, the kid from Butcher Creek eventually journeyed to every corner.

The greening prairie mounded all around under a cloud-clotted, gentle sky. Off west, white-capped peaks aligned over the distant city while north, south, and east, velvet hillocks humped to empty horizons. Settlements a short distance east, like Last Chance, perished in slow motion, life leached away until graveyards were fuller than the towns. Yet just to the west, a heedless, yearning metropolis flourished under the Rockies. Gabe was headed home to Leif, Mary Anne, and Jamie—

South High Street, not Last Chance—afloat in a sky as infinite and dappled as possibility itself.

It was so clear off west Gabe could detect notches and striations in the snow melting on Indian Peaks. Beyond the Longs Peak massif, unseen, Poudre Canyon cut through the range, where that trail led to the demolished glade. Today would be one of the first afternoons warm enough for some young couple to hike up to some new marshy gap, to make love above the budding many-toed flax.

He hoped they were so absorbed by their kisses and the tickle of grasses on their bare skins that they didn't give a thought to immortal love. He hoped they would keep making love all afternoon, lost in attachment, lost to love without wondering whether love would last.

About the Author

A native of California's Mendocino Coast, Lee Patton has enjoyed life in Colorado since college. His fiction and poetry have been widely published and his plays produced nationwide. His novels include *Every Summer Day* from Bold Strokes Books; *Nothing Gold Can Stay*, a Lambda Literary Award finalist; *Love and Genetic Weaponry*; and *My Aim Is True*. *Faith of Power*, a novella, is featured in Main Street Rag's 2017 anthology, *In the Middle*. He received an MA in fiction from the University of Denver's Writing Program.

Books Available From Bold Strokes Books

Coming to Life on South High by Lee Patton. Twenty-one-year-old gay virgin Gabe Rafferty's first adult decade unfolds as an unpredictable journey into sex, love, and livelihood. (978-1-63555-906-4)

Death's Prelude by David S. Pederson. In this prequel to the Detective Heath Barrington Mystery series, Heath discovers that first love changes you forever and drives you to become the person you're destined to be. (978-1-63555-786-2)

His Brother's Viscount by Stephanie Lake. Hector Somerville wants to rekindle his illicit love affair with Viscount Wentworth, but he must overcome one problem: Wentworth still loves Hector's brother. (978-1-63555-805-0)

The Dubious Gift of Dragon Blood by J. Marshall Freeman. One day Crispin is a lonely high school student—the next he is fighting a war in a land ruled by dragons, his otherworldly boyfriend at his side. (978-1-63555-725-1)

Quake City by St John Karp. Can Andre find his best friend Amy before the night devolves into a nightmare of broken hearts, malevolent drag queens, and spontaneous human combustion? Or has it always happened this way, every night, at Aunty Bob's Quake City Club? (978-1-63555-723-7)

Death Overdue by David S. Pederson. Did Heath turn to murder in an alcohol-induced haze to solve the problem of his blackmailer, or was it someone else who brought about a death overdue? (978-1-63555-711-4)

Every Summer Day by Lee Patton. Meant to celebrate every summer day, Luke's journal instead chronicles a love affair as fast-moving and possibly as fatal as his brother's brain tumor. (978-1-63555-706-0)

Everyday People by Louis Barr. When film star Diana Danning hires private eye Clint Steele to find her son, Clint turns to his former West Point barracks mate, and ex-buddy with benefits, Mars Hauser to lend his cyber espionage and digital black ops skills to the case.(978-1-63555-698-8)

Cirque des Freaks and Other Tales of Horror by Julian Lopez. Explore the pleasure of horror in this compilation that delivers like the horror classics…good ole tales of terror. (978-1-63555-689-6)

Royal Street Reveillon by Greg Herren. In this Scotty Bradley mystery, someone is killing the stars of a reality show, and it's up to Scotty Bradley and the boys to find out who. (978-1-63555-545-5)

Death Takes a Bow by David S. Pederson. Alan Keys takes part in a local stage production, but when the leading man is murdered, his partner Detective Heath Barrington is thrust into the limelight to find the killer. (978-1-63555-472-4)

Accidental Prophet by Bud Gundy. Days after his grandmother dies, Drew Morten learns his true identity and finds himself racing against time to save civilization from the apocalypse. (978-1-63555-452-6)

In Case You Forgot by Fredrick Smith and Chaz Lamar. Zaire and Kenny, two newly single, Black, queer, and socially aware men, start again—in love, career, and life—in the West Hollywood neighborhood of LA. (978-1-63555-493-9)

Counting for Thunder by Phillip Irwin Cooper. A struggling actor returns to the Deep South to manage a family crisis but finds love and ultimately his own voice as his mother is regaining hers for possibly the last time. (978-1-63555-450-2)

Survivor's Guilt and Other Stories by Greg Herren. Award-winning author Greg Herren's short stories are finally pulled together into a single collection, including the Macavity Award–nominated title story and the first-ever Chanse MacLeod short story. (978-1-63555-413-7)

Exit Plans for Teenage Freaks by 'Nathan Burgoine. Cole always has a plan—especially for escaping his small-town reputation as "that kid who was kidnapped when he was four"—but when he teleports to a museum, it's time to face facts: it's possible he's a total freak after all. (978-1-163555-098-6)

Of Echoes Born by 'Nathan Burgoine. A collection of queer fantasy short stories set in Canada from Lambda Literary Award finalist 'Nathan Burgoine. (978-1-63555-096-2)

www.ingramcontent.com/pod-product-compliance
Lightning Source LLC
LaVergne TN
LVHW091047080826
845145LV00002B/652

* 9 7 8 1 6 3 5 5 5 9 0 6 4 *